ALSO BY K. PATRICK CONNER

Blood Moon

Kingdom Road

Dying Words

a novel by

K. Patrick Conner

NaCl Press San Francisco 2012

 Published in the United States by NaCl Press, San Francisco.

ISBN 978-0-9856312-0-8

For Christine

Dying Words

CHAPTER ONE

GRAYDON HUBBELL CRACKED his knuckles, then shook out his sore hands and squinted down at his keyboard. He began to write:

"Mildred Duvall Bancroft, widow of shipping magnate Jonathan Bancroft and a passionate advocate for animal rights, died at her home in Pacific Heights Tuesday after a long illness."

Hubbell lifted his eyes and leaned forward to read what he had just typed, peering through the reading glasses perched on the tip of his nose, tracking the words across his computer screen with a fingertip. Satisfied with his lead, he sat back in his chair and picked up the notes he had taken while reading through the folder of articles containing references to Ms. Bancroft, provided by the newsroom's research librarians, drawing from back issues preserved on microfilm and more recent stories in the computer archives. After thumbing through his notes, he took a sip of coffee, then began working up the body of the obituary, chronologically recounting the arc of Ms. Bancroft's life.

She had enjoyed, by any measure, a life of comfort and privilege, beginning with her birth in San Francisco ninety-two years ago, the only daughter of a wealthy importer of Asian textiles and his socialite wife. After attending private schools on the East Coast, she returned to graduate from U.C. Berkeley with a degree in music history. She met her future husband at the San Francisco Symphony's opening night gala in 1949, and they were married the following New Year's Eve, quickly becoming a favored couple within the city's highest social circles, generous benefactors of the performing arts as well as shrewd collectors of modern art, their lives dutifully recorded in the Chronicle's gossip columns and society pages.

When her husband died, now more than ten years ago, Ms. Bancroft quietly retreated to their Broadway mansion and devoted the rest of her life to supporting organizations dedicated to caring for animals. Upon learning of Ms. Bancroft's death, both the Humane Society and the Zoological Society had faxed statements to the Chronicle, mourning her passing and hailing her as "a woman of surpassing kindness and uncommon largesse," both organizations hoping, obviously, that by publicly offering their heartfelt condolences, Ms. Bancroft's children might elect to preserve their mother's legacy with further contributions made in her name.

But Hubbell knew that wasn't likely. In recent years, as Ms. Bancroft had grown increasingly daft and disoriented, her escalating financial contributions to those and other organizations had become a source of intense frustration to her son and daughter, who had their own plans for the family money. Two years ago, they had gone so far as to petition the court to declare their mother incapable of managing her own affairs, withdrawing their request only when the old woman, in a moment of rare lucidity, threatened to cut them out of her will entirely. As Hubbell inserted the statements from the Humane Society and the Zoological Society into the body of the obituary, he had little doubt that Ms. Bancroft's son and daughter were today discreetly celebrating their mother's belated demise, reveling in the fortune so long in coming to them, even as they donned the solemn masks of bereaved family members.

He reached for his notebook and flipped back to the notes he had taken during a telephone conversation with their attorney earlier that afternoon, requiring only a moment to locate the statement the attorney had phoned in on their behalf:

"We grieve the passing of our dear mother, but we take solace in the knowledge that she lived a full and rewarding life. She shall live on in our hearts forever."

It was a tepid remembrance, to say the least, but Hubbell dutifully inserted it near the bottom of the obituary, and after adding the extended list of surviving family members and noting that a memorial service would be held at Grace Cathedral, the obituary was finished. In twelve column inches, he had captured the essence of Mildred Bancroft's life and bid her a fond farewell, and even if the obituary was less than a masterpiece of modern journalism, he could say in all honesty that he had done the best he could with what he had, upholding, as always, the time-honored conventions of the genre. He was, after all, a consummate professional, and after carefully reading the obituary down, not once but twice, after checking every fact and quote against their sources, after poring over each sentence to make sure the obituary didn't just read but sang, Hubbell reached out and pressed the key to send it to his editor.

HUBBELL HAD BEEN WRITING obituaries for the past eleven years, ever since he suffered a heart attack, albeit a mild one, in the pressroom at the Hall of Justice. For more than forty years, he had covered the police department and the district attorney's office, and he had wanted to return to the hall after his convalescence. But his doctor did not want him working under intense deadline pressure, so Hubbell, facing an imposed retirement, negotiated an arrangement in which he would become the paper's full-time obituary writer, convincing his doctor that there is little in the way of deadline pressure to be encountered while covering the deceased.

That is not to suggest that Hubbell was particularly enthused about his new assignment. Like most of his colleagues, he regarded writing obituaries as a morbid job made all the more unpleasant by having to deal with the grieving families of the dead. But he was back in the newsroom, which was all that really mattered, as far as he was concerned, and over time, his perspective changed. He came to appreciate the obituary as both a staple of daily journalism and an art form in its own right, and he now considered himself as good at writing obituaries as he had been at covering the Hall of Justice, as capable of writing a final salute to the rich and powerful as of composing a simple farewell for the eccentric and the notorious.

His desk was located in the back of the newsroom in a corner casually referred to as Section Eight, an oblique reference to that section of the U.S. military code that provides for a discharge on the grounds of insanity. For as long as Hubbell could remember, Section Eight had been occupied by an eclectic group of senior reporters who were at once admired and deeply resented by their younger colleagues for their ability to kick virtually any assignment they found even remotely distasteful. More than a dozen reporters used to occupy Section Eight, but now only Hubbell and three others remained: Mitchell Wiggins, known as "the Senator," a bear of a man with long black hair that piled up on the shoulders of his dark brown suits, one of the shrewdest political reporters at City Hall before he effectively retired from reporting to accommodate his responsibilities as the newsroom's guild steward; Eugene "Poopdeck" Leggett, a squat, bearded, bowlegged feature writer who liked to prowl the newsroom as if it were the deck of a ship, refusing to accept any story that didn't have a strong nautical angle; and Elliott Jennings, bald, pale and legally blind, the paper's distinguished, longtime medical reporter, who in recent years had begun contracting the symptoms of the medical conditions he wrote about, narcolepsy being his current affliction.

They reported to Myron Carroll, an annoying little runt of a man, not quite thirty years old, which is to say less than half their ages, and asinine in the extreme. They had been reporting to Myron for more than two years now, though it seemed much longer than that, ever since he was promoted from the copy desk and made an assistant city editor. They had objected in the strongest possible terms, but their pleas, delivered en mass to Harold Robertson, the managing editor, brought them no relief, leaving them no recourse but to do everything they could to make Myron's job as difficult and as frustrating as possible, hoping against hope that he would request another assignment or return to the copy desk. Unfortunately, Myron had been treated with little or no respect all his life, which rendered him largely immune to their mockery and invective, as well as the occasional threat of physical violence, and so their efforts had thus far had little meaningful impact.

As Hubbell slipped his notes into the folder of articles from the library, he saw Myron storming back to Section Eight in his black trousers and white short-sleeve shirt, his thin black tie swinging out in front of him as his wingtips slapped the linoleum floor. He planted himself in front of Hubbell's desk, a tuft of brown hair rising from the crest of his forehead, his dark eyes dilated behind the lenses of his gold wire-rimmed glasses.

"Where's the fucking dog?" he demanded.

Hubbell leaned back in his chair.

"May I assume you're referring to Bootsie, the grieving Pomeranian?"

"The old lady's attorney just called Harold and told him you refused to include her dog in the list of surviving family members."

"That is true."

"He made it explicitly clear that the old woman wanted the dog listed with her son and daughter."

"That may also be true, Myron, but, as per the official policy of the San Francisco Chronicle, we do not include pets of any kind among the surviving family members."

"What policy? What the fuck are you talking about?"

"It comes up more often than you might think," Hubbell told him. "We finally had to draw the line."

"Why haven't I heard about this policy?"

"Think about it, Myron – first it's a dog, and then it's a cat. The next thing you know, it's parrots and ferrets and then it's some poor bastard's ant farm."

Myron reached up and rubbed his forehead.

"I can't believe this," he said.

"Our concern is merely to preserve the dignity of the deceased," Hubbell assured him.

"Fuck the deceased," Myron said. "Can't you just give me a break here?"

"I'm not putting Bootsie in the obituary – period," Hubbell told him. "And if you put the dog in the obit after I leave, I want you to pull my byline."

Myron could only shake his head.

"Under the guild contract, I have that right, Myron, and I intend to exercise it."

That was all Myron could bear. He turned and started back to his desk.

"For the love of Christ," he muttered. "Why me?"

AS HUBBELL PLACED the folder on the stack on his desk, he was sorry to deny Ms. Bancroft her dying wish, but policy was policy, and to the extent that he had been instrumental in the formation of that policy, he was disinclined to cast it aside without good cause. Nor did he intend to wait around for the benefit of Myron's final edits, much less to watch him insert Bootsie into the obituary, so he reached out to turn off his computer – just as a message appeared across the top of his screen: Harold wanted to see him. Hubbell allowed himself a laugh. Of course, Harold wanted to see him. He didn't have to guess why.

He rose from his desk and started down the aisle leading through the newsroom, through the warren of waist-high cubicles, his younger colleagues slumped down in front of their computer terminals, surrounded by dusty file cabinets and overloaded bookcases, stacks of cardboard boxes and old newspapers, droning televisions and wire baskets filled with unopened mail and unread press releases. He had known Harold for more than fifty years now. They had started as copyboys together, running errands for the reporters working the night shift until they were eventually promoted to become reporters themselves. When Hubbell was sent down to the Hall of Justice, Harold was sent down to City Hall, and over the years, they became close friends, collegial rivals, even, their stories competing for the front page.

Their relationship was strained, naturally, when Harold left the guild to become the city editor and later managing editor, but it was Harold with whom Hubbell had negotiated his return to the newsroom after his heart attack, a move that was less than enthusiastically received by other editors at the newspaper, who viewed Hubbell and his aging comrades less as seasoned, if somewhat eccentric, reporters and more as temperamental windbags who had long ago ceased to carry their own weight – a perspective that was closer than one might think to Hubbell's own view that Section Eight had become at least as much of a state of mind as a corner of the newsroom, perhaps even a school of thought.

Hubbell leaned in through the door of Harold's office. In a light blue shirt with thin gray stripes, his dark blue tie loosened around his neck, Harold was sitting at his mahogany desk, reading down the stories slated for tomorrow's front page.

"You wanted to see me?"

Harold looked up, his thick gray hair combed straight back above his broad forehead, his eyes gunmetal blue beneath the ridge of his brow. He pointed at the black leather chairs arranged in front of his desk.

"Sit down," he said.

Hubbell crossed his office and sat in the chair on the left, sinking into the distressed leather.

"What can I do for you?" he asked, as if he didn't know.

"I understand you instructed Myron to take your byline off the Bancroft obituary."

"Only if he inserts Bootsie into the list of surviving family members," Hubbell said.

"Doesn't that seem a little melodramatic?" Harold asked.

"It's a flagrant violation of established policy."

"I'm aware of our policy," Harold said.

"We established that policy after a great deal of discussion. Surely you recall our lengthy deliberations."

"How could I forget?"

"But you told Myron to put the dog in the Bancroft obit anyway?"

"It seems to me that in this case, we can make an exception."

"Because their lawyer would run this up to the editor-in-chief?"

"If I've learned anything over the years, it's when to pick my battles," Harold said.

"It's a precedent, Hal."

"I understand."

"What's going to happen the next time this comes up? What's going to happen when some old woman wants her husband's beloved gerbil listed in the obituary?"

An amused smile leaked out the corner of Harold's mouth.

"I do appreciate your concern about the paper's broader editorial issues," he said.

"I wanted to make a point," Hubbell said.

"And indeed you have, but pulling your byline still strikes me as over the top."

"Call it whatever you like," Hubbell said.

"After all these years, you're still a pain in the ass."

"It's a matter of principle, Hal."

"Of course, it is."

HUBBELL STEPPED out onto the sidewalk, a misty breeze pressing in from the ocean. After tugging down the brim of his hat, he walked down to Market Street and turned onto the broad brick sidewalk lining the city's main boulevard, negotiating his way through the crush of people rushing toward the underground BART and Muni stations, past the flower vendors and the street artists, the raving preachers and the blind guitarist, the thickset beat cop wearily surveying his domain. At Third Street, he caught the 30 Stockton, climbing aboard the bus and squeezing into the passengers standing in the aisle between the rows of seats along the windows, grabbing the overhead handrail and holding on tightly as the bus snaked through the Stockton Tunnel into Chinatown and finally crossed Broadway into North Beach.

When the bus arrived at Washington Square, he got off and walked down to Filbert Street and then started up the hill. He had lived on Russian Hill for more than fifty years now, ever since he and Maria purchased a two-story, blue-gray Edwardian shortly after they were married. They had moved into the building's upper flat with every intention of filling it with their children, but that, tragically, was not to be. Hubbell couldn't bear to live in the flat after Maria died, but neither could he bring himself to sell the property, so he moved into the cottage behind the Edwardian, and he had lived there ever since.

As he approached the Edwardian, he dug his keys out of his pocket and then let himself in through the gate that led back to his cottage. As he walked along the side of the Edwardian, he could hear music, if that's what it could be called – Ms. Gifford's music.

Ms. Gifford had been renting the bottom flat from him for the past three years now, an aging flower child who had arrived in the city during the Summer of Love and, like so many of her motley tribe, never left, still considering herself to be a free spirit, which, by observation, Hubbell understood to mean someone who spends the better part of every day smoking marijuana, drinking tequila and listening to bootleg recordings of Grateful Dead concerts.

Ms. Gifford liked to play her music while she worked in the garden, tending the small plot where she planted herbs and vegetables. She must have heard him closing the gate. As he stepped into the garden, she was waiting for him.

"Good evening, Graydon."

"Hello, Lydia."

She was wearing faded blue jeans and a long-sleeve denim shirt buttoned tightly around her wrists, oversized garden gloves and a floppy straw hat, the brim sagging down onto her forehead. Her long gray-blond hair was woven into a thick braid that lay across her right shoulder. Her eyes were pale blue, though her right eye often seemed reluctant to participate in her vision, veering off in all directions as if it had a mind of its own.

"So who died today?" she asked him.

"I wrote an obituary for a woman named Mildred Bancroft," he said.

"Never heard of her."

"Her husband owned a fleet of container ships. She was an animal rights advocate."

"I had a cat once – a spooky white cat, very spooky, if you ask me. We never really got along. I mean, I fed him, but he was a very finicky eater. I had no idea cats could be so finicky. Sometimes he would just go crazy, climbing up the curtains or tearing up the rug. It was a Persian rug. I loved that rug. Anyway, I think it might have been the music. I had to make a choice between the music or the cat."

"I see," Hubbell said, though, of course, he didn't.

"I love music, Graydon."

"Yes, I know you do."

"Let's just say it's a major part of my life. I listen to my music morning, noon and night."

"So I've heard," he said.

"You don't mind my music, do you?"

"Of course not."

"I like to play it loud – concert volume. I like to re-create the moment."

"Indeed."

"Do you know how many times I saw the Dead play?"

"I have no idea."

"I don't even remember," she said. "I went to Egypt with the band in 1978. I certainly remember that. I was there when they played the pyramids. Do you have any idea what kind of a trip that was?"

As she turned away and walked over to her garden, Hubbell realized that Ms. Gifford didn't expect an answer from him. It was a rhetorical question. Many of Ms. Gifford's questions were rhetorical in nature, although Hubbell often didn't realize that until he attempted to form a response. In fact, in retrospect, he had had whole conversations with Ms. Gifford that would have to be regarded as rhetorical.

"I planted my tomatoes this morning," she told him.

She pulled off her gloves and leaned down to inspect the young plants, enclosed in wire hoops.

"I like to plant them early," she said. "The earlier, the better, I say. The longer they grow, the bigger they get, and the bigger the plant, the more tomatoes. That's my philosophy, anyway."

"That's very sound thinking, it seems to me."

"You've tasted my tomato sauce," she reminded him.

"Yes, I have."

"And you liked it."

"I'm sure I did."

She turned back to him.

"Now there's an idea."

The brim of her hat flopped down over her eyes. She pushed it back up, and there went her right eye, angling away as if chasing a flying insect. She smiled at Hubbell, which always made him nervous.

"I still have several quarts of that sauce," she said. "How about I make dinner for us one of these nights?"

Hubbell despaired. He had no ready excuse.

"How about Saturday night?" she asked.

He summoned a smile, knowing he couldn't decline her invitation, concealing his dread.

"Saturday night sounds fine, Lydia. I look forward to it."

HUBBELL CLIMBED the stairs leading up the side of the hill to the door of his cottage, the planks creaking loudly beneath him with every step. At the landing at the top of the stairs, he opened the door and stepped into the kitchen. The cottage was still warm from the afternoon sun, so he crossed the kitchen and raised the window above the sink to let the cool evening air move in.

After putting away his coat and hat, he returned to the kitchen and opened the refrigerator. He leaned in and grabbed a wedge of cheese and a chug of salami, then he carried them over to the table, setting them down beside a shallow wicker basket that contained a slender baguette. As he pulled out a chair and sat down, he looked out across the bay, at the last of the sunlight illuminating the soft blond hills of Marin. He had always loved the evening. He had always loved the fading hours of the day. As he tore off a piece of the baguette, he couldn't help but recall the evenings spent with Maria in the Edwardian's upper flat, watching her prepare their dinner, sipping a glass of wine as they discussed the events of the day. Yes, he knew that could be considered old-fashioned. Yes, he knew that he could be fairly called a male chauvinist. But he wasn't ashamed. He made no apology. That was who he was, and that was who he intended to remain. Those were, quite simply, the best days of his life.

When he finished his dinner, he walked down the hall to his bedroom, where he removed his clothes and padded barefoot into the bathroom. He swept aside the clear plastic shower curtain and turned on the water. He gave the water a moment to warm up, then stepped into the ancient, clawfooted tub and let the water pour down onto the base of his neck. He stood there until the water began to lose its heat, then he turned it off and stepped out of the tub. After drying off, he used the towel to wipe the steam from the mirror above the pedestal sink and studied his watery reflection. His thinning hair had long since faded from gray to white. Veins blossomed on his cheeks. Creases curled around his mouth, furrowed his forehead, radiated from the corners of his eyes. He looked – and felt – every day of his seventy-six years.

He hung up the towel, then returned to his bedroom, where he drew back the blankets and turned out the light and slipped into bed. As he lay on his back, he could hear the low moan of the foghorns. He could feel the chilled air seeping in through the open window. He was tired, exhausted. In addition to the obituary for Mildred Bancroft, he had also written, over the course of the past week alone, obituaries for the daughter of a wealthy industrialist who decided to join a convent and spent the rest of her life teaching school in Madagascar; an insurance agent who had been a highly decorated naval pilot during World War II; and the founder of a line of sportswear for elite athletes who spent his fortune purchasing and protecting groves of old-growth redwoods along the North Coast. As Hubbell sank back into the mattress, he wondered how many obituaries he had written since he returned to the newsroom eleven years ago – hundreds, certainly, a thousand perhaps, perhaps even more than that. He had written more obituaries than he could count, far more than he could possibly remember. But as he stared up into the darkness, he knew that number didn't matter – that number wasn't important. All that mattered was the number of obituaries that remained to him, the number he would write in the days to come, before he finally succumbed to the afflictions and indignities of his age.

CHAPTER TWO

HUBBELL STOOD on the sidewalk as the yellow cab turned down Filbert Street and pulled up in front of him. As he opened the back door and slid across the seat, the driver turned and looked back at him – a Russian with a huge pink head, his eyes thin slits, stiff blond hair protruding from his scalp. It wasn't that Hubbell disliked Russians. He didn't have anything against them, not per se. He liked to think that he was open to the possibility that there were good Russians, too, as opposed to the virulent communists bent on world domination. But in Hubbell's personal experience, as limited as that might have been, he had found Russians to be a coarse and vulgar people, predisposed to bombast and confrontation, and, as a rule, he avoided them assiduously. This morning, however, he had no choice.

"I need to get to the California Pacific Medical Center," he said. "And I'm in a bit of a rush."

That was all, apparently, the Russian needed to know. He spun back to the wheel, dropped the cab into gear and stomped down on the accelerator. The tires howled on the pavement as they pulled away from the curb, the sudden acceleration throwing Hubbell back in the seat with such force that his hat flew off and bowled up against the back window. He reached back and grabbed the hat as the driver turned up Leavenworth and then onto Union. He gripped the top of the seat in front of him as they raced down the hill. When they reached Van Ness, the Russian jerked the wheel hard to the left, cutting directly in front of an oncoming delivery truck and scattering a group of screaming schoolgirls in the crosswalk. Hubbell couldn't bear to watch as the cab driver began weaving through the three lanes of southbound traffic, his left arm thrust out the window, gesturing wildly for the other drivers to get out of his way, all the while shouting into the cell phone wrapped around his right ear, arranging, for all Hubbell knew, the sale of enriched uranium to some obscure terrorist organization.

After streaking down California Street, running through a series of red lights, the driver turned onto Webster and pulled up in front of the medical center, brakes locked, tires screeching, a cloud of blue smoke boiling out from beneath the cab as it came to a complete stop.

The Russian stabbed the meter with his index finger.

"Eight dollars and forty-five cents," he said.

With his heart still pounding in his chest, Hubbell withdrew his wallet and produced a ten-dollar bill. He handed it to the driver, glad to still be alive.

"Just take it all," he said.

HUBBELL CLIMBED out of the cab and crossed the sidewalk to the medical center, the large glass doors sliding open as he entered the lobby. Several years had passed since he had last seen Dr. Martin. It had not been a conscious decision to avoid him or any other doctor. It was simply that Hubbell wanted to believe that he was in relatively good health, particularly for a man of his age.

But late last night, shortly before three o'clock, he had awakened to find himself dripping with sweat, his cotton undershirt soaked. It was not the first time he had been awakened by the night sweats. They had been occurring with a distressing increase in frequency. Initially, he simply assumed that he had contracted a mild fever, but several weeks later, he was stricken again. He was concerned, of course. Still, it didn't seem like an acute medical crisis. But lately, the night sweats were waking him more and more often, disrupting his sleep nearly every night. The time had come to find out what was going on.

He took the elevator up to the fifth floor and walked down the hallway to Dr. Martin's office, then reached down and let himself into the waiting room. He removed his hat and stepped up to the receptionist's window. The receptionist, her hair dyed a dark metallic blue, looked up at him.

"Good morning. My name is Graydon Hubbell. I'm hoping to see Dr. Martin this morning."

"Do you have an appointment?" she asked.

"No, I'm afraid I don't."

"Is this an urgent medical issue?"

"I can't sleep," Hubbell said, having learned long ago that when seeking relief there is little benefit to understating the problem. "I haven't slept for days."

"Oh my," she said. "You must be exhausted."

"Exactly."

"Why don't you have a seat, Mr. Hubbell, and I'll let the doctor know you'd like to see him."

"Thank you," he said.

Hubbell sat across the room from the receptionist's window, his feet together, his hat on his lap. He sat there for nearly thirty minutes before the door beside the window opened, and a young nurse in a crisp blue uniform called his name. He raised his hand and followed her down the hall to a small examination room, where she instructed him to remove his coat and step onto the standing scale. As she recorded his weight and height in his medical file, Hubbell stepped down from the scale and crossed the office to sit on the examination table. She wrapped the blood pressure cuff around his bicep and pumped it full of air, studying her watch as she released the pressure, the air hissing away. His blood pressure was 142 over 80, slightly higher than the nurse would have liked, though it must be said that Hubbell, at his age, was glad to have any blood pressure at all.

Dr. Martin knocked twice before he opened the door and entered the examination room. In his white lab coat, he was tall and lean with light blond hair and a deep tan. He had been Hubbell's primary physician for nearly twenty years, overseeing his recuperation from his heart attack and the terms of his return to the newsroom, the arrangement in which Hubbell became the Chronicle's obituary writer.

The doctor thrust out his hand.

"It's been a while, Graydon, which I generally take to be a good sign."

"I've been doing pretty well for a man my age," Hubbell told him.

"I understand you've been having trouble sleeping?"

"That's right. That's why I'm here. I keep waking up in the middle of the night, soaked with sweat."

"How long has this been going on?"

"I suppose it started a year or so ago, maybe longer than that," Hubbell said. "Lately it's been happening almost every night."

He watched as the doctor made a note in his chart, then slipped his pen into the pocket of his coat.

"Unfortunately, sleep hyperhidrosis is fairly common," Dr. Martin said. "Night sweats can be utterly harmless, nothing more than a temporary nuisance. Often they disappear without so much as a wave good-bye. On the other hand, they might be a symptom of something more worrisome. But you say you've been feeling all right in general?"

"Well, at my age, feeling all right is pretty much a memory, but I don't have any specific complaints, if that's what you mean."

"Excellent," the doctor said. "Why don't you take off your shirt and let me listen to your heart and lungs?"

Hubbell slid off the examination table and removed his shirt. After hanging it on the hook on the door, he climbed back onto the table. The doctor lifted his sleeveless undershirt and pressed the stethoscope against his chest.

"Take a deep breath and then let it out slowly," he said.

Hubbell followed Dr. Martin's instruction as the doctor worked his way around to his back. When Dr. Martin was finished, he stepped back and let the stethoscope hang from around his neck.

"Everything sounds fine," he said.

But it was then that the doctor noticed the purplish bruise on the inside of Hubbell's right forearm. He reached out and took Hubbell's wrist and gently raised his arm to study the bruise.

"How did you manage to do this?" he asked.

Hubbell looked down at his forearm, noticing the bruise for the first time.

"I have no idea," he said.

"Really?" the doctor asked. "This must have hurt."

"I'm a lot tougher than I look."

"Do you have any other bruises?"

"Not that I know of."

"Why don't you take off your undershirt and let me take a look."

Hubbell pulled his undershirt up and over his head. The doctor circled him slowly, as if inspecting a used car.

"You have several more bruises on your lower back," Dr. Martin said. "Do you recall how you might have gotten those?"

"I have no idea," Hubbell said.

"All right," the doctor said. "You can put your shirt back on."

He walked over to the counter and picked up a paper form listing scores of medical tests.

"I'm going to send you down to the lab," he said, checking off a number of the open boxes, indicating the specific tests he wanted performed. "Let's get a complete blood workup and see what that tells us."

The doctor handed the sheet to Hubbell.

"Other than those bruises, you look like you're in pretty good shape," he said.

"For a seventy-six-year-old man?"

The doctor conceded a smile.

"For a seventy-six-year-old-man, you look like a million bucks."

AFTER STOPPING by the lab to have his blood drawn, five vials, no less, Hubbell passed back through the lobby and walked out of the medical center. A cab was parked along the curb. Hubbell ducked down to make sure the driver wasn't a Russian. When he saw the driver was wearing a red bandanna on his head, pulled down tight and tied at the back of his neck, he opened the back door and slid across the seat. To the best of Hubbell's knowledge, few Russians wore red bandannas, fewer still, he was confident in assuming, while driving a cab.

"Fifth and Mission," he said.

Without so much as a word, the driver reached down and started the engine, then he wheeled the cab around and headed downtown. As Hubbell sat back and gazed out the window, he was relieved that Dr. Martin hadn't seemed overly concerned about his night sweats. Still, he couldn't help but wonder what the blood tests might show. It seemed to Hubbell that every time he submitted himself to a medical test he was diagnosed with a new infirmity and prescribed a new medication to treat it. His daily regimen currently consisted of prescriptions to lower his cholesterol, thin his blood, suppress the acid in his stomach and prevent migraines, the pills and capsules all but filling the palm of his hand as he swallowed them every evening. Soon, he supposed, he would be taking something else to address the cause of his night sweats.

When the cab pulled up in front of the Chronicle, Hubbell climbed out and pushed through the heavy, tinted-glass doors into the lobby. As he walked over to the elevators, he flashed his identification card at Leonard, standing glumly behind the counter in his navy blue blazer and smart black cap, an ever-vigilant member of the private security force that served as the newspaper's first line of defense – turning away enraged subscribers demanding their money back, dragging out the clinically insane as they screamed their conspiracy theories, chasing away protesters with their whistles, air horns and portable loudspeakers. It was an assignment that routinely taxed the limitations of Leonard's aptitude and training, and as Hubbell waited for his elevator, he couldn't help but overhear Leonard pleading with a bike messenger to take back the package he was trying to deliver to one of the reporters, all-too-aware that he would be blamed when the package inevitably failed to make it to its intended recipient.

Hubbell took the elevator up to the third floor, then walked past the wood-paneled entrance to the publisher's suite and ducked into the men's room. After placing his satchel on the shelf beside the door, he stepped up to the broad mirror above the row of sinks. He raised the knot in his red-and-black-striped tie and tugged down the cuffs of his white shirt. He straightened the lapels of his tweed coat and adjusted the brim of his brown fedora. He was, as always, properly attired for the newsroom. In Hubbell's view, journalism was nothing less than a profession, and he, like his colleagues in Section Eight, was determined to uphold the newsroom's long-established sartorial tradition – and if, over the years, it had been observed that he occasionally treated his younger colleagues with a degree of disdain, that sniffish attitude may very well have derived, at least in part, from the manner in which they dressed, their slovenly clothing reflecting little respect for the occupation. Plus, Hubbell thought most of his younger colleagues were idiots.

He grabbed his satchel and left the bathroom and walked down to the newsroom and then back to Section Eight. As he hung up his coat, he heard the dreaded cadence of Myron's wingtips on the linoleum. When he turned around, Myron was standing beside his desk.

"We're going to need the Cassidy obit for tomorrow," he said. "Apparently the chief croaked late last night."

"All right," Hubbell said.

"When do you think you'll be able to file it?" Myron asked.

"I'll have it for you in ten or fifteen minutes – twenty minutes, at the most," Hubbell said.

But Myron knew better.

"Sure you will," he said, turning away. "Sure you will."

Hubbell watched Myron walk back to his desk, then he pulled out his chair and sat down. He turned on his computer, then reached for his keyboard and called up the obituary that he had begun working up for the former police chief several days ago, when they learned that his condition was rapidly deteriorating.

Joseph Cassidy was a native of the city, the son of Irish immigrants and a graduate of St. Ignatius, who had studied the administration of justice at City College before entering the Police Academy. After joining the force, he was assigned to walk a beat in Chinatown, and from there he worked his way up through the ranks, spending time on the vice squad and the homicide detail before eventually being promoted to captain and appointed to run Central Station in North Beach. When he was named chief, he vowed at his inauguration to always remain a cop's cop, which meant, above all else, that he would turn a blind eye to the myriad forms of misconduct and illegal activity the rank and file routinely engaged in, from the gambling rackets they protected in the Mission District to the prostitution rings they shook down in the Tenderloin, as well as overlook the occasional use of what the feckless members of the civilian oversight board liked to call excessive force.

For six years, Cassidy served as police chief, liberally indulging his fondness for strong drink and randy limericks, but nothing thrilled the chief so much as racing across the city with his lights flashing and siren wailing. Unfortunately, it was while rushing to the scene of an officer-involved shooting outside a liquor store on Potrero Hill that the chief lost control of his vehicle, sideswiping three parked cars before striking a light standard, the impact propelling the chief through the windshield and onto the street, where he was run over not once but twice by officers following in their patrol cars. Miraculously, the chief survived, but as a quadriplegic, unable to speak other than to produce the occasional monosyllabic grunt. The general consensus was that the chief, in his diminished capacity, might not be able to continue to run the department, so he was formally retired in a grand ceremony in the rotunda at City Hall and then dispatched to spend the rest of his life in a nursing home near the Presidio, where, apparently, he had just passed away.

Hubbell read his working draft of the obituary, then rose from his desk and walked back through the newsroom to the fax machine. He thumbed through the faxes in the tray, eventually finding the official statements sent over by the mayor and the current chief of police, hailing Cassidy as an honest cop and thanking him for his years of public service, and even if their praise wasn't entirely true, much less sincere, Hubbell knew it would suffice, at least for the purpose of his obituary.

He carried the faxes back to his desk, needing only a comment from the chief's family to finish the obituary. But that wasn't necessarily going to be easy. Protocol called for seeking comment about the deceased from the immediate family, of course, preferably the surviving spouse, or, in these modern times, the surviving domestic partner. And, in cases in which the subject of the obituary had been married more than once, protocol called for seeking comment from the most recent spouse or domestic partner, thereby avoiding the possibility that hard feelings may have followed the dissolution of the earlier relationships and could promote intemperate remarks about the not-so-dearly departed, comments that might be at variance with the purpose of the obituary, which was to note the deceased's passing and bid them good-bye.

Cassidy had been married only once, exchanging vows with his high school sweetheart at St. Mary's shortly after he joined the police department. But after being promoted to the vice squad, Cassidy left his wife and two children to consort with an exotic dancer named Brandy, whose act at the Mitchell Brothers O'Farrell Theater featured, among other accoutrements, a red pork pie hat, which was said to be the source of Cassidy's carnal infatuation and endured, apparently, until his tragic accident. The chief and his leggy paramour had lived together for nearly ten years, and, as such, protocol obligated Hubbell to seek comment from her. Unfortunately, Hubbell had no idea where Brandy might be. She had left the city shortly after the chief was moved into the nursing home, quietly selling off anything of value in the apartment they had shared on Nob Hill, and even though Hubbell had heard rumors that she was plying her trade in Mexicali, he didn't even know her last name, and, it is fair to say, there were as many questions about the veracity of her first name as there were about the authenticity of her breasts.

Which left Hubbell little choice but to turn to the wife the chief had abandoned but never formally divorced, hoping against hope, as he dialed the number for the house in the Sunset District where she still lived, that the passage of time did indeed heal old wounds, even as he was unable to recall a single instance in which that had actually proven to be true, particularly among those of Irish ancestry.

He let the telephone ring and then ring some more. He was just about to give up, when she finally answered.

"Yeah, hello," she said, her voice throttled deep in her throat.

"Ms. Cassidy, this is Graydon Hubbell at the Chronicle. I'm very sorry to disturb you during this very difficult time, but I'm working on an obituary for Chief Cassidy, and I was hoping to get a minute of your time."

He heard her light a cigarette, the lighter snapping shut, the first husky inhalation. A television was playing in the background. He could hear the studio laughter.

"And, please, let me extend our condolences from everyone here at the paper," he said.

"Yeah, thanks," she said. "Those condolences really mean a lot to me, coming from whoever the fuck you are."

Hubbell sat back in his chair, fairly certain the chief's widow had chosen to observe the occasion of her husband's death with an alcoholic beverage.

"I'm a reporter for the Chronicle," he gently reminded her. "I'm working on the obituary for your husband."

"Oh, him?" she asked.

A joke. She laughed, as sharp as a cough, then she took a drink, ice cubes rattling in her glass.

"So what do you want from me?" she asked.

"We always try to include a comment about the deceased from a member of the immediate family," he explained. "We're always looking to include a poignant observation or memory."

"A poignant observation? A poignant memory?"

"Well, sincere," Hubbell said.

"Like what?"

"That's really up to you."

She took another drag on her cigarette, sucking the smoke deep into her lungs and then releasing it slowly.

"You mean like, 'The man was a saint, a loving husband and a devoted father, until he ditched us for that fucking hooker?'"

"Maybe not in those exact words," Hubbell said.

"Well, fuck you, then," she said. "What's wrong with those exact words?"

Hubbell set his notebook aside. He was beginning to think the call to Ms. Cassidy was not going to be as productive as he had initially hoped.

"What do I get out of this – besides your fucking condolences?" she wanted to know.

"Perhaps this wasn't a good time to call," Hubbell said.

"Nothing – not a fucking thing, as usual."

"I'm sorry to have troubled you," he said.

"What about my poignant observation?" she asked. "What about my poignant memory?"

"I'm afraid I have to get back to work."

"Wait a minute! Where the hell are you going?"

"I'm on deadline, I'm afraid."

"I don't give a fuck about your deadline," she said. "I'm talking to you!"

"I really do thank you for your time."

"Don't you hang up on me!"

But Hubbell did. That's exactly what he did.

"Jesus," he said. "Jesus Christ."

AS A MATTER OF HABIT, Hubbell liked to drink a cup of coffee before he began working up an obituary, so he rose from his desk and walked back through the newsroom to the alcove off the mailroom. He placed his mug on the counter beside the coffee machine, then discreetly glanced around the mailroom. When he was sure no one was watching him, he reached for the pot to fill his mug, declining, as always, to drop fifty cents through the slot in the top of the coin box, as the sign on the wall instructed. For years, Hubbell and his colleagues in Section Eight had refused to pay for the coffee as a matter of principle, believing the company should pay for anything that had the predictable effect of making the reporters in the newsroom work harder. It was a small crime, certainly, but he didn't want to get caught – he was well aware that his position, however rational it might be, would not serve as a strong defense, nor was it likely to elicit broad support from his younger colleagues, who might very well agree with him, at least on a theoretical basis, but who had been paying for their own coffee regardless.

After filling his mug, he turned and started back to his desk. Unfortunately, Myron spotted him.

"Where are we?" he asked.

"I'm just about finished," Hubbell told him.

But Myron knew better.

"No, you're not, are you?"

And that was the nature of Hubbell's relationship with Myron. Myron continued to operate under the delusion that Hubbell would do exactly what he asked, when he wanted Hubbell to do it. But that was absurd. Hubbell had worked in the newsroom for more than half a century, nearly twice as long as Myron had been alive. He needed no advice or direction from Myron. And he knew well that the more time an editor had to work with a story, the greater the likelihood he or she would find a way to screw it up.

So, as always, Hubbell took his time, giving Cassidy far more respect in death than he deserved in life. After working up the obituary, he read it down carefully, checking and double-checking the names and dates, making sure that the quotes he had used were consistent with his notes and the faxes, polishing and refining every sentence, and only then, when he was satisfied that the obituary didn't just read but sang, did he file it to Myron. That gave Myron ten minutes to read the obituary before he had to move it to the news desk. As far as Hubbell was concerned, that was more than enough time.

As he turned off his computer and prepared to leave for the day, the Senator gripped the top edge of his cubicle wall and pulled himself up to stand. His face flushed from the effort, his long black hair coiled on his shoulders, he unbuckled his belt and unzipped his trousers and began tucking in the tail of his white shirt, scarcely able contain his bulging paunch.

"Gentlemen, may I interest you in a libation? There's a matter I would like to discuss with you – a matter of the utmost urgency."

Hubbell glanced over to Poopdeck, who pawed at his beard and shrugged as if to say he didn't know what the Senator was talking about, either.

"I'd be delighted to join you," Hubbell said.

"Aye," Poopdeck said.

When Hubbell looked over to Jennings, he saw that he was dead asleep, his head tilted back, his mouth open, arms hanging slack along the sides of his chair, his feet dangling several inches above the floor. Hubbell gently shook the arm of the chair, and Jennings snorted and blinked, fighting through his confusion, requiring a moment before he realized where he was.

"We're going out for a drink," Hubbell told him. "Would you like to join us?"

Jennings reached up and ran the palm of his right hand across his head, flattening the few sparse hairs that still clung to his scalp.

"Yes, it's been a long day, hasn't it?"

Hubbell put on his coat and hat, and with the Senator leading, they started down the aisle leading through the newsroom and then down the corridor to the elevators. After departing the building through the Fifth Street guard station, they made their way down the sidewalk and then turned into the alley that ran behind the loading dock. A block down the alley was a bar called the Tempest, which occupied the bottom floor of the three-story brick building owned by the Newspaper Guild. As the guild steward for the newsroom, the Senator drank there every evening, reasoning that at least a small percentage of the money he spent there would be returned to the guild in the form of the bar's rent, and so, by extension, the more he drank, the greater his selfless contribution to the guild's long-term financial stability.

He entered the Tempest first, a man who liked dramatic entrances, his huge frame filling the doorway, his deep voice booming out his salutations, and it would have been a grand entrance indeed had anyone but the bartender and a waitress named Abby been there to witness it. Hubbell and his colleagues followed the Senator over to the table he preferred, situated directly in front of the long wooden bar. They had no sooner removed their coats and draped them over the backs of their chairs when Abby arrived at the table to deliver the martini the bartender had taken the liberty of preparing for the Senator.

"You're an angel," he said.

Abby stood beside the Senator as he lowered himself into his chair.

"I'll take a rum and coke," Poopdeck said.

"I'd like a glass of red wine," Jennings said.

"That sounds fine to me," Hubbell told her.

As Abby walked back to the bar, they turned toward the Senator, watching as he took a sip of his martini.

"So what are you hearing?" Hubbell asked him.

"I'm hearing the company is going to ask for another round of layoffs," the Senator said.

"You've got to be kidding," Hubbell said.

"I wish I was."

"Why?" Hubbell asked. "They laid off nearly a hundred people just last year."

"I'm hearing they want to lay off fifty more."

"Good Christ," Poopdeck groaned.

"Circulation is in a free fall," the Senator told them. "The classifieds are gone forever. Retail advertising is being killed by the recession. The company claims they're losing a million dollars a week."

"They can't take another fifty people out of the newsroom,"

Hubbell said. "Who do they think is going to put out the paper?"

"Not us," Poopdeck declared.

"The newsroom is not the reason the paper is losing money," Hubbell said.

Raising both hands, the Senator rocked back in his chair.

"You'll get no argument from me," he said.

"But we get fucked every time," Hubbell said. "The morons in circulation don't know what they're doing. The clowns in advertising are even worse."

The Senator took another sip of his martini.

"Make no mistake about it, gentlemen – we're a dying breed. We're a dying breed at a dying newspaper in a dying industry."

HUBBELL REMAINED at the Tempest long enough to drink another glass of wine, then caught the 30 Stockton back to North Beach. After walking up the hill, he let himself in through the gate and started back to his cottage, the pungent aroma of marijuana greeting him as he entered the garden. It had to be Ms. Gifford's marijuana. On more than one occasion, he had observed Ms. Gifford smoking marijuana in the garden. She was rather casual about it, actually, entirely untroubled by the fact that it was illegal, not to mention the provision in the rental contract she had signed that authorized him to evict her if she engaged in unlawful activity of any kind.

But he didn't see her, so he started across the yard to his cottage. He had just reached the steps leading to the upper level of the garden when he heard the door of her flat open behind him. When he turned around, Ms. Gifford was standing in the doorway, a shot glass in her left hand, no doubt filled with tequila, her beverage of choice.

"Good evening, Graydon."

"Good evening, Lydia."

"And how was work today?" she asked.

"It was fine, thank you."

"Did anyone die today?"

"I wrote an obituary for a man named Joseph Cassidy. Mr. Cassidy used to be chief of police."

"Oh," she said.

She sipped at her tequila.

"I've never cared much for the police, if you must know," she said.

"I wasn't aware of that," Hubbell said.

"They arrested me once, more than once, actually, but who's counting, certainly not me."

"It probably doesn't matter," Hubbell said.

"All I was doing was smoking a little pot," she said.

Hubbell allowed himself to smile. It was gratifying to know that Ms. Gifford had learned her lesson.

"I had just gotten here," she said. "I came on the Greyhound, all the way from Toledo, Ohio. I rode that bus straight on through."

"How interesting."

"I was seventeen years old, fresh out of parochial school."

She cocked her head and grinned at Hubbell.

"A virgin, but not for long."

"I see," Hubbell said, heat rising into his face, eager to leave the story of Ms. Gifford's lost virginity for another day, perhaps another lifetime.

"Graydon, may I ask you something?"

And there went her right eye again, careening off to the side, beyond him, searching for what, Hubbell didn't know.

"Do you find me to be a little too forward?" she asked. "I want you to tell me the truth."

"Forward?" he asked. "In what way?"

"Promise me you'll tell me the truth."

"I promise."

"Sometimes I wonder if I'm a little too forward, is all."

"No, I don't think so."

"I'm just trying to be open. I just want people to know what I'm thinking."

"There's nothing wrong with that."

"I just want to be honest, totally honest. Do you know what I mean?"

"Yes, I do."

"So, I'm asking, are you comfortable with me being who I am?"

Hubbell had to think. He wondered if this might be another of Ms. Gifford's rhetorical questions.

"Who else would you be?" he ventured to ask.

"That's why I don't hold anything back. That's why I just let it rip. Do you know what I mean?"

"Yes, I do."

But of course she had lost him. He had tried to stay with her. He had tried to understand what she was talking about, but he had no idea. The whole conversation confused him.

"Graydon, sometimes I think that you're the only one who understands me."

"Really?"

"You might be the only one who ever understood me."

"Really?"

She raised her shot glass.

"Listen," she said. "Would you like to come in for a shooter or two?"

"Thank you," Hubbell said. "Thank you very much. But can I take a rain check? It was a long day, and I'm afraid I'm beat."

"Of course," she said. "Of course, you can take a rain check. But whenever you feel like doing a shooter, just come on over. I'm always up for it."

"I will," he promised. "I will."

HUBBELL CLIMBED the stairs and let himself into his cottage. After putting away his coat and hat, he walked down the hall to his bedroom and changed into a pair of khakis and a gray flannel shirt. When he returned to the kitchen, he poured himself a glass of wine. As he took a sip, he looked out upon the blue-black bay. Darkness was falling. He could see the first lights on the distant shoreline.

But then his eye was drawn down into the yard below, through the double glass doors at the back of Ms. Gifford's flat. She was dancing in her kitchen. Ms. Gifford was always dancing, which is not to say that Hubbell fully understood her curious movements, twirling around in circles and flinging her arms in all directions. He had to assume she had poured herself another shooter or two. No doubt, she had smoked some more of her marijuana.

He had never known a woman like Ms. Gifford. She was a hedonist by nature, an opportunist in practice. She knew what she liked, and she spent every day in pursuit of those supple pleasures. There was nothing wrong with that, of course. Hubbell was willing to acknowledge that there was much to admire about Ms. Gifford's approach to life, at least in a purely philosophical context, and he would never presume to deny her the right to enjoy every minute of every day. But that didn't mean he wanted to be a part of it. That was what Ms. Gifford didn't seem to understand.

She had been insinuating herself into his life ever since she answered the ad for the vacant flat that he had placed in the Chronicle classifieds. She worked, or as Hubbell was to learn later, she had worked as a part-time substitute school teacher, but district officials declined to bring her back after learning that the lessons she offered the city's elementary schoolchildren consisted primarily of instruction in the art of juggling. As far as Hubbell could tell, Ms. Gifford wasn't working anywhere right now. He had no idea where she got what little money she had, and he was loath to ask, if for no other reason than she might tell him. He was prepared to admit that he might be better off if he didn't know.

In all fairness, she had willingly confessed that she was not very good with money when she arrived to inspect the unoccupied flat, and Hubbell had found her candor refreshing. It might very well have been the reason he rented the flat to her, as opposed to several more conventional, and more qualified, applicants. That she was bad with money turned out to be something of an understatement, of course. Her rent checks had bounced on any number of occasions, and Hubbell had no idea how many months she was currently behind. He recalled only that the last time she had troubled to pay her rent, she had done so in cash, producing a wad of crumpled bills held together with a rubber band, accompanied by two rolls of quarters. Still, she was short, though by just twenty dollars, which, as he recalled, was better than she had done the month before and was certainly better than nothing.

He could have asked her to leave, of course. He had every right to evict her, if not for failure to pay her rent, then for her use of marijuana. Certainly that would have been the prudent move, at least from a financial perspective. But money was not one of Hubbell's primary concerns. The mortgage on the two flats and his cottage had been paid off years ago. He wasn't counting on the rental income to pay his current bills. And so, for reasons he didn't fully understand, he let Ms. Gifford stay, even as she fell further and further behind in her rent, even as she smoked her marijuana cigarettes, even as a voice in the back of his head warned that he was making a terrible mistake.

CHAPTER THREE

HUBBELL WOKE to sunlight flooding through his bedroom window, the glare so intense he had to roll away from it. As he lay on his back and stared up at the ceiling, a deep yawn washed over him. He stretched his arms and then his legs. Slowly, he began to realize that he had slept through the night, untroubled, mercifully, by the night sweats.

He had dreamt about Maria again, as always, his dreams little more than fragments of memory now, refracted through the prism of time. He dreamt about the first time he saw her, all those years ago, standing before the Municipal Court judge in a dark blue coat and white blouse, small and slight, her long black hair a mass of curls that fell to her shoulders. He had just been sent down to the Hall of Justice, and she was working for a small law firm on Sutter Street. Her client was being arraigned for the burglary of an automotive body shop in the Mission District.

He waited for her outside the courtroom. When she stepped into the corridor, he introduced himself as a reporter for the Chronicle.

"I was wondering if I could buy you a cup of coffee," he said.

"And why would you want to do that?" she asked.

"Or lunch," he said.

She smiled, but he knew the answer was no.

"Maybe some other time," she said.

Hubbell had no intention of giving up. He knew a lawyer who worked at the same firm and discreetly inquired about her. He learned she had gone to U.C. Berkeley and had studied law at Hastings in the city. He learned she was devoted to her clients – the seamier the client, the harder she worked on his or her behalf, prompting her colleagues in the office to call her "Sister Maria," a nickname she rather enjoyed. Her only passion outside the office, he learned, was baseball, one of her uncles having played briefly in the Pacific Coast League.

That was all Hubbell needed to know. He bought a pair of tickets for the first Giants game of the season at Candlestick Park and caught up to Maria the following morning as she was walking into court.

"I thought I'd try once more to see if you might consider letting me take you to lunch," he said.

Before she could turn him down, he reached into his coat pocket and produced the tickets.

"Opening Day – hot dogs and beer on me."

"I'd be delighted," she said.

The following day, they took a cab down Third Street, through the city's bleak industrial wasteland to the new stadium, a sprawling concrete bowl built on the windswept flats near the Hunters Point Naval Shipyard, then slipped into the crowd surging toward the main gate, passing through the turnstiles and into the stadium. As they walked down the open concourse, they could hear the rumbling crowd, restlessly stamping their feet, then they turned into the narrow corridor and stepped up into the sunlight, the vast green expanse of the playing field spreading out before them.

As they settled into their seats, she turned to him.

"This is wonderful," she said.

He watched as she wrote down the starting lineups in her program, explaining that she had learned the arcane science of keeping score from her father, who used to listen to the Seals games on the radio and took her to Sunday double-headers when she was a schoolgirl, and when the game began, she recorded it on her scorecard as if she intended to re-create the whole of the game for her father that evening. Hubbell loved how tense she was in the early innings when the score was close, how she winced every time a Giants player made an out, how she leapt up out of her seat and threw her arms in the air when the Giants scored a run. He loved how she pulled her cap down over her hair, the bill shading her dark brown eyes, how easily she smiled and how freely she laughed, how her voice grew coarse and all but disappeared by the end of the game.

As Hubbell sat up and swung his legs over the edge of the mattress, he couldn't believe how much he still missed her, even after all these years.

HUBBELL WALKED up Fifth Street, past the Vietnamese sandwich shop and the broad concrete steps of the old Mint, the solemn gray edifice of the Chronicle building looming across Mission Street. Beneath its ragged flag, the stunted clock tower showed the time to be shortly after four o'clock, but that wasn't right, of course. The clock on the tower had been wrong for years, certainly for as long as Hubbell could remember, so far off, in fact, that it was impossible to determine whether the clock was running fast or slow.

After waiting for the streetlight to change, Hubbell crossed Mission and pushed through the heavy glass doors. As he entered the lobby, he saw a man in a long black peacoat and a red, white and blue top hat, his face caked with silver paint, laughing hysterically as he urinated into the bed of gold moss at the base of one of the potted palms. Fortunately, Leonard seemed to have the situation under control, which is to say he was begging the man to stop, his hands clamped to the sides of his head.

Hubbell took the elevator up to the third floor and walked down the corridor to the newsroom. The instant he started back to Section Eight, he saw there was trouble. The Senator had pulled himself up to stand and was leaning heavily on the back of his chair. Poopdeck was pacing back and forth in front of the window, tugging at his beard. Jennings was staring up at the water stains in the acoustic tile ceiling, running his open palm across his oblong head.

"What happened?" Hubbell asked.

"Cleopatra died," the Senator told him.

"Elizabeth Taylor?"

"The Queen of fucking Egypt," Poopdeck said.

Jennings peered up at Hubbell through his large glasses, tusks of black hair protruding from his nostrils.

"Congestive heart failure," he said. "She'd been battling it for several years."

"Do you want the bad news?" the Senator asked.

"Who won?" Hubbell asked.

"Myron says he won."

"Is that a bitch?" Poopdeck asked. "Or is that a bitch?"

"I'll check," Hubbell said.

He walked over to his desk and took off his coat and hat, then he sat down and unlocked his bottom drawer, reaching in and withdrawing a yellow legal pad. Ever since he returned to the newsroom to become the paper's obituary writer, Hubbell had been in charge of the ghoul pool, in which members of the newsroom placed bets on the next celebrity to die. The wager was a dollar per celebrity with no limit on the number of bets one can place. The winner collected the whole pot.

Hubbell ran the tip of his index finger down the list of names, and, sadly enough, there was Myron. He had indeed bet on Taylor. Hubbell looked up at his colleagues. He didn't have to say anything.

"Goddamn it," the Senator said.

Poopdeck spun away.

"Is that a bitch, or is that a fucking bitch?"

"I thought there was a rule prohibiting management from participating," the Senator said. "I thought we were betting among ourselves – guild members only."

"Sorry," Hubbell said.

"Well, there should be a rule," Poopdeck declared. "I say we draft a new rule right now."

"And there's nothing to say the new rule can't be applied retroactively," the Senator said.

"I'd like to keelhaul the little prick," Poopdeck said.

"Here he comes now," the Senator said.

Hubbell turned and watched as Myron made his way back to Section Eight, grinning broadly as he approached.

"Yes!" he shouted, throwing both arms in the air. "I won!"

"Put your fucking arms down," Poopdeck told him.

"How much did I win?" Myron asked.

Hubbell handed him the envelope stuffed with cash.

"Ninety-four dollars."

"I can't believe it," he said. "I never win. I never win anything."

"Myron, I think we can all stipulate that you're a loser of the first order," Hubbell said.

"Amen," the Senator said.

Myron opened the envelope and withdrew his winnings. He raised the thick wad of bills to his ear, fanning them with his thumb.

"Just listen to that," he said. "Don't you love the sound of money?"

That was enough for Poopdeck.

"Just take the fucking money and get the fuck out of here," he said.

Myron knew better than to press his luck. He turned to walk back to his desk, throwing his arms in the air one last time.

"I'm rich!" he shouted. "I'm rich!"

HUBBELL SPENT the rest of the morning recording the newsroom's next round of wagers. His colleagues in Section Eight pressed their earlier bets, each of them maintaining their own unique approach to the selection process. The Senator favored wagering on comedians, particularly those whose acts he had never found even remotely humorous, making it that much easier to hope for their swift demise. Over the years, he had won with Buddy Hackett, Don Knotts, and, in a truly inspired choice, Soupy Sales, so he gave Hubbell a five-dollar bill and renewed his wagers on Jonathan Winters, Phyllis Diller, Don Rickles, Jim Nabors, and no less than Bill Dana.

Jennings focused more narrowly on former talk show hosts, a subject of some familiarity as a result of his wife's lifelong insomnia. Jack Paar and Johnny Carson had paid off handsomely in the past, so he doubled down on Mike Douglas, Phil Donahue, and in an unguarded moment of wishful thinking, Larry King.

Poopdeck liked to bet on blonds, real or otherwise, putting his money, yet again, on Kim Novak, Doris Day and Tippi Hedrin.

"And give me Zsa Zsa Gabor," he said.

He reached for his wallet and handed Hubbell four crumpled dollar bills.

"She's been dead for twenty years, but no one's had the nerve to tell her."

Hubbell, for his part, hadn't won the pool since Bob Hope died. But last Labor Day, while absently flipping through the channels on the television, he had stumbled upon the Jerry Lewis Muscular Dystrophy Telethon. He was stunned when he saw the host, the once lanky, hyperactive comedian now bloated and perspiring, gasping for breath. With a little research, he learned that Lewis had survived two heart attacks and prostate cancer and was currently suffering from diabetes and pulmonary fibrosis. As Hubbell slipped his dollar into the envelope, he had to believe that it was only a matter of time before the Nutty Professor did the right thing.

As he returned the legal pad and envelope to his bottom drawer, his telephone rang. He reached over and picked it up.

"Hello, Mr. Hubbell. This is Cynthia from Dr. Martin's office."

"Hello, Cynthia," he said.

"Dr. Martin asked me to call to tell you that he has your test results. He'd like to talk to you."

"Shall I make an appointment?"

"Dr. Martin would like to talk to you today, if that's possible."

"Today?"

"He'd like to talk to you as soon as possible."

Hubbell sat back in his chair.

"I suppose I could come in," he said.

"Could you come in now?" she asked.

"Right now?"

"Or as soon as you can."

Hubbell reached up and rubbed his forehead.

"All right," he said. "I'll come in right now."

HUBBELL GRABBED his coat and hat and walked down the aisle leading through the newsroom, stopping at the editorial assistant's desk near the fax machines to check out one of the city desk's cars. After signing the logbook, he slipped the keys into his coat pocket and started down the corridor to the elevators.

He left the building through the Fifth Street guard station and walked down the sidewalk to the parking lot across the alley from the loading dock. He let himself in through the gate in the chain-link fence that enclosed the lot, then crossed the crumbling pavement to the city desk's fleet of aging Chevrolet Novas. He unlocked the door of the light blue Nova in space number fourteen and slipped behind the wheel, then backed out of the space and guided the Nova out of the lot and down the alley to Fifth Street.

He drove across the city to the medical center and parked in the underground garage, then he took the elevator up to the fifth floor and walked down the hall to Dr. Martin's office. After removing his hat, he opened the door and stepped up to the receptionist's window.

Cynthia looked up at him.

"Hello, Mr. Hubbell. I'll tell Dr. Martin that you're here."

The waiting room was empty. He walked over and sat down in a chair beside a small wooden table. As he flipped through the stack of old magazines, Dr. Martin opened the door beside the receptionist's window.

"Hello, Graydon. Come on in."

Hubbell followed him down the interior hall to the same examination room he had been in yesterday.

"I have to admit that I'm a little surprised you got my test results back so quickly," he said.

The doctor closed the door and motioned toward the examination table.

"Yes, I asked for expedited results," he said.

As Hubbell stepped up to the examination table, the doctor sat on the stool at the foot of the table, holding Hubbell's medical chart in his hands.

"May I ask why?" Hubbell asked.

"I was concerned about your bruises," the doctor said. "Bruising can be a symptom of a serious medical issue, much like the sleep hyperhidrosis, so I asked for a complete blood count."

"All right," Hubbell said cautiously.

"The CBC shows that you have an unusually high number of abnormal white blood cells. A high white blood cell count could mean any number of things, but, Graydon, I have to tell you that I'm very concerned that you may have a form of blood cancer."

Hubbell couldn't suppress a caustic laugh.

"Are you serious?"

"Let me emphasize that I am only an internist," Dr. Martin said. "I am not an oncologist, but I'm quite concerned."

"So you think I should see an oncologist?"

"Yes, absolutely," Dr. Martin said. "I took the liberty of contacting Dr. Humiko Ishihara on your behalf. I had the CBC results sent to her. She's an excellent oncologist. I told her that I would recommend that you see her today."

Hubbell forced himself to smile.

"I have to tell you that you're making this sound rather ominous."

"It may very well be serious, Graydon. I don't want to mislead you. But, again, I'm not an oncologist."

Hubbell sat there for a moment. He allowed himself a nervous laugh.

"Well, I suppose I should go then," he said. "I suppose I should go talk to Dr. Ishihara."

"Let's hear what she says," Dr. Martin said. "Let's hear what she recommends, and we'll go from there."

HUBBELL SAT on the examination table in Dr. Ishihara's office, holding his hat in his hands, his fingers working their way around the soft felt brim. He couldn't believe he might have cancer. He felt fine, perfectly fine. It didn't make any sense. There had to be a mistake.

The room was warm, uncomfortably warm. When he reached up to loosen his collar, he found it moist with perspiration, so he slipped off the table and walked over to open the window. As he reached for the latch, Dr. Ishihara knocked on the door and stepped into the room.

"Mr. Hubbell?"

"You got here just in time," he said. "I was just about to jump."

She didn't laugh. She closed the door and motioned toward the table.

"Please, have a seat," she said.

Hubbell returned to the table.

"I wasn't really going to jump," he told her.

"I'm pleased to hear that," she said.

She was wearing a light blue lab coat and dark gray slacks, her long black hair clipped back off her face. She pulled over a chair and sat down in front of him, her knees pressed together, her fingers laced on his medical chart.

"How are you feeling?" she asked him.

Hubbell turned both palms up.

"I feel great for a man who just learned that he may have cancer."

"Yes, I'm afraid that's entirely possible," she said. "I've looked at the results of the tests Dr. Martin ordered, and I believe you very likely have a cancer of the white blood cells called chronic myelogenous leukemia."

"Leukemia?"

"Of course, we'll need a bone marrow aspiration and biopsy to be certain," she said. "We'll need to take a piece of bone marrow from your hip and examine it under a microscope to be absolutely sure."

"You've got to be kidding me."

"No, I'm afraid I'm not," she said.

"And I just got this out of the blue?"

"In all probability, you've had CML for some time," she said. "It can be a very insidious disease. In as many as forty percent of all CML cases, the disease may not present any symptoms for years."

"I see," Hubbell said, as if he had to say something.

"The disease progresses slowly through three phases, which are determined by the percentage of abnormal white blood cells in your blood and bone marrow."

"Do I dare ask what phase I'm in?"

"I'm afraid your blood count indicates that you are in the third phase of the disease."

"The third of three phases?"

"It's called blast crisis. It means your blood and bone marrow contain more than twenty percent of those abnormal white blood cells – or blasts."

Hubbell looked out the window but saw only the empty sky. He turned back to Dr. Ishihara.

"So what does all this mean?" he asked. "How do we proceed from here?"

"I'm afraid our treatment options are quite limited," she said. "The best option in terms of battling CML at this stage would be high-dose chemotherapy – using a combination of very powerful drugs to kill the abnormal cells in your blood and bone marrow. Unfortunately, the side effects of an intense chemotherapy regimen are quite severe. They would certainly degrade your quality of life, and I have to tell you that I'm not confident that even high-dose chemotherapy would significantly increase your long-term prognosis, particularly given your age."

Hubbell could feel beads of perspiration forming on his upper lip. He reached up and wiped them away with his index finger.

"But that's really our only course of action," she said. "In recent years, with the introduction of a new class of drugs called tyrosine kinase inhibitors, we've had a high degree of success treating CML in the early phases of the disease. Unfortunately, the drugs that are so effective in the chronic and even the accelerated phases are not nearly as effective when CML has progressed to the blast crisis phase."

Hubbell could only stare at her.

"Of course, the other option is to do nothing at all," she said. "By that I mean providing palliative care, of course. Dr. Martin and I would do everything we can to preserve your quality of life. We would very aggressively treat the symptoms of the disease as it progresses."

Hubbell could only nod. He didn't know what else to say or ask.

"How you wish to proceed is entirely your decision," she said. "But time is of the essence, obviously."

"How much time have I got?"

"It's very difficult to say," she said.

"Are we talking about months? Or weeks? Days?"

Dr. Ishihara let her shoulders fall forward.

"I wish I could tell you otherwise, but your disease is highly advanced."

Hubbell nodded once more. He understood.

"Is there anything else?" he asked her.

She shook her head.

"No," she said. "Dr. Martin and I just need to know how you wish to proceed. Think about it. Talk with your family and friends. Let me know what you decide as soon as possible."

AS HUBBELL CROSSED the underground garage to the Nova, he could feel a smile breaking across his face. He had no idea why he was smiling, grinning, actually, from ear to ear, but he couldn't help himself. He opened the door and eased himself behind the wheel, then glanced up into the rear-view mirror. He looked as if he had gone mad – synapses misfiring deep in his cranium, ricocheting off the interior walls of his skull, sparks flying, tufts of smoke drifting out his ears.

Perhaps his grin was only natural, a perfectly rational response to the absurdity of it all. He had gone to Dr. Martin simply because he was having difficulty sleeping – only to learn from Dr. Ishihara that he was in the terminal phase of an insidious disease. And there was little they could do about it. He had to laugh. It was a joke, a terrible joke, a cosmic joke. His options were to wage a battle that he had virtually no chance of winning, and to pay a terrible price while doing so, or to raise a white flag and go on as if nothing were wrong, even in the slightest, treating only the symptoms of the disease as it spread through his body to savage his vital organs.

Hubbell shook his head. It was all too much, more than he could comprehend. He needed time to think. But not now. He needed to pull himself together. He had to get back to the paper. Somehow, he had to get through the day. He had no intention of telling anyone that he had just learned that he had a form of leukemia, not even his colleagues in Section Eight. They were journalists, after all, which is to say they were constitutionally incapable of protecting privileged information of any kind. To tell his colleagues in Section Eight about his diagnosis would be to tell everyone in the newsroom, and Hubbell didn't want anyone to know that his demise might very well be imminent, not before he had sorted it all out for himself.

He closed his eyes and sat back in his seat. With both hands on the steering wheel, he took a deep breath. He held it in his lungs for as long as he could and then slowly released it. After a moment, he could feel the muscles in his face beginning to relax, the grin beginning to subside. He reached down and started the engine, then backed the Nova out of the parking space and drove up to exit the garage, pulling in beside the parking attendant's booth. He handed his ticket to the attendant and gave him a twenty-dollar bill, then tossed his change onto the passenger's seat and pulled out of the garage.

Traffic was heavy as he drove back downtown, taking Van Ness down to Eddy Street, passing through the Tenderloin before he crossed Market and drove up Fifth Street to the Chronicle. After crossing Mission, he turned into the alley that ran behind the loading dock – the wrong way, of course, but he didn't care. Unfortunately, such was the nature of his day that one of the paper's delivery trucks had just pulled away from the loading dock and was driving toward him, so Hubbell slowed and pulled up onto the sidewalk, giving the truck as much room as he could, even as the side of the Nova scraped against the chain-link fence.

When the delivery truck drove by, Hubbell continued down the sidewalk, the fence shuddering as he rolled past, then he reached up for the clicker clipped to the underside of the sun visor and pressed the button to open the gate to the parking lot. As the gate drew back, he pulled into the lot and turned down the aisle on the left and drove down to the parking spaces reserved for the city desk cars. Space number fourteen, where he had found the Nova, was still empty, but the cars on either side had encroached upon the space to the extent that he had to brake before slowly easing the car into the space.

The loud snap puzzled him, then the sound of broken glass falling to the pavement. He had no idea what had just happened, but he stopped and put the Nova in reverse and backed out of the space, noticing only then the damage to the car on the right, its side-view mirror dangling by a cord along the driver's-side door panel. And it was then, as he considered the possibility that he might very well have caused that damage, that he felt the heavy thump behind the Nova, his head bumping back against the head rest as he heard, once again, the sound of broken glass raining on the asphalt and realized that he had backed into the car on the opposite side of the aisle.

That was enough. Enough was enough. He drove down the aisle until he found a significantly larger parking space. As he pulled the Nova into the space, he didn't care that it was not one of those reserved for the city desk cars. He didn't care that it was reserved for someone else. With no little relief, he killed the engine and grabbed his coat and climbed out of the car. Without looking back, he walked across the parking lot and let himself out the gate. He didn't care what might have just happened. He didn't care what he might have just done. That was the least of his problems.

AFTER RETURNING the Nova's keys to the strongbox and signing out in the logbook, Hubbell walked back to Section Eight, followed closely by Myron.

"Where the hell have you been?" Myron asked.

Hubbell hung up his coat, then turned back to Myron, noticing that his round, wire-rimmed glasses rode at a slight angle across the bridge of his nose, giving him the look of a man who had just been slapped on the side of the head.

"I had a doctor's appointment," Hubbell told him.

"You could have let me know," Myron said.

"I wasn't aware that I needed your permission to see the doctor."

"Is something wrong?" Myron asked.

Hubbell wanted to laugh.

"Myron, don't you think I would tell you if something was wrong?"

Myron wasn't sure how to answer that.

"You're my editor, aren't you?"

Myron took a step back, shoving both hands into his pockets.

"Yes, I am."

"You sign my timecard every week, don't you?"

"Yes, I do."

"So doesn't it stand to reason that you would be the first person I'd tell if something was wrong, if I had a serious medical issue?"

Myron hesitated.

"Yes, I suppose so."

"Now, is there anything else?" Hubbell asked him. "I've got work to do, if that's all right with you."

"No, that's fine," Myron said. "That's all."

As Myron started back to his desk, Hubbell pulled out his chair and sat down, longing for the days when he and his colleagues in Section Eight reported to Robert McCaleb, a twenty-year veteran of the desk, and, notably, the founder of the ghoul pool. McCaleb had been determined to retire the day he turned fifty-five and thus became eligible to collect an early pension, and the closer that date appeared on the horizon, the more actively he had discouraged Hubbell and his colleagues from filing stories, or obituaries, that he would be subsequently obligated to edit. McCaleb didn't care where his reporters were, much less what they might be working on – a desire to be kept in the dark that earned him the nickname "Mushroom Bob." It was a sad day in Section Eight when Mushroom Bob retired and departed for Baja, where he planned to spend the rest of his life living in a single-wide trailer along the Sea of Cortez, enjoying a lifestyle that revolved around cocktails at daybreak and small arms practice at dusk.

Hubbell didn't quite know what to do. He supposed he could resume work on his hold-for-release obituaries, by any measure a simple task requiring nothing more than a review of articles provided by the library, but even as he reached for the manila folders containing those articles, he found it impossible to focus. He got up and helped himself to a cup of coffee in the alcove off the mailroom, as if that might strengthen his powers of concentration. He took a break and walked up the stairs to the patio on the roof of the building, as if a breath of fresh air would clear his mind. But all he could think about was Dr. Ishihara's diagnosis. His thoughts swung wildly from utter disbelief to abject resignation, from refusing to accept Dr. Ishihara's reading of his blood tests to realizing he had no good reason to believe she might be in error.

Finally, shortly after five o'clock, Hubbell gave up. He turned off his computer and rose from his desk to put on his coat and hat.

"Gentlemen, I'm taking my leave a little early this evening," he said. "I hope you have a fine weekend, and I shall see you on Monday."

AFTER TAKING the 30 Stockton back to North Beach, Hubbell let himself into his cottage. He put away his coat and hat and walked down the hall to his bedroom, where he stripped off his clothes and crossed the hall into the bathroom. He drew the shower curtain aside and turned on the water. He had just stepped into the tub when he heard a sharp knock on the cottage door.

"Hello? Graydon?"

It was Ms. Gifford, of course.

Hubbell turned off the water and put on his robe and walked down the hall to the kitchen. She had opened the door and was leaning in from the landing at the top of the stairs, wearing a loose

Grateful Dead sweatshirt featuring an illustration of a red, white and blue skull that appeared to contain a bolt of lightning, the sleeves rolled up nearly to her elbows, her long hair flowing out from beneath a blue stocking cap.

"I'm sorry, Graydon. Were you taking a shower?"

"I was just about to," he said.

She gave him a toothy smile, her right eye wandering off like an errant child.

"I much prefer a bath, if you must know," she said. "I love taking a long hot bath, with candles and incense, of course, and a shooter of tequila. There's nothing better than that, in my humble opinion."

As she stepped in through the door, Hubbell tried not to envision her reposing in the bath.

"So how are you today, Graydon?"

It was a fair question, but not one he intended to answer truthfully.

"I'm fine, thank you."

"Did anyone die today, anyone that I should know about?"

He had to think for a moment.

"I'm afraid Elizabeth Taylor passed away," he said.

"The Elizabeth Taylor?"

"The one and only."

"I'm very sorry to hear that," she said. "I was a very big fan of hers."

"I wasn't aware of that."

"Oh, yes, I followed her career very closely – the marriages, anyway."

"She was quite an actress, one of the finest actresses of her generation, I would say."

"And one of the early feminists, I mean, besides the jewelry. But who could blame her? Women love diamonds. I mean, I love diamonds, and I'm a woman."

"Of course," Hubbell said.

But she had lost him, again. He had no idea what she was talking about. For that matter, he had no idea what she was doing in his kitchen.

"Was there a reason you dropped by?" he asked.

"Of course, there was," she said.

"And what was that?"

"I don't believe we set a time."

"A time for what?"

"A time for dinner tomorrow night."

He had forgotten.

"What time would you like me to come over?" he asked.

"The truth is, I'm always late," she said. "I've been late all my life. I just can't help it. I think it may be genetic, as in my genetic makeup, so to speak. My mother was always late, and, well, I'm her daughter, so it only stands to reason."

Hubbell's head was beginning to hurt. A dull ache pressed against the backs of his eyes.

"How about seven o'clock?" he suggested.

"That's exactly what I was thinking."

"Fine," Hubbell said. "I'll see you then."

HUBBELL CLOSED the door and returned to the bathroom. As he turned on the water and stepped back into the tub, it occurred to him that his just having learned that he was in the final phase of a terminal disease might actually make a plausible excuse to get out of dinner with Ms. Gifford tomorrow night. He could tell her about Dr. Ishihara's diagnosis. He could tell her he needed the time to be alone. He could ask if they could postpone the engagement until a later date. She would have to understand. She would have to agree. And suddenly it occurred to Hubbell that if he died quickly, he might get out of dinner altogether. It was an intriguing possibility. He wasn't prepared to go so far as to view his cancer as a blessing in disguise, but there was no reason the cancer couldn't make itself useful, so long as it was going to all the trouble of sending him to the ever-after.

He had known this day was coming. Of course he had. This day came for everyone, eventually, and in the context of human mortality, Hubbell expected no preferential treatment. But he had always assumed that he would die of a heart attack – not cancer. He would never forget the day, eleven years ago, when he was stricken in the pressroom at the Hall of Justice. He was sitting at his desk, working on a story, when he suddenly felt a heavy pressure on his chest. He sat back in his chair, hoping that it would pass, but then a bolt of pain shot down his left arm. He stood up, but the room began revolving around him. As he sank to his knees, the other reporters in the pressroom rushed to his side and called for an ambulance. He was taken to San Francisco General Hospital, where the doctors determined that he had experienced a mild myocardial infarction. They told him it could have been worse. They also told him it could happen again, at any time. And so, based on that admonition, Hubbell had always believed that someday he would be stricken again, just as suddenly but far more seriously, perhaps even dropping dead at his desk in the newsroom.

It had happened before. It had happened in Section Eight just two years ago, when Leonard Ellison, the paper's legal affairs reporter, suffered a massive cerebral aneurysm and collapsed at his desk, issuing a loud grunt before plunging his face into his keyboard. The paramedics didn't even try to resuscitate him. Instead, they heaved his dead body onto a stretcher, and as they wheeled him out of the newsroom, the whole of the staff stood and gave Ellison a standing ovation. Yes, it was melodramatic, perhaps even excessively so, Hubbell was willing to concede as much. But it was nonetheless an honorable way to die, far better, in Hubbell's opinion, than wasting away in a rest home, dying alone wearing nothing but a soiled diaper.

But now Hubbell realized that he wasn't going to die of a heart attack in the newsroom, and to the extent that there would be no sustained applause when he passed away, he couldn't help but feel somewhat disappointed. Instead, if Dr. Ishihara was to be believed, he was going to die of blood cancer. But as the water poured down onto the back of his neck, Hubbell reminded himself that his time had not come yet, not quite. He was still alive, at least for now, and he had to be grateful for that. He would discuss it all tomorrow with Maria. Surely she knew what had happened. Given her privileged vantage point, she might very well have known this was coming, in which case, she might very well know how it was all going to play out. Certainly she could help him decide what to do. He would seek her sage counsel tomorrow, as he had so many times in the past.

CHAPTER FOUR

HUBBELL FOLDED DOWN the ironing board, mounted in a cabinet recessed into the bathroom wall. After plugging in the iron, he returned to the bedroom and reached into the closet for his best suit – a three-piece, charcoal gray suit made of fine Italian wool. He always wore his best suit when he went to visit Maria. That was the reason he bought it. He bought it to lend an air of formality to the occasion, and, of course, he wanted Maria to see him handsomely dressed on her behalf. He wanted her to see that he was looking good and doing well, or at least as well as might be expected, given the fact that he had just been diagnosed with terminal cancer.

After ironing his shirt and getting dressed, he walked down the stairs and through the garden to the door on the side of the Edwardian that led down to the garage. He descended the interior stairs and crossed the garage to his Mustang, parked along the opposite wall. He had purchased the Mustang in 1967, and the signs of its age were impossible to ignore. The yellow paint had faded nearly to white on the hood, roof and trunk, and thick scabs of rust grew along the windshield trim. The bucket seats were coming apart at the seams, and the radio emitted nothing but static. The brakes squealed, and the clutch slipped, and the front end pulled hard to the right. But Hubbell didn't mind. He was well acquainted with the infirmities of age. He liked to think he knew how the Mustang felt.

The door groaned as Hubbell pulled it open and slipped behind the wheel. He turned the key in the ignition, and the engine reluctantly rumbled to life. After pulling out of the garage, he drove up and over the crest of Russian Hill and then down to Van Ness, slowly making his way south through the city and down the Peninsula to Colma, the quiet community of the dead on the back of San Bruno Mountain. He knew he was taking the long route, down Mission and El Camino Real, stopping at light after light and getting caught behind buses and double-parked delivery trucks. But he didn't care. He was in no hurry, and he was not such a fool that he would test his vision and reflexes on the freeway, not anymore. Those days were long past.

After stopping at a floral shop to buy a dozen white roses, Hubbell turned in through the gate leading into the Italian cemetery. He slowed down and quietly rolled past the rows of old stone chapels that lined the main road, past the black ash trees planted between the chapels, stopping when he reached the marble angel, high on a slender column rising from a hedge-lined island in the middle of the road, her shoulders slumped beneath her burden of sorrow, the side of her face resting in the palm of her right hand as she contemplated the fates of all those buried below. She was beautiful, cool white against the misty sky, and over the years, as Hubbell had come to visit Maria, the angel had become a comforting presence to him, even as he knew she was waiting for him to join them. But today was not the day. He was sorry to disappoint her, but she would have to wait a little longer.

He turned left and followed the single lane of buckled asphalt as it passed a long row of marble vaults, then he pulled over to the side and parked on the dirt shoulder. He gathered up the roses, then climbed out of the car and opened the trunk. With the roses in his left hand, he reached in for the metal folding chair and then carried the chair and the roses out into the field of headstones, planted in geometric precision across the gently rolling slope, across the recently mown grass to Maria's grave, surrounded by the graves of her mother and father, her aunts and uncles.

Hubbell placed the chair at the foot of Maria's grave, then knelt down and unwrapped the roses and arranged them in the marble vase in front of her headstone. Maria loved roses. Her father had planted a rose garden in the yard behind their flat in North Beach. He grew roses of every color, and Maria loved them all. But white roses were her favorite. Hubbell stepped back to study the arrangement, the small white buds just beginning to unfurl, releasing the fullness of their color as they spilled over the lip of the vase. After pronouncing himself satisfied, he sat down in the metal chair.

"Hello," he said.

At the sound of his own voice, he looked around and saw that he was the only person in that section of the cemetery, the only living soul among the quiet congregation of the dead. He was often the only one there. He enjoyed the silence. The silence made it so much easier to communicate with Maria.

"How are you?" he asked.

He smiled, appreciating the absurdity of the question. Maria was fine. Of course, she was fine. She had been dead for almost forty years.

He took off his hat and looked up at the sky.

"What a day! What an afternoon! Can you believe what a beautiful day it is?"

HUBBELL SLIPPED his hand into his coat pocket and withdrew a slender, tightly rolled cigar. He peeled off the cellophane wrapper and passed the cigar beneath his nose, closing his eyes to fully appreciate its rich aroma. He bit off the tip, struck a match and sucked the flame deep into the cigar, holding the match there until the tobacco began to glow, then he tilted his head back and released a thin stream of smoke, watching it slowly dissipate in the cool spring air. He always smoked a cigar when he visited Maria's grave. The cigars had become a central element of his ritual visits, and he smoked them slowly, enjoying each moment, celebrating her memory, and now, finally, anticipating their imminent reunion.

"As you may very well know, I have been diagnosed with a cancer of the white blood cells called chronic myelogenous leukemia. Apparently I have had this disease for quite some time."

Hubbell tapped the cigar with his fingertip, watching the ash fall into the grass.

"My options are few," he told her. "I can submit myself to a regimen of high-dose chemotherapy to try to kill the cancerous cells in my blood and bone marrow, or I can let the disease run its natural course, treating the symptoms as they present themselves."

Hubbell shrugged.

"It's really not much of a choice," he said. "I have no intention of spending the time that remains to me lying in a hospital bed, barely conscious with chemicals dripping into my veins."

He raised the cigar and took a drag, then released the smoke slowly.

"It isn't clear how much time I have, how much time before I join you. But that doesn't worry me. I'm not afraid of dying. The fact is, I'm looking forward to seeing you. I look forward to seeing you and your family."

Hubbell allowed himself a laugh, recalling the first time he met Maria's family, several months after they attended Opening Day at Candlestick. He and Maria had seen each other often that summer, frequently meeting for dinner after work, watching movies at the Fox Theater on Market Street, strolling through Golden Gate Park on the weekends, and in September, Maria invited him to dinner at her family's third-floor flat on Taylor Street.

Hubbell knocked on the door. When Maria opened it, he could hear laughter and shouting in the flat above. She grabbed his arm and led him up the stairs and down the hall to the dining room, where she introduced him to her father, a short thick man with a face as red as a blister and a coarse black moustache, a fisherman who worked the bay with his dory and hand-sewn nets and crab pots. In a blue cotton dress, a gray sweater draped over her shoulders, her mother carried in a large kettle of cioppino and placed it on the table. She was as small and slight as Maria, her long black hair threaded with silver, her eyes as dark as her daughter's.

They sat down at the table, and after her mother led them in saying grace, her father began ladling the cioppino into bowls. Hubbell picked up his spoon and tasted the cioppino, thick with clams and mussels, coiled shrimp and pieces of rock cod. He devoured that bowl and then another, mopping the bowl clean with a piece of bread torn from a still-warm loaf. As he leaned back in his chair and took a sip of the red wine they fermented in barrels in the basement, Maria's father rose and walked into the living room and sat down at the stand-up piano against the far wall, joined on the bench by her uncle carrying an acoustic guitar. Hubbell couldn't help but smile as they began playing an enthusiastic, if off-key, rendition of "Over the Rainbow," but when Maria's aunts began chasing the children into the living room to dance, he despaired at what he knew would come next.

"Please," he pleaded.

"You must," Maria said.

"I can't."

She laughed at him and took his hand.

"Of course you can," she said. "Everybody can dance."

"I can't dance. I can't sing. I can't even whistle."

But it was no use. She pulled him up to stand and led him into the living room. He had no choice. He gave it his best effort, but he had never felt so awkward or embarrassed in his life. His only consolation was that Maria's brothers were no better dancers than he was. At least he was not the only one making a fool of himself.

They danced in the living room until Maria's father and uncle ran out of songs to play. By that time, Hubbell had danced with every woman in Maria's family, from her mother and aunts to all seven of her nieces. Maria led him back down the stairs and stepped out onto the porch, closing the door behind her.

"Thank you for coming tonight," she said.

"Do you humiliate all your men this way?" Hubbell asked.

She threw her arms around his neck.

"I'm hoping you'll be the last," she said.

The following Sunday morning, Hubbell was waiting for her outside Sts. Peter and Paul as Mass ended and the parishioners descended the church steps. Maria's family was the last to emerge from the vestibule. At the top of the steps, Maria saw him and stopped, knowing exactly what he had come for, the only conceivable reason he would be wearing a tuxedo. Suddenly, one of her aunts spotted him, too. She gasped, her hand fluttering up to her mouth, and then the rest of the family, as well as Father Adonzio, were also looking down at him. Maria's father turned to her and placed his hands on the sides of her face, gently drawing her to him and kissing her lightly on the forehead. Maria turned to her mother and took both of her hands, squeezing them tightly before she turned to Hubbell and started down the steps.

Hubbell wanted to do it right. He wanted to respect her family. He wanted to respect her faith. He wanted to respect the institution of marriage. So he dropped to a knee and reached out and kissed the back of her hand. He looked up at her.

"I asked if you would consent to become my wife, and you said you would."

Hubbell could only smile.

"That was the finest day of my life," he said.

He looked up at the sky, as if he might see her face.

"We had eight glorious years before you were taken away from me. For eight years, I was the luckiest man on earth, the happiest man alive. I count my blessings, even now, even as I prepare to depart this mortal world."

HUBBELL DROVE back to the city. After parking the Mustang in the garage, he walked through the garden and let himself into his cottage. He changed out of his suit, putting on a pair of old khakis and a gray sweatshirt, then he returned to the kitchen and poured himself a glass of water. He liked to think that he had had a good visit with Maria. The visit was sad, certainly. The visits were always sad. But they were also restorative. He always left with a sense of serenity, his earthly concerns in proper perspective.

But as he took a sip of water, he wondered if he should have told Maria about his dinner with Ms. Gifford. It certainly wouldn't be the first time he had gone to dinner with a woman in the years since Maria died. His life had not been monastic, by any means. As Maria knew, he had submitted himself to an untold number of liaisons with other women over the years, most of them arranged by the wives of his colleagues in Section Eight, who seemed incapable of understanding that he was perfectly comfortable living alone. He turned down the overwhelming majority of their invitations, but he couldn't be so rude as to decline every offer they extended. The fact is, the more of their invitations he rejected, the greater they assumed his loneliness to be. So, periodically, he consented to meet their lonely friends, most of them only recently having become single, though never, the wives of his colleagues emphatically assured him, through any fault of their own. Hubbell did his best. He was always generous. He never failed to be polite and accommodating. He didn't want to embarrass anyone, least of all himself. But they were uniformly dreary affairs, and no one was ever foolish enough to believe otherwise. To Hubbell's great relief, his colleagues' wives eventually pronounced him a hopeless case and gave up.

He had no reason to believe that dinner with Ms. Gifford would be anything other than another dismal evening. Still, he couldn't help but feel that he should have told Maria about her invitation. It was not a deliberate omission. He certainly wasn't trying to conceal the dinner from Maria, if, in fact, it was possible to conceal anything from her. He would have made sure Maria understood that the dinner was not his idea. He would have made sure she knew that he was dreading it. He had accepted Ms. Gifford's invitation only because she was his tenant, her invitation solely to share the bounty of the garden. He was having dinner with Ms. Gifford strictly in the service of a good tenant-landlord relationship. It would be all business. Furthermore, he was not going to stay a moment longer than necessary. Already, he wished the dinner were over.

HUBBELL WOKE with a start. It was only as he sat up on the sofa that he realized that he had fallen asleep while listening to the Giants game on the radio. He pushed up to stand and walked into the kitchen. When he looked up at the clock above the door, he saw it was nearly six o'clock – time to begin getting ready for dinner with Ms. Gifford.

He walked down the hall to his bedroom and took off his clothes to take a shower, his hands and hair still smelling faintly of the cigar he had smoked at the cemetery. He knew Ms. Gifford to be a passionate advocate for the use of marijuana, but he didn't know what her position was with regard to tobacco products. It had been Hubbell's experience that some women found the smell of a cigar to be distasteful, offensive, even, while others found the smell uniquely masculine, perhaps even enticing. Hubbell didn't want to chance it, either way.

After showering, he stood in front of his open closet, trying to decide what to wear. The dinner with Ms. Gifford was hardly a formal affair, but he wanted the occasion to be as businesslike as possible, so he selected a pair of gray wool trousers and a blue long-sleeve shirt with a dark blue tie. After raising the knot to his collar, he withdrew a bulky blue-gray sweater from his bureau drawer and pulled it down over his head. Leaning into the mirror on his bureau, he combed his hair with his fingers, parting the thin gray strands above his right ear, then he slipped his feet into a pair of black loafers and returned to the kitchen.

When he glanced up at the clock, he saw that it was precisely seven o'clock. The time had come. He grabbed a bottle of Pinot Noir from the counter and made his way down the stairs and through the garden to Ms. Gifford's flat. The door was slightly ajar. He knocked on the doorframe.

"Graydon, is that you?" she called from down the hall.

"Good evening, Lydia."

"Come on in," she said. "I'll be right there."

He stepped into the jungle of her kitchen – huge ferns, arching palms, a tall, glossy rubber plant in red clay pots on the floor along the double-glass doors, spider plants and asparagus ferns in wicker baskets hanging from the ceiling, wandering jews and devil's ivy growing down the side of her refrigerator. As Hubbell stood beside the table, he had to admire Ms. Gifford's considerable botanical skills. He had little doubt that somewhere in the flat, if not in the garden, right before his very eyes, she was growing her marijuana. He didn't want to know about it.

A door closed down the hall, and a moment later, Ms. Gifford entered the kitchen wearing a pair of loose white cotton pants and a tie-dyed T-shirt, a design that Hubbell believed might very well serve as a schematic diagram of her inner mind, the chaotic patterns and riot of color clearly illustrating the long-term consequences of the indiscriminate use of high-potency recreational drugs.

"I took the liberty of bringing a bottle of wine," he said.

"Why thank you, Graydon. Shall I open it?"

"By all means," he said.

He sat at the table while Ms. Gifford opened one of the counter drawers and withdrew a corkscrew. He watched as she peeled the foil off the top of the bottle.

"You certainly have a green thumb," he said. "You have your own indoor rainforest here."

But Ms. Gifford had focused her attention on the bottle of wine, clutching it between her thighs and, after no little effort, wrestling out the cork, most of it, anyway.

"Damn," she said.

She held up the corkscrew and studied the broken cork, relying solely on her good eye, of course, her right eye apparently feeling no obligation whatsoever to participate in the inspection.

"Why do I always get the bad corks?" she asked.

"A fair question," Hubbell said.

"But it's still drinkable," she said. "It's still vino."

Yes, Hubbell thought, it's still – vino.

She stabbed a butter knife into the neck of the bottle, forcing what remained of the cork down into the wine.

"Voilà," she said.

She took two wine glasses down from the cabinet above the counter, then carried them over to the table and filled them with wine, a few stray crumbs of cork floating on the surface.

"A toast," she said, lifting her glass.

Hubbell raised his glass, too.

"To us," she said, clinking her glass against his, so hard he feared the stem might snap off in his hand.

"Yes, to us," he said.

He took a sip of the wine, straining it through his teeth, then he picked the stray pieces of cork from the tip of his tongue. The cork fragments didn't appear to bother Ms. Gifford. Of course, it was entirely possible, Hubbell told himself, that all the vino Ms. Gifford drank contained flotsam of some kind.

"This is very nice," she said.

"I'm sure it will pair well with the pasta," he said.

Her shoulders sank.

"Oh, Graydon. I'm so sorry, but I couldn't find any of the sauce I made last year. I thought I had a couple quarts left, but I must have used them all."

For a fleeting moment, hope rose in Hubbell's chest. He wondered if that might be a serviceable reason to get out of dinner. But just as quickly he realized it was far too late for that.

"So I'm making you my specialty," she said.

"And what might that be?" Hubbell asked.

"Stir-fried vegetables over brown rice," she said. "It's delicious, especially with soy sauce. You see, Graydon, I'm a vegetarian."

"I didn't know that," he said.

"At least I'm pretty much a vegetarian. I'm not a perfect vegetarian. I eat only fruits and vegetables and grains, though I do have a weakness for country ham. I mean what's wrong with a slice of country ham every once in a while? It's not like it's poisonous."

"Of course not," Hubbell said.

"I mean, how many people ever died from eating a slice of country ham?"

"You make a good point," he said.

She smiled and took another swallow of wine.

"But not tonight," she said. "Tonight, I'm making you my specialty."

HUBBELL SIPPED his wine while Ms. Gifford worked over the stove, the lid on the pot of brown rice burping steam, the oil in the wok hissing and spitting as she stirred the snow peas, sliced carrots and chopped peppers, the florets of broccoli and cauliflower. With a dishtowel wrapped around her left hand, she lifted the lid of the pot and stirred the rice with a wooden spoon, then she turned back to the vegetables sizzling in the wok. She certainly seemed to know what she was doing, and as Hubbell relaxed and leaned back in his chair, he couldn't remember the last time a woman had cooked dinner for him. It was not entirely unpleasant.

"It smells wonderful," he said.

Ms. Gifford turned to him.

"Why thank you, Graydon."

It was then, however, that Hubbell noticed the corner of the dishtowel had caught fire. Fortunately, Ms. Gifford noticed it, too.

"Oh my," she said.

She waved the dishtowel in front of her as if signaling distress. When that served only to fan the flames, leaping up at her wrist, she spun around and flung the towel into the sink, then lunged for the faucet and turned on the water, successfully dousing the flames. It was then, however, that she noticed that the vegetables in the wok had begun to burn. She reached down and turned off the burner and began furiously scooping the vegetables into a large glass bowl, the wooden spoon clanging on the wok as the oil crackled, the smoke in the kitchen so thick it stung Hubbell's eyes. As he took another sip of wine, he made a mental note to check his fire insurance.

With the vegetables in the bowl, Ms. Gifford turned to Hubbell and shrugged her shoulders, offering him a loopy smile.

"Well, I think we're ready to eat," she said.

But then the smoke alarm went off, a shrill, ear-piercing siren so loud that Hubbell's teeth hurt. He stood up and dragged his chair down the hall and positioned it beneath the alarm mounted high on the wall. Gripping the back of the chair, he raised his right foot and placed it on the seat, then he stepped up onto the chair. With both feet on the seat, he slowly straightened up, his hands walking up the wall until he could just reach the alarm. Rising up onto his toes, he released the alarm from the plate screwed into the plaster, then he tugged apart the electrical harness, instantly shutting off the alarm.

"Bravo, Graydon! Bravo!"

With the alarm in his left hand, he slowly leaned down to grab the back of the chair. He had nearly reached the chair when he sensed his weight shifting to the right, when he realized that, in fact, he was losing his balance. He dropped the alarm and grabbed the back of the chair – but too late. All he could do was let go and leap down. He did so successfully, at least to the extent that he managed to plant both feet on the hardwood floor. Still, he couldn't check his momentum, couldn't prevent himself from plunging forward, onto his hands and knees, ramming his forehead into the hard plaster wall, just above the baseboard.

"Graydon!" Ms. Gifford screamed.

"Urmph," he said.

For a moment, Hubbell saw only flashes of light, but he managed to blink them away. He could feel Ms. Gifford kneeling beside him, her arm across his back.

"Graydon, are you all right?"

Slowly, he sat back on his heels, reaching up to his right temple, gingerly probing the point of impact.

"Yes, I think so," he said.

"Let's get you into the kitchen," she said.

She helped him rise to his feet and led him back down the hall into the kitchen, still filled with drifting smoke. She pulled out a chair, and he sat down heavily.

"You just sit right here," she said.

She disappeared down the hall and then returned with a moist washcloth and began cleaning off the pieces of plaster imbedded in the abrasion on his forehead.

"There," she said, placing a bandage over the abrasion and tapping it with the tip of her finger. "As good as new."

"Thank you, Lydia."

She glanced around the kitchen, waving away the haze of smoke, then she turned back to Hubbell.

"Why don't we eat out on the patio?" she said.

Hubbell shrugged. It made no difference to him.

"Whatever you say," he said.

HUBBELL ROSE from the chair, picked up his glass and the bottle of wine and stepped unsteadily out the door. He crossed the brick patio and sat down in one of the canvas chairs arranged around the wooden table. Through the double-glass doors in the back of her flat, he watched as Ms. Gifford prepared their dinner, flopping mounds of brown rice onto plates and then burying the rice beneath an avalanche of vegetables. As she carried the plates out to the patio and placed them on the table, Hubbell observed that presentation was not a central concern in the preparation of her signature dish.

"This looks swell," he said.

"Thank you, Graydon. Be sure to use some of the soy sauce. That's the secret ingredient."

He reached for the bottle and sprinkled a few drops onto his vegetables, noticing, as he picked up his fork, that many of the vegetables appeared to have been scorched in the near catastrophe in the kitchen. He speared a piece of carrot and raised it to his mouth, his teeth crunching through the charred crust.

Ms. Gifford watched him closely, as closely as she could, anyway, given her right eye's fleeting attention span.

"Well?"

He swallowed hard, as quickly as he could, the taste of ash, unfortunately, lingering on his tongue.

"It's delicious," he said.

She smiled, her mouth, as always, slanting down to the right.

"I'm so glad you like it," she said.

Hubbell reached for his glass of wine. As he took a sip, he watched

Ms. Gifford pour a river of soy sauce onto the rice and vegetables heaped onto her plate and realized that the role of Ms. Gifford's secret ingredient was not to enhance the taste of the rice and the vegetables so much as to drown it. When she set the bottle down, he reached for it and splashed at least as much of the soy sauce onto his own plate, then he picked up his fork and scooped up some rice and a floret of broccoli, and, yes, that did taste better, helping him overcome his initial fear that he couldn't take another bite.

"You looked quite handsome today in your three-piece suit," Ms. Gifford said.

"That's very kind of you to say," Hubbell said.

"You looked like you were going to a funeral."

"I was going to the cemetery, actually."

"To visit your wife?"

"Yes, that's right."

Ms. Gifford stabbed several of the snap peas with her fork, dragged them through the pool of soy sauce, then raised them to her mouth and took them in her teeth. She chewed thoughtfully.

"Do you visit your wife's grave often?"

"I try to visit her on a regular basis."

"You must have loved her very much."

"Yes, I did."

"I was married once myself," Ms. Gifford said.

"I didn't know that."

"Oh, yes," she said. "Morgan and I were married in Golden Gate Park on July 11, 1969. We had a Native American ceremony with log drums and reed whistles and carved flutes. I wore a lovely suede wedding dress with seagull feathers pinned in my hair. It was very spiritual, and I do mean very."

"Your husband was an Indian?" Hubbell asked.

"Oh, no. Morgan was Jewish."

"Oh," Hubbell said, as if he understood.

"Morgan was a poet," she said. "Morgan Willis. Perhaps you've heard of him?"

"I'm sorry, but no, I'm afraid I haven't," Hubbell said.

"City Lights published a chapbook of his poetry."

"I really should read more poetry," Hubbell conceded.

"That's where I met Morgan. I met him at a reading at City Lights. He was reading with Allen Ginsberg."

"I'm familiar with Mr. Ginsberg, of course."

"I fell in love with Morgan right there," she said. "It was love at first sight, so to speak. Of course it didn't last."

"I'm sorry to hear that."

"Nothing lasts forever, right?"

"No, I'm afraid not."

"Especially with poets," she said. "They're very sensitive – highly sensitive, you might say."

"I'm afraid I haven't known many poets in my day."

"And so is my daughter," Ms. Gifford said. "I mean highly, highly sensitive, sensitive to a fault."

"I didn't know you have a daughter," Hubbell said.

"Her name is Sonne," she said, spelling it out for him, letter by letter. "She married a dentist named Barney. I mean, can you imagine – Barney, the dentist?"

"I'm trying to," Hubbell said.

"They live in Pleasanton, of all places – the heart of suburbia. They have a huge, five-bedroom, four-bath house with a pool in the back. The place gives me the creeps, if you want to know the truth. I can't even go there. I haven't been there in years."

"It's a long drive," Hubbell said. "A good hour, I would guess."

"And you know I don't own a car anymore."

"Yes, of course," he said, recalling the afternoon several years ago when the repossession team sent by the bank took it back.

He took another sip of wine, noticing the look of disappointment that had abruptly come over Ms. Gifford.

"You didn't eat very much," she said.

Hubbell looked down at his plate. He had eaten as much as he could, which, unfortunately, was not a lot. When he looked across the table, he saw that Ms. Gifford's plate was empty but for a trace of the soy sauce. He was surprised she hadn't picked up the plate and licked it clean.

"It was absolutely delicious," he said. "But I'm afraid I had a late lunch, after I returned from the cemetery."

She didn't seem to have heard him, turning her attention back to his forehead, as if his collision with the wall might have caused a loss of appetite.

"Graydon, are you sure you're all right?"

He reached up and touched the bandage.

"Oh, yes," he said. "I'll be fine. A little bump on the head is the least of my concerns."

"The least of your concerns?"

"It's no big deal," he said. "I'm feeling fine, honestly."

"What other concerns, Graydon?"

Hubbell looked at her. He didn't know what to say, other than to simply tell her the truth. It was nothing to be ashamed of, nothing to hide. She would find out soon enough, anyway.

"I'm afraid I've been diagnosed with cancer," he said.

Ms. Gifford stared at him.

"Cancer?"

"Yes, I'm afraid so."

"May I ask what kind of cancer?"

"A form of leukemia," he said.

She took that in, thinking, apparently.

"And your doctor told you this?" she asked.

"My oncologist, yes."

"What else did your oncologist tell you?" Ms. Gifford asked.

"She said it's rather highly advanced. She said there's really not much they can do in terms of fighting it."

"There's not much they can do?"

"Apparently not."

"So that's that? That's all she wrote?"

"Yes, I suppose so."

Ms. Gifford shook her head and sat back in her chair.

"You see, Graydon, this is why I have so little faith in Western medicine."

"I'm not sure I follow you," he said.

"Frankly, I have no faith in Western medicine at all."

"I have no reason to believe my oncologist is wrong," Hubbell said. "She comes very highly recommended."

"I'm sure she does."

"She was recommended by my primary care physician."

Ms. Gifford shook her head.

"Honestly, Graydon, I never knew you to be such an apologist."

"What am I apologizing for?"

"Did it ever occur to you that Western medicine might not have all the answers? Did it ever occur to you that your oncologist, as highly recommended as she might be, might not know everything?"

Hubbell shrugged.

"I suppose I could get a second opinion," he said.

"Oh, Graydon, I'm not talking about a second opinion. I'm talking about a completely different approach. I'm talking about herbal medicine. I'm talking about herbal remedies the Chinese having been using for thousands of years."

"Herbal remedies for cancer?"

"Graydon, I'd like to discuss your case with my herbalist."

"There's really no need," Hubbell said.

"No need? You'd rather just give up and die – just to defend your oncologist's reputation?"

"That's not what I'm saying," he said.

"Then it's settled," she said. "I'll talk to my herbalist the first thing next week."

She smiled at him, her cheeks dimpled, as pink and chubby as a schoolgirl's. He couldn't fight her.

"Well, if it isn't too much trouble," he said. "I mean, why not?"

"You're going to be fine," Ms. Gifford said. "I'm sure of it, Graydon. I can feel it. Trust me."

CHAPTER FIVE

AS HUBBELL SAT on the examination table, idly gazing at the illustrated posters of the human anatomy tacked to the wall, he knew the first thing Dr. Martin would ask about was the bandage on his forehead. But Hubbell had no intention of recounting the patently absurd and highly embarrassing sequence of events that culminated with him ramming his head into the wall in Ms. Gifford's hallway. He had no intention of telling anyone that Ms. Gifford had invited him to dinner, or that he, against his better judgment, had spent the better part of an evening in her flat. He certainly didn't want anyone to know that he had confided to her that he had just been diagnosed with a form of blood cancer, and that he had tacitly consented to let her discuss his case with her Chinese herbalist. Dying was one thing. Getting laughed at was another.

In his white lab coat, Dr. Martin knocked twice, then opened the door and crossed the examination room to shake Hubbell's hand.

"Good morning, Graydon."

"Good morning," Hubbell said.

Dr. Martin sat on the stool at the foot of the examination table, placing Hubbell's medical chart in his lap and, just as Hubbell had anticipated, observed the bandage on his forehead.

"You appear to have injured yourself," he said.

"It's nothing," Hubbell said.

"Would you like me to take a look at it?"

"I don't believe that will be necessary."

"Would you like to tell me what happened?"

"As a matter of fact, no."

"I have to be honest with you, Graydon – I don't like it when my patients show up with head wounds."

"I understand your concern," Hubbell said. "But I can assure you that I'll be perfectly fine."

Dr. Martin permitted himself a smile, realizing there was little to be gained by pressing the issue further.

"So how do you feel, otherwise?" he asked.

"I feel fine, all things considered," Hubbell said.

"How was your appointment with Dr. Ishihara?"

"She gave me the bad news."

"By that I assume you mean she laid out your options?"

"Such as they are."

Dr. Martin nodded sympathetically.

"When I spoke with Dr. Ishihara, I asked specifically if you might be a candidate for a bone marrow transplant or any experimental drugs or new protocols currently being studied in clinical trials. Unfortunately, she wasn't aware of anything that might be appropriate."

"At this point, all I want to know is how much time I have left," Hubbell said.

"I don't know, Graydon – not as much time as any of us would like. That's all I can say with any degree of certainty."

"All I'm asking for is an educated guess."

Dr. Martin folded his hands on top of Hubbell's medical chart.

"A month, couple months – maybe more, maybe less."

Hubbell didn't blink.

"Believe me, I hope I'm wrong," Dr. Martin said. "I hope Dr. Ishihara is wrong. Obviously, I hope you have a lot longer than that."

"So how is this going to play out?" Hubbell asked him.

"Well, very likely you'll soon begin experiencing fatigue, perhaps even severe fatigue. It will be extremely important for you to make sure you get your proper rest and maintain a healthy diet – and to make sure you don't overly exert yourself."

"All right," Hubbell said.

"And I would expect that as the disease progresses, as the abnormal white blood cells begin to accumulate, you'll experience some swelling and tenderness in your liver and spleen and lymph glands. That's something we'll want to monitor very carefully."

"All right."

"But our most serious concern is going to be infection," Dr. Martin said. "The abundance of abnormal white blood cells compromises the body's immune system, the body's ability to defend itself against infection."

"All right," Hubbell said, once again, as if there was nothing else to say.

A leaden silence fell between them as they fully realized what lay ahead.

"Graydon, have you considered participating in a support group?"

"Of course not," Hubbell said.

"You're not alone, Graydon. Many other people are going through the same ordeal, making the same difficult choices."

"And I wish them all the best."

"You might benefit from their shared experiences."

"I doubt it," Hubbell said.

"You might surprise yourself."

"I doubt it."

Dr. Martin shook his head.

"All right, Graydon – suit yourself."

"I'm planning on working at the paper as long as I can," Hubbell informed him.

"That wouldn't be my recommendation, but I suppose that's all right, at least for now – just so long as you don't let it wear you down," Dr. Martin said.

"I won't."

"But you realize that there will come a point at which you won't be able to work any longer," Dr. Martin said.

"I understand," Hubbell said.

"The day you leave the Chronicle will very likely be difficult for you."

"I understand."

"I just don't want that day to be any harder than it has to be."

"I understand."

AFTER HANGING UP HIS COAT and placing his hat on his computer, Hubbell walked back through the newsroom, then leaned in through the door to Harold's office. Harold was seated at his desk, preparing for the daily story meeting, convened every morning in the main conference room, the meeting at which he and the paper's department heads discuss an initial lineup of stories for the next morning's front page, surrounded by a chorus of vacuous blowhards from around the newsroom, who sit in on the meeting solely to hear the sounds of their own voices, no matter how inane or sophomoric their observations and suggestions.

"Do you have a minute?"

Harold looked up.

"Sure, come on in," he said.

Hubbell stepped into his office, then closed the door behind him.

"May I take you into my confidence?" he asked.

"If you absolutely must."

He walked over and sat in one of the black leather chairs positioned in front of Harold's desk.

"It seems I have cancer," Hubbell said. "It seems I have a form of blood cancer."

"Jesus," Harold said. "When did you learn this?"

"Just the other day."

"How serious is it?"

"The disease progresses through three phases," Hubbell told him. "According to my oncologist, I'm in the third phase."

"That can't be good."

"It's not."

"So when will you begin treatment?" Harold asked.

"There won't be any treatment," Hubbell said. "The only option is high-dose chemotherapy, but my oncologist isn't convinced it would make any significant difference in terms of my prognosis."

"No treatment at all?"

"No."

Harold sat back in his chair, his thick gray hair combed back, his eyebrows converging above the bridge of his nose.

"So what does all this mean?" he asked.

"It means I'm dying, Hal. It's as simple as that."

Harold could only stare at him, as if he still couldn't believe what Hubbell was telling him.

"My plan is to keep on working as long as I can," Hubbell said.

"Are you out of your mind?"

"What else would I do?"

"Anything," Harold said. "Whatever you want. You could travel. You could go anywhere."

"Like where?"

"Like Paris," Harold said. "It's April. It's spring. Paris is beautiful in the spring. This is the perfect time to go."

"I have no intention of spending the days that remain to me in a country full of giggling Frenchmen," Hubbell said. " I may be dying, but I haven't lost my mind."

Harold suppressed a smile.

"I wasn't aware of your antipathy toward the French."

"They're as bad as the fucking Russians," Hubbell said.

Harold leaned forward, his forearms on his desk.

"So what can I do?"

"I need you to keep this to yourself," Hubbell said. "I don't want anyone else to know about this."

"All right, Graydon. I can do that. I'll do what I can to protect your privacy. But I think you're crazy."

"I appreciate that."

"Do you need anything else from me?"

"You could send Myron back to the copy desk."

"It's good to see you've managed to retain your sense of humor," Harold said.

"I'm serious," Hubbell said.

"So am I."

HUBBELL RETURNED to his desk. As he flipped through his mail, finding nothing of even conceivable interest, he noticed a young woman walking back to Section Eight. In blue jeans and a green turtleneck sweater, her red hair pulled back into a short ponytail, she looked vaguely familiar. Although he had no idea where he might have seen her before, he realized that it was entirely possible, given her presence in the newsroom and the absence of a visitor's badge, that she was one of his colleagues.

She seemed, in fact, to be walking directly back to him.

"Hello, Mr. Hubbell."

"Hello."

"Am I disturbing you?"

"Not yet," he said pleasantly.

She smiled, her eyes large and green, her cheeks dusted with freckles.

"I was wondering if you read my story this morning."

"What story was that?"

"My story about the double-homicide in the Tenderloin," she said. "It ran on the front of the Bay Area section."

"I'm afraid I must have missed it," he said.

"Maybe you saw my byline – Naomi Mitchell."

Hubbell shook his head.

"No, I'm sorry."

She shrugged and shoved her hands into her back pockets.

"I've been working the night shift," she said. "The shooting happened late last night. I barely made the late edition."

"Is that so."

"Do you remember Lt. Lawrence Wallace?" she asked.

"Larry Wallace?"

"Lt. Wallace was the watch commander down at the Hall of Justice last night."

"Cockroach Larry made lieutenant?"

"He told me to pass along his regards."

"I figured he would have been busted down to meter maid by now."

"He told me that you used to work out of the hall. He said you were a pretty fair reporter back then."

Hubbell wasn't sure where the conversation was heading, but he didn't necessarily want to argue.

"I'd like to think my career hasn't been a total waste," he said.

"He also said you were a real son of a bitch."

Hubbell didn't deny it.

"Cockroach Larry may be right about that, too," he said.

She reached up and tucked a loose strand of hair behind her ear.

"I had the library pull some of your old stories," she said.

"And why would you do that?"

"I loved the series you wrote about the department's field training officers. I loved how you exposed them all as a bunch of thugs."

Hubbell leaned back in his chair. It was gratifying to know his work met with the approval of at least one of his younger colleagues.

"I'm glad you enjoyed it," he said.

"That must have taken months of reporting," she said.

"As a matter of fact, it did," Hubbell said.

"I'd like to get a chance to sink my teeth into a story like that someday."

"Perhaps you should express this desire to your editor, rather than to me," Hubbell said.

"My editor is a douche bag."

"I see."

"It's too bad that all you do is write obituaries anymore. Otherwise, we could maybe team up on something big."

"Yes, that's a shame, isn't it?"

"I mean, how do you stand it – writing about dead people every day?"

"As a rule, I write about what they did while they were alive."

"Still."

Hubbell smiled politely.

"Is there anything, specifically, that I can do for you this morning, Ms. Mitchell?"

She shook her head.

"No," she said. "I just wanted to pass along Lt. Wallace's regards."

"And I thank you for that," Hubbell said.

"Is there anything you'd like me to tell the lieutenant when I go back down to the hall tonight?"

"Just tell Cockroach Larry that I'm looking forward to writing his obituary," Hubbell said.

Ms. Mitchell smiled. She liked that.

"I will," she said. "I'll tell him."

HUBBELL REMEMBERED his series about the department's field training officers well, of course. He liked to think his stories about those officers responsible for training rookie cops how to deal with the public represented some of his finest work, and he couldn't help but appreciate the fact that Ms. Mitchell had asked the library to retrieve them from the archives for her. If nothing else, Ms. Mitchell possessed a degree of initiative uncommon among the reporters of her generation.

He had developed the series after learning that one of the field training officers, a lieutenant by the name of Morris Buford, had been arrested for punching his ex-girlfriend in the face and then stealing her car, crashing it, ultimately, into one of the koi ponds at the Japanese Tea Garden in Golden Gate Park. The incident prompted Hubbell to wonder if any of Buford's fellow officers might have been involved in any similar off-duty misadventures, so he spent several months carefully checking the names of each of the field training officers against state and federal court records, as well as internal department disciplinary proceedings.

The results of his reporting might very well have shocked a young, less experienced reporter like, say, Ms. Mitchell, but Hubbell was hardly surprised to learn nearly half the department's field training officers had been charged with, and in many cases convicted of, engaging in a litany of criminal activities ranging from aggravated assault to possession of stolen property. His personal favorites included one officer, a lieutenant by the name of Aloysius Buckley, who was arrested after going berserk following a minor traffic accident on Broadway, drawing his service revolver and pistol-whipping the 63-year-old piano teacher who had rear-ended him, then shooting out every window in the old man's car. Another officer, Detective Marty Hogue, had been taken into custody following a dispute with a prostitute over the price of a sex act she had performed on him in one of the changing booths at Neiman Marcus, slapping the poor hooker senseless in front of the lipstick counter. And then there was Sergeant Felix Woolsey, who was jailed after coming unglued at a pub in the Sunset District, so enraged when the bartender refused to pour him one last shot after closing time that he picked up a jar of pickled eggs and broke it over the bartender's head, fracturing his skull and causing serious facial lacerations.

Needless to say, Hubbell's exhaustive, and, yes, colorful recounting of the off-duty escapades of the department's field training officers made for good reading, although not necessarily at the Hall of Justice, where the chief called a hasty press conference to dismiss the incidents reported in Hubbell's series as nothing more than the "harmless hijinks of a few officers blowing off a little steam" and to take umbrage with the implication that his officers were anything less than men and women of the highest moral timber. The chief was wise enough, however, to announce that he would form a blue-ribbon committee to conduct a thorough review of the issues raised in Hubbell's series and would initiate reforms where appropriate. Of course, the committee never actually troubled to meet, much less conduct a review of any kind, but that is not to suggest that Hubbell's series was written in vain. Hubbell's reporting won him the enduring enmity of virtually every officer on the force, and in the context of his assignment, he could think of no higher accolade.

As Hubbell reached down and turned on his computer, he realized that nearly twenty years had passed since he had written that series. It was hard to believe that it had been that long, but that was the truth. He was proud of the investigative stories he had written while covering the police department and district attorney's office, exposing the corruption, cronyism and sheer incompetence endemic at the Hall of Justice, but the days of those bold headlines, stripped across the front page, had long since passed. As Ms. Mitchell was in the process of learning, the Chronicle rarely engaged in investigative journalism anymore, and with another wave of buyouts and layoffs coming, it was increasingly unlikely that the paper would support much of that kind of enterprise reporting in the future.

As his computer crackled to life, his telephone rang. He picked up the receiver.

"This is Graydon Hubbell at the San Francisco Chronicle. How may I help you?"

"Hello, Mr. Hubbell. This is Katrina Reisner. I was hoping to get a moment of your time."

"Certainly, Katrina. What can I do for you?"

"I was hoping you might have a moment to come over to my office."

"I'd be glad to," he said.

"Are you available now?"

"I'm on the way," Hubbell said.

AS HE ROSE from his desk, Hubbell knew exactly what Ms. Reisner wanted to talk about. Ms. Reisner had worked as the newsroom's financial manager for as long as Hubbell could remember, and, for the record, he had nothing against her personally. He understood that Ms. Reisner had a job to do. He understood that her job was to monitor newsroom expenses. But over the course of the past several years, the paper's dire financial condition had emboldened Ms. Reisner and her servile minions to question, if not challenge, virtually every request for reimbursement submitted by the newsroom, which, in turn, served only to stiffen the resolve of every reporter to demand reimbursement for every expense incurred while covering a story, no matter how niggling or far-fetched – a campaign championed, much to Ms. Reisner's dismay, by Hubbell and his colleagues in Section Eight.

She occupied a small office on the far side of the old Business and Sports departments, now a vast expanse of empty desks, vacated over the past few years as the staff of the newsroom contracted through a series of mass layoffs, buyouts and resignations. He knocked once, then reached down and opened her office door. She was sitting at her desk, a heavyset woman with a thick neck and an uncommonly large head, her broad shoulders filling out her blue-black flannel shirt, the sleeves rolled up to reveal her meaty forearms. She looked up as Hubbell stood in the doorway, her blond hair cropped short, a dark gap between her two front teeth, a scar in the form of a crescent adorning her blunt chin.

"Hello, Katrina," he said.

"Have a seat," she told him.

As Hubbell sat in one of the hard wooden chairs in front of Ms. Reisner's desk, he offered her a pleasant but thoroughly professional smile. She didn't return it. Instead, she looked down at the yellow legal pad on the desk in front of her, covered with her handwritten notes.

"Mr. Hubbell, did you check out one of the city desk cars last week?"

"Yes, I did," Hubbell said.

"According to the logbook, you checked out one of the cars last Friday morning."

"That is correct," Hubbell said.

"And you returned it that afternoon?"

"That is also correct."

She looked up at him.

"Did you return the car to one of the spaces reserved for the city desk cars?"

Hubbell smiled.

"I thought that might be where this is going."

"Is that a yes or a no?"

And that really was Ms. Reisner – all business, all the time. He admired that about Ms. Reisner. She never lost her focus.

"No, I did not," he conceded.

"And may I ask why not?"

"Yes, you may."

She waited. He let her wait. Ms. Reisner could ask whatever she wanted to ask, and he was more than willing to answer her truthfully, as truthfully as he could, anyway, so long as he didn't have to incriminate himself, either by admission or implication. He felt no obligation to abandon his constitutional rights, nor, for that matter, did he feel any obligation to assist Ms. Reisner in the formation, much less the direction, of her questions.

"So, please tell me why you didn't return the car to the parking space in which you found it?"

"The space was too tight," Hubbell said. "I didn't think the car would fit."

And that was true, or at least partly true. It was certainly sufficiently true for the purpose of the conversation.

"So where did you park the car?" she asked.

"I parked it down the aisle on the left, near the back of the lot," Hubbell said.

"In Mr. Woodbury's space?"

"Mr. Woodbury?"

"Robert Woodbury," Ms. Reisner said. "Mr. Woodbury is a senior account executive in the advertising department."

"I'm afraid I don't know Mr. Woodbury."

"He was not pleased when he returned from a sales call on Friday afternoon and found the car in his parking space," Ms. Reisner said. "He was quite upset, actually. He called to have the car towed away."

"I had no idea our advertising executives were that excitable," Hubbell said. "Perhaps Mr. Woodbury would be wise to avail himself to some professional counseling. A session or two about anger management might be appropriate."

"Fortunately, one of our security guards saw the Press placard on the dashboard and sent the tow truck back."

"Yes, that was fortunate, wasn't it?"

"Did you notice anything unusual about the car when you checked it out?" she asked.

"Unusual?"

"Damage," she said.

"No."

"Did you notice any damage to the car when you returned it?"

"No, I did not."

"So you didn't see that the right side of the car had been badly damaged?"

"No, I did not," Hubbell said.

And that was true, literally, though, of course, it was not inconceivable that the side of the car might have been damaged slightly when he pulled up onto the sidewalk to let the delivery truck pass and scraped the chain-link fence behind the loading dock. But Hubbell had seen no evidence to confirm that, and he was disinclined to engage in baseless speculation, particularly the kind of speculation that might suggest that he was in any way responsible for the damage that Ms. Reisner was referring to.

"You were, however, according to the logbook, the last one to drive the car," she said.

"That's entirely possible," Hubbell said. "It's also possible that someone else used the car after I did and failed to record it in the logbook."

Ms. Reisner didn't argue with him. She knew he was right. She knew that was possible. And when she leaned back in her chair and clasped her hands over the thick folds of her stomach, Hubbell knew the conversation was effectively over.

"Will there be anything else?" he asked.

"No, that's it," she said.

AFTER STOPPING in the alcove off the mailroom for a cup of coffee, Hubbell walked back to Section Eight. The Senator looked up, raking his long black hair back with his fingers as Hubbell stood in front of his desk.

"I just had a meeting with Katrina Reisner," Hubbell told him.

"What's her problem?" the Senator asked.

"She's upset because I parked one of the city desk cars in a space reserved for one of the account executives in the advertising department named Robert Woodbury."

"Never heard of him," the Senator said.

"Apparently he pitched a fit," Hubbell said.

"So who cares?" the Senator asked.

"She may also try to blame me for some damage to the right side of the car," Hubbell said. "I may need the representation of the guild, if she decides to press the matter further."

"And the representation of the guild, you shall have," the Senator said. "I shall see to it personally."

The Senator glanced behind Hubbell, then turned back to his colleagues, discreetly taking them into his confidence.

"Are you gentlemen aware that Katrina Reisner is a lesbian?"

"A lesbian – as in having a peculiar fondness for women?" Poopdeck asked.

"That's exactly right," the Senator said.

"Where did you hear that?"

"Gentlemen, please, I cannot and I shall not divulge my sources," the Senator said. "Let me just say that in my capacity as an officer of the guild, I hear a great many things that are not necessarily for public consumption."

Hubbell wanted to laugh. The truth is, no one more fully appreciated the power and beauty of the wholly unsubstantiated rumor than the Senator. In a newsroom rife with ancient grudges, enduring prejudices and petty resentments, lascivious gossip was the coin of the realm.

"I believe my ex-wife was a lesbian, a closet lesbian – that's my theory, anyhow," Poopdeck said.

"Which ex-wife was that?" the Senator asked.

It was a good question. Poopdeck had to think. He had been

married three times, each culminating in a bitter divorce, the last of them leaving him with nothing but a dilapidated houseboat listing hard to starboard along the muddy banks of Mission Creek.

"All of them, come to think of it," he said.

"Lesbians do tend to hate men," the Senator said.

"Game, set, match," Hubbell said.

"What I'd like to know is how Ms. Reisner got that scar on her chin," the Senator said.

"A dog bite?" Hubbell wondered.

"That would have been one brave fucking dog," Poopdeck said.

"It looks more like a knife wound to me," the Senator said. "I wouldn't be surprised if she got it in a bar fight. I hear those dyke bars can get pretty rough, especially around closing time."

"I wouldn't want to tell Ms. Reisner she was done for the night," Poopdeck said.

"Nor would I," the Senator said. "But let me assure you, gentlemen, that if Ms. Reisner thinks she can shake down one of our guild brothers in some kind of tawdry extortion scheme, she is sadly mistaken. As your guild steward, let me assure you that, if necessary, I will open up an industrial-size can of Whup-Ass, and Ms. Reisner will surely rue the day she decided to tangle with Section Eight."

HUBBELL SPENT the rest of the day working up an obituary for a former minor league baseball player named Alfredo Viviano, a native of North Beach who had grown up with the DiMaggio brothers and played for nearly a decade with the San Francisco Seals. After he retired, Viviano opened a family-style Italian restaurant on Stockton Street, known across the city for its generous portions and inexpensive prices. He tended the adjoining bar virtually every night, its walls covered with memorabilia accumulated over the course of his career – framed black-and-white photographs of the old Pacific Coast League ballparks, autographed portraits of the Seals teams Viviano played on, yellowed newspaper clippings recalling Viviano's best days on the diamond. Hubbell knew Viviano to be a good man, who loved nothing more than a hearty laugh and a well-told story, a man whose character was shaped by the city, and a man, who, in turn, shaped the character of the city. He was genuinely sorry that Viviano had passed away.

It took longer than Hubbell thought to finish the obituary for Viviano, primarily because he had trouble tracking down any of his former teammates, most of them, unfortunately, having beaten Viviano to the grave. But Hubbell didn't mind working late, not on Viviano's behalf. He wanted Viviano to get his due recognition, and if that meant putting in a couple hours of overtime, that was fine with Hubbell, and the fact that he was also able to frustrate the whimpering Myron, who repeatedly walked back to Section Eight to implore him to finish the obituary as quickly as possible, was easily as rewarding to Hubbell as the modest increase he could expect to see on his next paycheck, provided, of course, that he was still alive.

He took the bus back to North Beach and walked up the hill to his cottage. After taking a quick shower, he returned to the kitchen and poured himself a glass of wine, then he opened the refrigerator and drew back the small aluminum door of the freezer compartment, wondering which of the three frozen delicacies wedged into the hoary white frost he desired tonight.

But then he heard someone climbing the stairs. He knew immediately that it was Ms. Gifford, that it couldn't be anyone else, so he closed the refrigerator and crossed the kitchen to open the door for her.

"Good evening, Graydon."

She was carrying a large brown paper bag. When she reached the landing at the top of the stairs, he stepped aside to let her enter the kitchen. She set the bag on the table and sat down heavily.

"Good evening, Lydia. May I offer you a glass of wine?"

She smiled brightly, her plump cheeks filling with color, her hair fashioned into a pair of gray-white pigtails sprouting from either side of her head, her right eye veering off across the kitchen.

"I'd love a glass of vino," she said.

"And may I ask what you have in the bag?"

"I went to see my herbalist today, just like I promised you. I can be very responsible, when I want to be."

"I'm sure that's true," he said.

"His name is Doon Wah Lee. At first, I thought his name was Doom, but his name is Doon – not Doom."

"Yes, that's much better," Hubbell said. "I would have had concerns about a Chinese herbalist named Doom."

"Oh, he's a Chinaman, all right. He's very old. I mean, very, very old, with a long gray beard. He's very small, but I'm sure he knows Kung Fu, though I've never asked him, not specifically."

"That's probably not necessary," Hubbell said.

"I told him about your prognosis or your diagnosis, whichever, and he knew exactly what you need."

Hubbell handed her a glass of wine.

"And what, pray tell, did he recommend?"

"A tea – an herbal tea."

"I don't really care for tea," Graydon said. "I'm more of a coffee drinker, actually."

But she paid him no mind as she began unloading the bag, lifting out clear plastic baggies containing various dried herbs.

"This is stinging nettle," she said, placing the baggie on the table.

"Stinging nettle?"

"And this is brooklime, and these are elder blossoms."

Hubbell could only watch as she emptied the bag, adding baggies filled with St. John's wort, sweet Woodbury, root extract of dandelion, calendula, wormwood and meadowsweet to the pile on the table.

"And that's it," she said.

Sitting across from her, Hubbell sipped his wine, beginning to regret that moment of weakness in which he agreed to listen to what Ms. Gifford's herbalist might recommend.

"I really don't know about this," he told her.

But Ms. Gifford seemed not to hear him.

"I'll need a large bowl and your measuring spoons," she said.

Reluctantly, Hubbell rose from the table. He reached into one of the lower cabinets and grabbed a large white bowl, then he opened the drawer beside the sink and picked out the measuring spoons. He carried them over to the table and sat down to watch as Ms. Gifford unfolded a sheet of creased white paper, her recipe, written in a large looping scrawl, and bent down to study the list of ingredients. She selected the tablespoon and dug it into the baggie of sweet woodruff.

"Two tablespoons of sweet woodruff," she said, emptying the spoon into the bowl. "One tablespoon of dandelion root extract. Two tablespoons of the calendula blossoms."

"Are you sure about this?" Hubbell asked her.

"Oh, Graydon. Don't be such a worrier. The Chinese have been using these medicinal herbs for thousands of years. What could go wrong?"

"That really is the question, isn't it?"

When she finished spooning the herbs into the bowl, she vigorously mixed them together, then she stood and crossed the kitchen and took one of the saucepans from the drying rack on the counter. After carefully measuring a cup of water, she poured it into the pan and placed it on the left front burner.

"There now," she said.

When the water came to a full boil, she picked up the bowl of mixed herbs and spooned a heaping teaspoon into the churning water.

"Now, we boil the tea for five minutes," she said.

"Then what?"

But he knew, of course. As he sat at the table, watching the steam rising from the saucepan, a foul smell began to fill the kitchen, not unlike, it occurred to Hubbell, the smell of a fire at a distant landfill. He couldn't imagine drinking anything that smelled that bad, but he knew he would have to try, if for no other reason than to compensate Ms. Gifford for all the trouble she had gone to on his behalf.

After precisely five minutes, Ms. Gifford rose from the table and poured the sputtering tea through a strainer into a porcelain mug.

"That's all there is to it," she said. "The tea is ready."

She picked up the mug and carried it over to the table and set it down in front of him.

"I'm very excited about this, Graydon."

He turned to her, and there went that eye again, careening off on its own. It was all he could to do prevent himself from turning to see what, if anything, had attracted its attention.

"I just know this is going to work," she said.

Hubbell looked down at the tea, watching as the fumes drifted away, realizing his time had come.

"Well, here goes," he said.

He raised the cup and took a tentative sip. It tasted far worse than he had imagined. It was all he could do to force himself to swallow it. He gasped, leaning forward to catch his breath.

"I don't know if I can do this," he said.

"Oh, Graydon – you can do it. I know you can. Now you know what it tastes like. It won't be a shock this time. Try it one more time."

Hubbell stared down at the mug. He would give it one more try. He would give it one more try for Ms. Gifford. He grabbed the mug with both hands and took a deep breath, then he raised the mug to his mouth and tipped his head back and gulped it all down in three deep swallows.

"Bravo, Graydon! Bravo!"

He set the mug down hard and gripped the edge of the table. He could feel the tea churning deep in his stomach, as if to surge back up his throat. He waited. He waited a moment more. Finally, a low staccato belch escaped him.

Ms. Gifford clapped her hands.

"Do you hear that, Graydon? It's working! It's working already!"

CHAPTER SIX

IN THE MORNING SUN, Hubbell walked up Columbus Avenue, across the street from the bustling refuge of Washington Square. As he passed the knot of people at the corner of Union Street, waiting for the bus to take them downtown, he could hear an opera playing, the lilting aria filling the high blue sky. He felt good, as good as he ever felt anymore, rested at the very least, having slept straight through the night. If nothing else, the night sweats were no longer tormenting him every night, a modest accomplishment when viewed in the context of his larger medical concerns, but as Hubbell slipped past the tables in front of the crowded sidewalk cafes, he appreciated it nonetheless.

At Stockton Street, he waited for the streetlight to turn green, then stepped down from the curb, into the crosswalk. The blare of the horn caught him entirely by surprise. He never saw the white delivery van. He leapt back out of the way, tripping over the curb and tumbling onto his hands and knees on the sidewalk. A bolt of pain shuddered through his chest. For a moment, he thought he was having another heart attack.

But he quickly caught his breath and pushed up to stand and spun around to the van that had nearly run him down.

"What the hell is wrong with you?" he shouted at the driver. "You damned near killed me!"

A dark blue wool cap was pulled down low over the driver's forehead, his eyes concealed behind metallic-blue, wraparound sunglasses. He smiled as Hubbell stood in front of the van, pointing through the windshield at him.

"Come out of there!" Hubbell shouted, pounding his fist on the glass. "I'm placing you under citizen's arrest!"

But the driver only laughed. When he hit the horn again, Hubbell wheeled around to the people standing at the bus stop.

"Somebody call the police!"

No one moved, of course. As the van began inching toward Hubbell, he placed both hands on the front of the van and pushed back with all his strength, but the van was slowly backing him up, step by step, into the traffic moving down Stockton Street. He slipped around to the driver's side and tried to pull the door open, but the door was locked. The driver laughed as Hubbell banged his fists on the window. There was nothing, ultimately, he could do as the van slowly pulled away – nothing but kick the left rear tire.

That was a mistake. The pain in his right foot was excruciating. He sank to a knee as the van accelerated into traffic, leaving him behind in a cloud of oily blue exhaust. Clutching his foot, he looked over to the people huddling in the bus stop, staring blankly at him, having viewed the entire incident without so much as raising a single voice.

"Thank you all," Hubbell said to them. "Thank you so very much for coming to my assistance."

He rose to his feet and snatched up his satchel, then he hobbled across the street, ignoring the red light and the cars braking hard to veer around him.

"Let me through," he barked at the people standing on the opposite sidewalk. "Coming through, coming through."

PIETRO LIBERATORE'S LAW OFFICE was just down the block on Columbus. Liberatore had been practicing law there for years, specializing in resolving disputes with a minimum of drama and publicity, whether that was persuading an indiscreet mistress to relocate to another state or facilitating the disposal of the occasional dead body, which is to say that little of Liberatore's practice took place in the courtroom or strictly adhered to state and federal legal canon, his reputed connections to influential members of the city's Italian crime families sufficient to lend an air of authority to his considered recommendations. Hubbell had required his services only once before, and Liberatore had dispatched a thoroughly unpleasant dispute with the Internal Revenue Service with a single telephone call. Liberatore, who was not a day younger than Hubbell, was largely retired now, but the last time Hubbell had run into him, sitting on a barstool and enjoying a glass of beer at Gino and Carlo's, Liberatore said he was still going to his office in the mornings, and Hubbell hoped that was still the case.

He opened the door and climbed the stairs leading up to Liberatore's office on the second floor, leaning heavily on the railing bolted to the wall, trying to place a minimum of weight on his throbbing foot. At the top of the stairs, he limped down the narrow hall to Liberatore's office, the gilded foil letters that spelled out his name peeling off the clouded glass door. Hubbell knocked. When he got no response, he rapped his knuckles on the door once more. After knocking a third time, he reached down and let himself in.

Beneath the long blades of the ceiling fan, stirring the stale air, Liberatore's office was small and cramped, barely large enough to accommodate his dark oak desk. Two threadbare club chairs were arranged in front of his desk, flanked by opposing banks of dark green metal file cabinets. On the wall beside his coat rack hung a gallery of framed, black-and-white photographs of some of Liberatore's most prominent clients over the years, many of them members of North Beach's oldest Italian families, long since laid to rest.

Hubbell had no idea where Liberatore might be or when he might return, so he decided to leave a note, asking Liberatore to call him at the Chronicle. But as he approached his desk, looking for a piece of paper, he heard footsteps in the hall behind him and turned around to see Liberatore standing in the doorway with a cup of coffee in his left hand, his baggy gray suit hanging from his hunched frame, a red bow tie clipped to the collar of his white shirt, his eyes bloodshot above the sacks sagging onto his hollow cheeks.

"Well, I'll be damned," Liberatore said.

"Hello, Pietro."

Liberatore gestured toward the chairs in front of his desk.

"Please, Graydon, make yourself comfortable."

As Hubbell eased himself into the chair on the left, Liberatore sat down behind his desk.

"So how have you been, Graydon?"

"I've been better, to be perfectly honest."

"Haven't we all?"

Liberatore took a sip of his coffee, holding the cup with both hands.

"So what brings you by this morning?"

Hubbell crossed his right leg over his left, hoping that might ease the throbbing in his foot.

"It looks as if I'm going to be needing a will," he said.

Liberatore peered at him, across the top of the cup.

"I have to tell you, Graydon, that it's been my experience that clients only need wills when they're preparing to depart for the afterlife."

"I'm afraid that seems to be the case," Hubbell said.

Liberatore leaned back in his chair, the coiled steel spring beneath the seat creaking softly.

"I'm sorry to hear that," he said.

"Not as sorry as I was," Hubbell said.

Liberatore nodded, conceding the point.

"Yes, I'm sure that's true," he said. "So, tell me, is this an urgent matter?"

"Who really knows?" Hubbell said.

Liberatore nodded.

"Yes, who can ever say for sure?"

Hubbell watched as Liberatore took another sip of coffee.

"Of course, the prudent course of action is always to prepare for the worst and hope for the best," Liberatore said. "So, yes, of course, I can help you prepare a will. You know I'd be glad to. You know I'll do whatever you need me to do."

Liberatore set his coffee down, then reached for a mechanical pencil and the yellow legal pad beside his telephone. He rocked back in the chair and folded over the top page on the legal pad.

"A will is a fairly simple document," he said. "Its sole function, obviously, is to direct the distribution of your estate. So, you'll need to provide me with a list of all your property and assets, as well as your liabilities, of course."

"The only thing I own that's worth anything is the property on Filbert – the two flats and my cottage in the back."

"I assume you'll be leaving the property to family members?"

"I don't know," Hubbell said. "I haven't selected a beneficiary yet."

"Do you have anyone in mind to serve as executor of your estate?"

"No," Hubbell said. "I'm sorry, but I don't – not yet."

Liberatore tapped the legal pad with the pencil's eraser.

"Graydon, may I offer you a little unsolicited advice?"

"By all means," Hubbell said.

"I've written a hell of a lot of wills over the years," Liberatore said. "I've handled the disposition of more estates than I could count. I couldn't tell you how many people I've seen reach the end of their natural lives. And the one thing I've learned is that dying is a bitch. You don't want to go through it alone."

Hubbell clasped his hands over his right knee.

"You need someone to help you through it," Liberatore said. "You need someone you can trust not just to oversee your financial affairs, but to oversee your medical directives, as well. You need someone who cares about you, Graydon – someone with only your interests at heart."

"I understand," Hubbell said.

Liberatore took another sip of coffee.

"Have you given any thought to those medical directives?" he asked.

"I'm not sure I know what you mean," Hubbell said.

"Have you thought about how you want your life to end?"

The question caught Hubbell by surprise.

"No, I don't suppose that I have, not the specific details," he said.

"Well, you need to, Graydon. It's just as important to get your medical issues in order as it is to take care of your financial affairs. You need to sit down and talk to your doctor. You need to go through the whole process. There are a lot of decisions to make – decisions you need to make now, before your mind and body begin to fail you. And then you need to find someone to make sure those decisions are carried out on your behalf."

"You're right, of course," Hubbell said. "You're right."

But he could see that hadn't fully placated Liberatore.

"You're not ready for this, are you, Graydon?"

"No," he had to admit. "No, I don't suppose I am."

HUBBELL LIMPED down the stairs and flagged a cab to deliver him to the paper. As the cab drove through the Financial District, he knew Liberatore was right. He did indeed need someone to help him through the last difficult days of his life. But there were few he could prevail upon. His colleagues in Section Eight would do whatever he asked of them, of course, but the Senator was involved in the guild negotiations for a new contract, and Jennings was already caring for his disabled wife, and Poopdeck, well, there was no telling what he might do in the presence of uniformed nurses. Hubbell supposed that he could contact Maria's brothers, Vince and Dominic, but he saw them rarely, which is to say, only if he couldn't avoid them, and they might very well be reluctant to assume any obligation that reduced the time they spent sitting on a bench in Washington Square or playing bocce ball behind the North Beach library. Ultimately, Hubbell knew just one person who might be willing to take on the grim duty of escorting him to the ever-after, and the thought that he might have to place his life, or at least what remained of it, in the hands of Ms. Gifford was, well, distressing, to say the least.

But time was of the essence, and Hubbell saw no other option. He had no doubt that Ms. Gifford was available, at least to the extent that she didn't appear to have any conflicting responsibilities or competing obligations, and, she was already familiar with both his diagnosis and his prognosis, even if she couldn't distinguish between them, even if she had little confidence in Western medicine. True, she was not in the habit of making rational decisions. True, the world she inhabited was irrational in the extreme. But at least she had a positive attitude, which was certainly more than could be said about Dr. Martin and Dr. Ishihara, and, perhaps, Hubbell told himself, that was more important than anything else.

When the cab pulled up in front of the paper, Hubbell climbed out and pushed into the lobby, then took the elevator up to the third floor and walked down the corridor to the newsroom. On the way back to Section Eight, he stopped and picked up a copy of the paper from the stack on the filing cabinet across from the Page One desk. He never read the Chronicle at home anymore. He and his colleagues in Section Eight had cancelled their subscriptions years ago, preferring, as a matter of fiscal prudence, the free copies made available in the newsroom every morning. It was a trend viewed unfavorably by the hapless executives in the circulation department, whose increasingly desperate attempt to halt the Chronicle's plunging circulation had come to rely, at least in part, on selling subscriptions to the paper to the very employees who produced it. It was an unorthodox strategy, to say the least, and, in retrospect, it is fair to say the plan had trouble gaining traction. Hubbell and his colleagues ridiculed the subscription drives the department initiated in the newsroom and cursed the telemarketers who called them at home, and if the company went so far as to stop providing the newsroom with free copies, well, Hubbell was prepared to take a stand on principle and quit reading the paper altogether. Frankly, he could live without the aggravation.

After hanging up his coat, he sat down at his desk to begin his shift with a leisurely reading of the Sports section. He had just folded the section back to the box scores when the telephone rang.

"Hello, Mr. Hubbell. This is Katrina Reisner."

Hubbell set the Sports section aside.

"Good morning, Katrina."

"I was hoping I might get a few more minutes of your time today," she said.

He didn't like the sound of that. He didn't like the sound of that at all.

"Of course," he said.

"Would you be available this afternoon?"

Hubbell reached up and massaged his forehead with his fingertips.

"Certainly," he said. "What time?"

"How about two o'clock?"

"I'll swing by your office then," he said.

"Excellent," she said.

HUBBELL REPLACED the receiver, then rose from his desk and walked over to the cubicle occupied by the Senator, seated at his desk, his dark brown coat draped over the back of his chair, the sleeves so long they brushed the linoleum floor.

"Katrina Reisner just called me," Hubbell said.

The Senator looked up.

"She wants to meet with me again this afternoon."

"That doesn't sound good," the Senator said.

"I may be needing guild representation sooner than I thought."

"Perhaps we should take a moment to discuss your case."

"That's what I was thinking."

"Shall we step into my office?"

Hubbell limped after the Senator as he lumbered down the aisle through the newsroom, then down the corridor that led past the mailroom to the central elevator. They took the elevator down to the basement and walked over to the open area the company liked to refer to as the employee cafeteria – a dozen or so tables arranged in front of a row of vending machines in varying stages of disrepair, the dimly lit space as gloomy and inhospitable as if it had been designed expressly to ensure that employees spent no more time there than absolutely necessary.

They made their way over to the table in the back corner, beneath a fluorescent light panel with a single flickering tube.

"Would you like anything?" the Senator asked, glancing over to the vending machines.

"I'm fine, thanks," Hubbell said

Hubbell sat in one of the hard plastic chairs and watched as the Senator passed slowly down the row of vending machines, carefully exploring his options before stopping and reaching for his wallet. He fed several bills into the machine in front of him and pressed the buttons to identify his choice. When the machine hesitated to deliver his selection, the Senator persuaded it otherwise with a series of stiff blows of his forearm, rocking the machine back against the wall behind it, then he leaned down and collected his sandwich from the tray below.

He carried the sandwich over to the table and tore the cellophane wrapper from the plastic package. As Hubbell watched, the Senator took out one of the diagonally sliced sandwich halves and lifted the top piece of white bread. Slathered in mayonnaise, a pale green lettuce leaf lay upon a slice of processed meat that Hubbell believed to be a form of bologna. The Senator peeled off the lettuce and flung it toward the plastic trashcan. He missed, of course. It really wasn't even close. With a quiet slap, the lettuce clung to the wall above the trashcan like a splash of cheap paint.

"So what does Katrina want this time?" he asked Hubbell.

Hubbell watched as the Senator put the sandwich back together, then raised it to his mouth and devoured it in three industrious bites.

"I don't know," Hubbell said. "She didn't say."

"This can't be about your parking in the space reserved for that jerk in advertising – not again."

"I don't think so," Hubbell said. "What's left to say?"

Hubbell watched as the Senator pulled apart the second half of the sandwich and flung another piece of lettuce at the trash can, missing again, naturally, the lettuce striking the side of the can and then flapping to the floor.

"It's probably about the damage to the car," Hubbell said.

"What kind of damage are we talking about?" the Senator asked.

"I don't really know – other than that the damage is on the right side of the car."

"You haven't seen it?"

"I never looked."

"Do you have any idea what might have caused the damage?" the Senator asked.

Hubbell shrugged.

"It's possible that I may have damaged the car when I scraped it against the fence behind the loading dock," he said.

"But you don't know that for certain?"

"Not for an absolute certainty – no," Hubbell said.

The Senator nodded thoughtfully, then took another huge bite of the sandwich, so large he had to tuck the soggy crust into his mouth with his finger. He chewed it twice, then swallowed hard.

"So how, exactly, is Katrina going to pin this on you?" he asked.

"I don't know," Hubbell said. "But if she can, she will."

The Senator looked down and saw that a large dollop of mayonnaise had dropped onto his brown-and-gold paisley tie. He wiped it off with the pad of his thumb, then licked his thumb clean.

"It doesn't sound like she's got much of a case," he said.

The Senator crumpled the sandwich wrapper into a ball and hurled it toward the trashcan. It sailed over the trashcan and dribbled across the floor in front of the vending machines.

"That might not be all," Hubbell confessed.

"That might not be all what?" the Senator asked.

Hubbell could feel his shoulders slump.

"The reason I parked in the space reserved for that clown in advertising is that the car wouldn't fit in the space reserved for the city desk," he said.

The Senator waited.

"I tried to ease the car into the space, but I may have broken the side-view mirror off the car on the right."

"You may have broken the mirror off?"

"And then when I backed out of the space, I may have backed into one of the cars on the opposite side of the aisle."

"You might have?"

"I'm pretty sure I did, actually."

"Why do you think that?"

"I felt it," Hubbell said. "I heard what sounded like broken glass."

"Oy," the Senator said. "Did Katrina mention the side-view mirror or the car on the opposite side of the aisle?"

"No," Hubbell said.

"Is it possible that she's put all this together?"
"I don't know."
"We'd better hope not," the Senator said.

AT PRECISELY TWO MINUTES after two o'clock, Hubbell stood in the hallway outside Ms. Reisner's office, wondering where the Senator was. The last time he saw the Senator, he was walking down the corridor to the men's room, and that was never a good sign. It was not uncommon for the Senator to spend several hours at a sitting in his favored stall, a man of insatiable thirst and prodigious appetites, and, alas, plagued by chronic constipation. His bowel movements, as rare as they were, were nonetheless the stuff of legend, inspirational feats of human willpower and endurance that struck despair in the heart of the building manager, who all too often had to send a team of professionals in afterward to snake the toilet and mop up the overflow. As Hubbell stood in front of the door to Ms. Reisner's office, he had no idea how long the Senator might be indisposed.

But then he spotted the Senator, striding through the abandoned Business and Sports departments, clearly a man at peace, at least temporarily, with his gastrointestinal system, his head held high, shoulders thrown back, a triumphant smile across his face. With his long black hair coiled upon his shoulders, he raised his right hand and slapped Hubbell a loud high-five.

"Are we ready?" the Senator asked.

"As ready as I'll ever be," Hubbell said.

"We can handle this," the Senator told him. "Trust me."

Hubbell reached down and opened the door and stepped into Ms. Reisner's office. She looked up from the bound volume of computer printouts lying open on her desk, no small effort given the size of her head, which, Hubbell was startled to see, she had completely shaved.

"I believe we have an appointment at two o'clock," he said.

"Yes, we do," she said.

Hubbell stood to the side as the Senator followed him into Ms. Reisner's office.

"I brought my guild representative, as is my right, per the contract."

"So I see."

The Senator crossed in front of Ms. Reisner's desk and sat down directly in front of her, grunting as his broad rump made contact with the wooden seat, his ample girth lapping over the arms of the chair. As Hubbell sat down beside the Senator, Ms. Reisner leaned back in her chair, her thick arms crossed over her chest, the sleeves of her green-and-black flannel shirt folded up to her elbows.

"Hello, Katrina," the Senator said. "And before we proceed to the matter at hand, may I take the liberty of complimenting you on your new hairdo – or, shall I say, the lack thereof? It's most becoming."

"I couldn't agree more," Hubbell said.

"How kind of you to notice," she said.

"So," the Senator said, rubbing his hands together. "My esteemed colleague, to wit, Mr. Graydon Hubbell, has informed me that you're upset with him for parking one of the city desk cars in a space reserved for one of our colleagues in advertising."

"Yes, that is true," she said.

"Well, let me state, for the record, that Graydon has assured me that will not happen again."

"I'm certainly glad to hear that, but that, I'm afraid, is not why I wanted to speak with Mr. Hubbell today."

"Then, what is it, exactly, that you'd like to discuss?" the Senator asked.

Ms. Reisner leaned forward, resting her muscled forearms on her desk.

"Were either of you gentlemen working here in 1994?" she asked. "Were either of you working here during the strike?"

Hubbell had to suppress a laugh. The Senator didn't bother, the ten-day walk-out representing one of the finest moments of his career, a glorious demonstration of the guild's strength and unity that may not have secured a meaningful increase in compensation for the membership but nonetheless cost the company millions of dollars in lost revenue, which, as far as the Senator was concerned, was nearly as gratifying.

"Of course we were," the Senator said.

Ms. Reisner smiled.

"For a couple of guild members like you two gentlemen, those must be fond memories, indeed."

"Oh, yes," the Senator said.

"It's my understanding that emotions ran rather high during the strike," Ms. Reisner said.

"Very high," the Senator assured her.

"It's my understanding that the company was very concerned about potential vandalism and violence."

"Management knew who they were dealing with," the Senator said.

"Which is why, I gather, the company installed a video surveillance system around the perimeter of the entire property, including the parking lots."

Hubbell's stomach clenched. A rush of heat rose into his face. He remembered the installation of the video cameras, of course. During the strike, he and his fellow guild members had spent hours in front of those cameras, shouting vulgar epithets and making obscene gestures for the benefit of the security personnel charged with monitoring them.

"Of course, I wasn't here then," Ms. Reisner said. "So I had no idea they had installed those cameras. In fact, if it hadn't been for Mr. Woodbury, I might never have known."

Hubbell was beginning to tire of Mr. Woodbury's ever-expanding role in the events of last Friday afternoon.

"Mr. Woodbury has quite a temper," Ms. Reisner said. "There was no calming him down last Friday. He insisted on filing a formal complaint with the security guards, and then, when a copy of the complaint crossed my desk, there they were – frame grabs from the videotape from those surveillance cameras, showing Mr. Hubbell parking in Mr. Woodbury's space and then climbing out of the car and walking out of the lot. Would you like to see the video? I've got it right here."

"I don't believe that will be necessary," the Senator said.

"You can also see that the right side of the city desk car has been completely trashed."

"Graydon has assured you that he has no knowledge of that damage," the Senator reminded her. "He has no more knowledge of that damage today than he had yesterday."

"Two other cars were damaged in the parking lot last Friday," Ms. Reisner said. "Were you aware of that?"

Hubbell felt his throat tighten. Sweat trickled out of his armpits and down his rib cage.

"One car had its side-view mirror broken off. Another car, owned by an executive in the circulation department, had its right front fender smashed in and the headlight broken out."

She smiled again.

"And do you know what?" she asked.

"I believe I can guess," the Senator said.

"That's right – it's all on the videotape. You're very sharp, for an officer of the guild."

The Senator was not amused.

"Shall we take a look?" she asked them.

"I don't believe that will be necessary," the Senator said.

"I've got it all set up. In fact, I've gone all the way back to when Mr. Hubbell turned into the alley – driving the wrong way, I might add."

She turned the computer monitor around so that Hubbell and

the Senator could see it.

"Like I said, I don't believe this is necessary," the Senator said.

But then the videotape began to play. A sickly feeling came over Hubbell as he stared at the computer screen, utterly powerless to stop the events of last Friday from unfolding before him. He sat transfixed, grinning helplessly as the Nova turned down the alley and plowed into the chain-link fence behind the loading dock, as he pulled into the parking lot and tried to park in the city desk space, snapping the side-view mirror off the car on the right, as he backed into the car on the opposite side of the aisle, as he drove down the aisle and parked in Mr. Woodbury's space. Mercifully, the mayhem was over in a matter of minutes, which seemed to be enough – even for Ms. Reisner.

She turned to Hubbell.

"So what the hell? Were you drunk?"

"Absolutely not!" Hubbell shouted.

The Senator reached over and placed a hand on Hubbell's forearm.

"I really don't believe that kind of remark is helpful," the Senator told Ms. Reisner.

"So this is how this is going to go," she said. "It's very simple. I'm going to get estimates for repairing each of the three cars Mr. Hubbell damaged, and as soon as I get those estimates, Mr. Hubbell is going to give me a check to cover the cost of those repairs. How does that sound?"

"I'm sure we can work something out," the Senator said.

But Ms. Reisner shook her head.

"There is nothing to work out. That is how it is going to be."

"Right now, I'd like to sit down with Graydon and talk about how we want to proceed," the Senator said. "And then we can meet again, of course, when you obtain the estimates."

"I expect to have those estimates within a few days."

"Very well then," the Senator said.

He pushed up from his chair and turned toward the door. Hubbell rose beside him.

"Thank you, gentlemen. It's been a pleasure," she said.

Without so much as a word, Hubbell followed the Senator into the hallway. In defeat, they began walking back to the newsroom. As they passed through the vacated Business department, the Senator loudly ventilated his bowels, a sustained but nonetheless deflating discharge. Hubbell couldn't have said it better himself.

"That didn't go very well, did it?"

"I don't know how it could have gone any worse," the Senator said.

"What are we going to do now?"

"I'm not visualizing a lot of options," the Senator said.

"Nor am I."

"It looks like you're fucked," the Senator said.

"That's certainly what it feels like."

AFTER GRABBING a cup of coffee from the alcove off the mailroom, Hubbell made his way back to Section Eight. He had no idea how much it was going to cost to repair those three cars. All he knew was that it wasn't going to be cheap. But he would pay it – whatever it cost. He had no choice. Katrina Reisner had her foot on his throat, and what made that so much more distressing was the degree to which she seemed to be enjoying herself, deriving an inordinate amount of pleasure from his misadventures in the parking lot. He had never known a lesbian to have a sense of humor, even at the expense of a heterosexual male, such as himself. He had been led to believe, and his personal experience had largely confirmed, that lesbians, in general, were a dour lot, prone to surly moods and prolonged scowling, averse even to amusement, much less the kind of delight that Ms. Reisner seemed to be taking. It was all too confusing for Hubbell. It made his head hurt.

And as if to make matters worse, he heard Myron walking back to Section Eight, the slap of his wingtips on the linoleum. He looked up as Myron stood behind his computer.

"Richard O'Malley died," Myron said.

"Of the O'Malleys?" Hubbell asked.

"How would I know?"

"Good question," Hubbell said.

Myron handed Hubbell a folder containing articles pulled by the research librarians.

"I was thinking ten to twelve inches?"

"If he's one of the O'Malleys, he deserves at least that much."

"Harold wants it to run tomorrow."

"I'll do what I can," Hubbell told him.

As Myron walked away, Hubbell opened the folder. It took only a minute to confirm that Richard O'Malley was indeed a descendant of Thomas O'Malley, patriarch of one of the city's oldest and most influential families. Thomas O'Malley had arrived in San Francisco in the early 1860s, too late for the Gold Rush but still in time to make a fortune in the North Coast lumber industry. His son William formed a construction company that built a number of the largest commercial buildings in the city's Financial District, and, in turn, his son Davis built scores of modest homes in the Sunset and Richmond districts. For decades, the O'Malleys had been prominent supporters of Democratic candidates for public office and causes championed by the Catholic archdiocese. Although Hubbell was not familiar with Richard O'Malley, specifically, he merited an obituary on the basis of his pedigree alone.

As Hubbell began reading through the clips in the folder, he quickly learned that Richard O'Malley had grown up in Tiburon, a wealthy enclave on the north shore of the bay, then graduated from the University of San Francisco, his admittance there assured by his family's ongoing contributions to the Jesuits' endowment fund. He was commissioned a lieutenant in the Army during the Korean

War but was stationed in Tokyo and never saw combat. After the war, he founded O'Malley Properties, a company that acquired and managed residential hotels primarily in the Tenderloin, one of the city's most distressed neighborhoods. Over the years, O'Malley and his company had been sued numerous times by tenants' rights organizations, as well as cited repeatedly for egregious violations of the city's health and building codes, and two of O'Malley's hotels had burned down under mysterious circumstances, allowing him to collect insurance claims rather than pay for the major renovations required by the city. But no arrests were ever made, Hubbell was not surprised to see, no charges ever filed.

It was a pattern that Hubbell had observed on any number of occasions – the unmistakable disintegration of the family gene pool, generation by generation, in this case from the family patriarch, a man of vision and ambition who made an honest fortune, to his spoiled great-grandson, an unprincipled slumlord who preyed upon the poor and the dispossessed. Fortunately, O'Malley had brought his family's genetic decline to a merciful conclusion, never having found the occasion to father a son and pass on his cynical legacy, and for that, Hubbell told himself, the city could be thankful. It would be a pleasure, and, indeed, a public service, to write his obituary and kiss him good-bye.

After reading through the clips, Hubbell reached for the telephone book to call O'Malley's wife at their condominium on Nob Hill. The telephone rang for what seemed an eternity before it was finally picked up.

"The O'Malley residence," a woman finally said, her voice as soft and faint as a whisper.

"Yes, this is Graydon Hubbell with the San Francisco Chronicle. I'm trying to reach Virginia O'Malley."

"This is Virginia O'Malley."

"Hello, Ms. O'Malley. I'm very sorry to disturb you at such a difficult time, but I'm writing an obituary for your husband, and we're hoping to run it tomorrow."

"I understand," she said.

"Of course, we were all very sorry to hear about Mr. O'Malley's death. You have our heartfelt sympathies."

"That's very kind," she said.

"I know this may be difficult right now, but perhaps you could tell me a little about your husband."

The line went silent. Hubbell waited a moment, allowing her to negotiate the haze of tranquilizers.

"Richard was the finest man I have ever known," she said. "He was so intelligent, so handsome, so charming. He accomplished so much. He had so many friends. He was such a wonderful man."

"I'm sure he was," Hubbell said.

"Richard could be difficult at times, of course he could. But that's true of all of us, isn't it?"

"Of course," Hubbell said.

"No one's perfect. I'm not perfect. Richard wasn't perfect."

"None of us are perfect," Hubbell said.

"Richard was discreet, or at least he tried to be," she said. "That's all I ever asked of him."

She fell silent for a moment. Hubbell waited until the sniffling stopped.

"How old was Mr. O'Malley?"

"Richard was seventy-eight."

"And can you give me the cause of death?"

"I'm sorry?"

"Can you tell me how Mr. O'Malley died?"

"I don't understand," she said. "What does it matter how he died?"

"It's routine," Hubbell assured her. "We always note the cause of death, unless there's a reason not to. Otherwise, readers will wonder."

"Readers will wonder how Richard died?"

"And that's not what you want," Hubbell told her. "There are good ways to die, and there are bad ways to die. And readers, God help them, are predisposed to think the worst."

She fell silent again.

"I promise you, the imagination can go terribly wrong," Hubbell said.

"Richard died at the Olympic Club," she said.

"I'll need a little more than that."

"They tell me it was an accident. They tell me Richard and his group were standing on the sixteenth tee when Richard's partner took a practice swing. He didn't know Richard was standing right behind him. His club struck Richard in the forehead. They rushed him to the hospital, but he never regained consciousness."

"Good Lord," Hubbell said.

"I got there as fast as I could, but it was too late."

"I'm very sorry," Hubbell said.

"I loved that man," she said. "I loved him with all my heart."

"Of course you did."

"I don't know what I'm going to do without him."

She began to cry. Again, there was nothing Hubbell could do but wait for her to turn off the waterworks.

"He was just such a wonderful man," she said. "I never could stay mad at him, no matter what he did. I always forgave him. I just couldn't help myself."

"But, just to be clear, they assured you that your husband's death was an accident?"

"Yes."

"So as far as you know, no police report was filed?"

"A police report?"

"Yes," Hubbell said. "No arrests were made, is that correct?"

"What are you talking about?"

"Golf can be a highly competitive sport," Hubbell told her. "Wagers are made, tempers flare, violence erupts."

"What on earth are you suggesting?" she asked, indignation rising in her voice.

"I'm not suggesting anything," Hubbell said.

"How dare you!" she shouted. "How dare you!"

She slammed down the telephone. Hubbell winced as he recoiled from the receiver. Apparently, he had upset Ms. O'Malley. That certainly wasn't his intention, but he made no apology for carrying out the fundamental obligations of his profession. The questions had to be asked. The hard questions always had to be asked, even if the family of the newly deceased took umbrage at his line of inquiry. But he could handle it. He didn't mind. If Hubbell had learned anything over the past eleven years, it was that writing obituaries was not a job for the meek or faint of heart.

IT DIDN'T TAKE LONG to finish the O'Malley obituary. Still, Hubbell held onto it for as long as he could. Myron was not pleased. In fact, it would be fair to say that Myron was more than a little upset, complaining to anyone who would listen, which is to say no one, that he had less than ten minutes to edit the obituary before he had to move it to the news desk. That, of course, was precisely the point. As Hubbell shut down his computer, he wondered if Myron would ever figure that out.

In deference to his aching foot, sparing himself the walk down to the bus stop and the climb up Filbert, Hubbell called for a cab to take him home. After paying the fare, he let himself through the gate and limped along the side of the Edwardian. He had just entered the garden when Ms. Gifford spotted him.

"My God, Graydon! What happened?"

"I'm fine," he assured her. "I'm perfectly fine."

But she could see that he was placing virtually all of his weight on his left foot.

"No, you're not, Graydon. You're hurt."

"It's not so bad," he said.

But she had already slipped her arm around his waist, and there was little he could do to resist her as she ushered him across the patio and through the door into her kitchen. She pulled out one of the chairs around the table and sat him down.

"Let me take a look," she said.

"I really don't think that's necessary," he said.

But she was already kneeling in front of him. He could only watch as she rolled up the cuff of his trousers and untied his shoelace, abruptly realizing how old his shoes were, the black leather creased and scuffed, the stitched seams splitting apart, the heel worn at a hard angle, the sole as thin as a sheet of newsprint. He couldn't help but feel embarrassed as she cupped his heel in her hand and gently eased the shoe off his aching foot, releasing its musty odor. As she set his shoe aside, Hubbell vowed to buy a new pair at his earliest convenience. He certainly needed a better pair to wear in the casket.

He sat back in the chair as she rolled down his sock, revealing his ancient foot, the skin pale and nearly translucent, a few tired hairs rooted amid the raised purple veins, his big toe bruised and swollen and crusted with dried blood, the long curved nail split down the middle.

"Oh, Graydon," she said.

He leaned forward to take a closer look.

"It doesn't look that bad to me."

"You're going to lose that nail."

"Don't be so sure," he told her. "I'm a very quick healer."

But she had already pushed up to stand. She walked over to the sink and turned on the faucet. After rinsing out a small dishtowel, she returned and knelt down in front of him and carefully began to wash his foot, gently wiping away the dried blood. And it was then that Hubbell found himself confronted by Ms. Gifford's splendid bosom, visible as she leaned forward and her blue denim shirt fell away from her breasts. He jerked his head up and sat back in the chair, but he could still see her breasts, even with his eyes closed. He could feel his heart galloping in his chest, which was not necessarily advisable for a man who had already experienced one myocardial infarction, and the harder he tried to force the sight of her breasts from his mind, the more clearly he saw them. Finally, to his immense relief, she stood up and walked over to the sink.

He watched as she opened one of the lower cabinet drawers and withdrew a large kettle, then crossed the kitchen to the refrigerator and pulled all the ice trays out of the freezer compartment and emptied them into the kettle. She carried the kettle over to him. He forced himself to look away as she knelt down and wrapped his foot in a towel before lifting it up and submerging it in the ice.

"We'll ice it down for fifteen or twenty minutes," she said.

"All right," Hubbell said, as if he had a choice.

"So how did you do this?" she asked.

"I was nearly run over by a delivery van. I was in a crosswalk. The light was green. It was not my fault."

"Where were you?" she asked. "Where were you going?"

"I was crossing Stockton," he said. "I was on my way to see a lawyer."

"A lawyer?"

Hubbell shrugged.

"I figure I should get a will drawn up."

"I see," she said.

"I'm going to need one soon enough."

"A will just sounds so legal."

"Yes, I suppose that's true."

"I've never been a very big fan of the legal system," she said. "The legal system is just so technical. It's the technicalities that always get me. I mean, how are you supposed to keep track? How are you supposed to always know what the law is?"

"Well, I've known Pietro Liberatore for many years," Hubbell said.

"Pietro Liberatore?"

"He's the lawyer I went to see this morning."

"I don't know any lawyers – not by name, anyhow. I'd like to keep it that way."

"I'm going to ask Pietro to serve as the executor of my estate. I'm going to ask him to handle all the financial matters."

"Money, money, money. I mean, really – what does it matter?"

Hubbell couldn't argue with her. He didn't care about money, either, not anymore, except, of course, the money he was going to have to pay to repair the cars he had damaged in the Chronicle parking lot. That still frosted his ass.

"I'm also going to need someone to help me with the medical issues," he said. "I'm going to need someone to help me, as the cancer progresses."

She set her glass down and glared at him, as if he had just uttered the utterly unspeakable.

"That's just such negative thinking," she said.

"I'm just trying to be practical," he said.

"Did you drink your tea this morning?"

"Yes, I did."

"Did you notice anything different today? Did you feel any different?"

"No, not really," he said.

"But not any worse."

"No, not any worse."

"Well that counts for something, doesn't it?"

"I suppose so."

"Don't you see, Graydon – you could live for months, or even longer. There's no telling how much longer you might live."

"But even so, at some point, as my mind and body begin to fail, I'm going to need someone…"

"Oh, Graydon, just listen to you."

"I was hoping that you…"

"Me? You want me to help you die?"

"I wouldn't put it quite like that."

"Well, I won't do it, Graydon. I'm not going to do any such thing."

Hubbell could only stare at her.

"I'll do anything for you, Graydon, anything you want me to do. But I'm not going to help you die. You can just forget about it."

CHAPTER SEVEN

THE IDEA CAME to Hubbell while he was drinking his morning cup of tea, which was not to suggest, he hastened to remind himself, that the noxious brew prescribed by Ms. Gifford's Chinese herbalist was in any way responsible for that moment of enlightenment, but it was an epiphany nevertheless: he would plead poverty. He would tell Ms. Reisner that he simply didn't have the money to pay for the damage to all three cars – not all at once, not in one lump sum. He would have to pay off the repair bills over time. He would ask the Senator, as his guild representative, to negotiate the longest possible payment schedule, spread out over months, if not years, and if, regrettably, he happened to depart for the afterlife before he fulfilled his fiduciary obligations to the Chronicle, well, that would be a shame.

He limped down the sidewalk, then pushed in through the door of Hennessey's coffee shop and made his way down the row of padded red vinyl booths, passing behind the few solitary customers planted on stools along the speckled formica counter. The Senator was sitting in his regular booth, the last booth, his uncombed hair tangled upon his shoulders, his eyes swollen and bagged, hunched over the crossword puzzle in the Chronicle's Datebook section. The Senator worked the crossword puzzle every morning, although, to the best of Hubbell's knowledge, he had never successfully completed any of them. The exercise was purely academic, if not masochistic, invariably concluding with the Senator wadding the page into a ball and hurling it in the general direction of the door to the kitchen.

"May I join you?" Hubbell asked.

"Be my guest," the Senator said.

Hubbell slipped off his coat and slid across the ruptured seat, then leaned back as the waitress placed a porcelain mug on the table in front of him and filled it with coffee.

"Would you like a menu?" she asked.

"No, not this morning," he said.

Hubbell picked up his mug and took a sip as the Senator reached for the sugar jar and began pouring a thick stream into his coffee. Over the years, Hubbell had come to observe that the more sugar the Senator poured into his coffee, the later he had stayed at the Tempest the night before, and as the sugar piled up on surface of the coffee, Hubbell could see the Senator had had a long night.

He watched as the Senator stirred the sugar into his coffee, then raised the mug to his mouth and gulped the syrupy solution down, his whole body shuddering as he set the empty mug back on the table.

"So to what, may I ask, do I owe the pleasure of your company this morning?"

"I've been thinking about our meeting with Katrina Reisner yesterday," Hubbell said.

"As have I," the Senator said. "I keep asking myself – what earthly reason could a woman possibly have for shaving her fucking head?"

Hubbell sat back as the waitress delivered the Senator's breakfast

– a platter with six fried eggs, a double-order of hash browns and eight sausage links, accompanied by a smaller plate with a stack of six slices of toasted white bread.

"Perhaps a shaved head is regarded as attractive among women of her persuasion," Hubbell said.

"It certainly does little for the male of the species, which, I suppose, may very well be the point," the Senator said. "But surely the shaving of Katrina's head is not the reason that you chose to join me this morning."

"No," Hubbell said. "That's not it."

"What's on your mind?"

Hubbell wrapped both hands around his mug, watching as the Senator twisted the cap off a bottle of ketchup and began slopping it onto his eggs and hash browns, even the sausage links, pounding the bottom of the bottle with the heel of his hand.

"It looks as if I'm going to have to pay for the damage to those three cars," he said.

"I'm afraid so."

"It's going to cost me a small fortune."

"True," the Senator said. "And, if I may, all things being equal, I'm glad it's coming out of your wallet and not mine."

Hubbell watched as the Senator picked up a slice of toast, then used his fork to slide one of the fried eggs onto it. After putting his fork down, he folded the slice of toast in half and took a voracious bite, the ketchup and egg yolk running out the corners of his mouth and down his unshaven chin.

"I was wondering if there might be a way to negotiate some kind of extended payment plan," Hubbell said.

With another two bites, the Senator devoured the rest of the piece of toast, then wiped his chin with the back of his hand.

"Ordinarily, I would say yes. Ordinarily, I would say that shouldn't be a problem. But that's not what I'm worried about."

"What do you mean?"

"I'm worried about that videotape," the Senator said. "I'm worried about who else might get their hands on it."

"Like who?" Hubbell asked.

"I don't know," the Senator said. "But let's just lie low for a few days. Let's keep a low profile and wait for this to blow over – and when it does, we'll go in and talk to Katrina about some kind of payment schedule."

Hubbell didn't like it. He wanted to negotiate the payment schedule as soon as possible, if for no other reason than to get it off his mind. But if the Senator thought they should wait a couple days, he would defer to his recommendation.

"All right," he said.

HUBBELL STEPPED out of the elevator and walked down the corridor to the newsroom. As he passed through the bands of sunlight slanting through the blinds, making his way past the walls and columns covered with old political posters, defaced publicity stills and placards announcing various earnest but idiotic newsroom initiatives launched over the years, he found himself following Ms. Mitchell, walking back to Section Eight, her ponytail swishing across the backs of her slender shoulders. As a matter of professional courtesy, Hubbell had gone back and read the article she had written about the double homicide in the Tenderloin, and he was prepared to concede that it was perfectly competent for a reporter of her tender age and limited experience. In addition to being brash and ambitious, perhaps even slightly obnoxious, Ms. Mitchell was not entirely without talent.

She was carrying a large cardboard box with what appeared to be the long metal arm of a desk lamp protruding over her left shoulder. As Hubbell set down his satchel, he watched Ms. Mitchell place the box on the desk in the cubicle across the aisle from him. Several other boxes, all hers, presumably, already resided on the desk formerly occupied by Carleton Plank, the paper's longtime religion writer – until the day he fell out of a paddleboat on Stow Lake in Golden Gate Park and drowned in water no deeper than his knees.

After removing his coat and placing his hat on his computer, Hubbell walked over to Ms. Mitchell.

"Good morning," he said.

"Good morning, Mr. Hubbell."

"For a reporter working the night shift, you're in rather early this morning."

"I'm moving," she said. "I'm moving back here."

"So I see."

"You don't mind, do you?"

"Of course not," he said. "Why would I mind?"

"I'm trying to get as far away from my editor as I possibly can," she said.

"That's certainly understandable."

She looked up at him, a strand of hair drifting across her right eye.

"I'm also hoping I might be able to learn a thing or two from you gentlemen."

Hubbell was not immune to flattery, particularly, he was not ashamed to admit, when offered by a woman – and an attractive woman, at that.

"I suppose that's possible," he modestly allowed. "We do have a wealth of experience among us."

"I want to pick your brains."

"Of course."

"I want to learn what I can before it's too late."

"Too late?"

"I mean, while you're still around."

Hubbell smiled through his teeth. Ah, yes – the clear, pitiless eye of youth, unburdened by decorum, untroubled by sentiment.

"Yes, of course – while we're still around."

He spread his arms.

"Please," he said. "Permit me to welcome you to Section Eight."

AS HUBBELL SAT DOWN, he noticed the red light blinking on his telephone, indicating that a caller had left a message. He picked up the receiver and tapped in his access code.

"Hello, Mr. Hubbell. This is Abigail Tuttle. We're having a meeting of the diversity committee's executive council later this morning, and we're hoping that you might be available to join us. The meeting will be held in the main conference room at eleven o'clock. We hope to see you there."

Hubbell replaced the receiver, then sat back in his chair. He knew little about the diversity committee, other than that it was an unintended byproduct of the company's attempt to hire and promote what the human resources department liked to call journalists of color. The hope was that the staff of the newsroom would come to more accurately reflect the broader demographic composition of the greater Bay Area, thereby expanding the paper's coverage of the region's many racial and ethnic groups, and, subsequently increasing the paper's circulation in those same communities. It was a noble goal, certainly, but it was also problematic in that the Chronicle's ever-dwindling readership was largely composed of elderly white readers, whose parochial interest in those communities of color was primarily as a source of manual labor and inexpensive cuisine, and, in turn, the residents of those communities had little interest in subscribing to a newspaper that so shamelessly championed the nation's enduring imperialist ambitions.

Still, the campaign to diversify the newsroom had enjoyed a measure of success in recent years, at least to the extent that there were soon enough journalists of color to form the diversity committee. It was a spirited group that promptly established itself as the unofficial conscience of the newsroom and soon began sending out daily critiques of the paper, sharing the committee's enlightened opinions about the coverage of local news, and, in the kindest possible way, of course, pointing out the ignorance and insensitivities of their pale colleagues. It was fair to say that the committee's insights were not always appreciated in a newsroom still struggling to adjust to the presence of women, much less journalists of color. But little, if anything, had been said in objection to any of the committee's missives, as Harold had made it clear that the group was operating with his approval, realizing, of course, that anyone, including himself, with the temerity to challenge or question anything the diversity committee did, no matter how naïve or idiotic, would be forever branded an enemy of the people.

Ms. Tuttle was the de facto leader of the diversity committee. She was said to be a Native American, a Pomo by tribal affiliation, hired straight out of the journalism program at U.C. Berkeley, which is to say without any experience whatsoever at a daily metropolitan newspaper. She had been assigned to the City Desk, where, the Senator had famously and perhaps too loudly observed, she swiftly demonstrated why her people, living for thousands of years in the lush coastal hills of Northern California, had failed to develop a written language. And so, by default, Ms. Tuttle was allowed to devote the vast majority of her time and energy to the execution of her duties as leader of the committee, including penning the daily critiques that had warmed the hearts of so many of her colleagues.

Which is all to say that Ms. Tuttle was a pain in the ass. But if she wanted Hubbell to attend a meeting of the committee's executive council, he was willing, if not eager, to accommodate her. He had nothing to hide. He had nothing to fear. And he had a ready defense. If the executive council had a problem with his obituaries, Hubbell would simply blame it on Myron. For once, the little rodent could make himself useful.

SHORTLY AFTER eleven o'clock, Hubbell crossed the newsroom to the main conference room. He reached down and opened the door and leaned inside.

"Good morning," he said.

Ms. Tuttle was seated at the head of the long table, flanked by a contingent of her solemn associates. She was short and stout, her black hair parted down the middle of her scalp and woven into two long braids, her eyes dark brown above her sharp cheekbones, her mouth barely capable of containing her large teeth, notably her left front tooth, which was adorned with a silver cap.

"Please, come in, Mr. Hubbell."

Hubbell stepped into the conference room, then closed the door and took a seat at the far end of the table, opposite Ms. Tuttle.

"Do you know the members of our executive council?" she asked.

"No, I don't believe I do," Hubbell said.

Ms. Tuttle turned to her left and introduced Amelio Juarez, a thickset copy editor on the Datebook staff with a crew cut and a large gold crucifix hanging from around the stump of his neck, and Darnel Johnston, a writer in the Features department with a heavy-lidded glare and a mass of untamed dreadlocks. She then turned to her right and introduced Eileen Chin, a rail-thin editorial assistant in the Food section, dabbing her mousy nostrils with a tissue, and Victoria McAdams, a tall, lanky, red-headed librarian, who bore, it abruptly occurred to Hubbell, an uncommon resemblance to Victor McAdams, who had worked in the library before her.

"It's a pleasure," Hubbell said.

"Well," Ms. Tuttle began, "as you may know, we on the diversity committee's executive council have been meeting with reporters from throughout the newsroom. Our goal is to foster an ongoing dialogue about how we, as journalists, and as a newsroom, cover local news, and, by that, I mean specifically how we cover the many racial and ethnic communities that constitute the greater Bay Area."

She paused to smile as if basking in applause, closing her eyes, her silver-capped tooth gleaming like a newly minted dime.

"Our goal is solely to improve the paper," she said. "Our goal is to create a better experience for our readers."

"How exciting," Hubbell said. "I'm looking forward to it already."

She smiled again, her eyes slits above her cheekbones.

"And we certainly appreciate your enthusiasm, Mr. Hubbell."

"So what can I do for you?" he asked.

"My fellow committee members and I invited you here this morning with the hope that we could begin a dialog about the paper's approach to our local obituaries," she said.

"And what, may I ask, prompted your sudden interest in our obituaries?"

"A very good question," Ms. Tuttle said. "They caught my attention this morning, when I read the obituary you wrote for Richard O'Malley. You see, I have some familiarity with Mr. O'Malley. Mr. O'Malley was my landlord."

"I see," Hubbell said.

"Mr. O'Malley was a slumlord of the lowest order, so why, I asked myself, did the Chronicle write an obituary for him?"

Hubbell had been a journalist long enough to recognize a loaded question when he heard one, but he ventured to answer it anyway, assuming that was why Ms. Tuttle had invited him to the meeting.

"We wrote an obituary for Mr. O'Malley because he was a member of one of the oldest families in the city."

But Ms. Tuttle, it turns out, wasn't interested in his explanation.

"Yes, I read that – whatever," she said, waving off his explanation as if it were an insect.

She reached for the newspapers stacked on the table in front of her, a selection of Bay Area sections, each of them folded back to the obituaries.

"So I decided to go back and see who else we've written obituaries about over the past few weeks."

She arranged the obituaries across the table.

"Here we have Mr. O'Malley, and here we have Mildred Bancroft and Alfredo Viviano, and here, of course, is the obituary for Chief Cassidy."

She studied the obituaries for a moment longer, then looked up at Hubbell.

"Do you know what the subjects of these obituaries have in common?" she asked.

"They're all dead?" Hubbell guessed.

She smiled again, her eyes compressed, her lips drawn back to bare the silver-capped tooth.

"I should hope so," she said. "But that was not the point I was trying to make."

"I'm sorry," Hubbell said. "I thought you were asking a question. I didn't realize you were trying to make a point."

"They're all white," she said.

"Ah," Hubbell said. "May I assume that's the point you were trying to make?"

"Yes," she said. "You may assume exactly that."

"That's very interesting," Hubbell said. "I'll certainly bring this to the attention of my editor. I'm sure Myron will find this very interesting."

But Ms. Tuttle wasn't finished.

"That, of course, led me to ask myself if these obituaries of the past few weeks reflected a larger pattern, so I asked Victoria to go back and audit our obituaries over the past year and develop a breakdown of those obituaries by the race and ethnic background of the deceased."

She smiled again, her eyes sealed shut, the tooth shining.

"And would you like to guess what she found?"

Hubbell knew better than to try.

"Victoria found that the subjects of our obituaries have been white no less than eighty-seven percent of the time. And of that eighty-seven percent, the subjects have been men no less than seventy-three percent of the time."

That didn't sound good, even to Hubbell.

"That's also very interesting," he said.

"Interesting?" Ms. Tuttle asked. "I wouldn't call those figures interesting. I'd call those figures rather distressing."

"Well, yes, distressing, too, from a negative point of view."

"I'd call those figures disturbing, frankly, and I'm quite sure Harold will agree with me."

"Harold?"

"After each of our meetings, I provide Harold with a memorandum, summarizing our discussion," Ms. Tuttle said. "And, after Harold has had a chance to review the memorandum, the committee's executive council and I sit down with him and discuss how we should proceed."

Hubbell had to wonder if Harold had any idea what he had turned loose in the newsroom. But of course, he did.

"Now, please, I don't want you to get the wrong impression," Ms. Tuttle said. "We don't view the figures Victoria worked up, as, in and of themselves, irrefutable evidence of racial or ethnic bias."

"That's certainly a relief," Hubbell said.

"We want to make it perfectly clear that we are not accusing you of harboring any kind of racial or ethnic prejudice, certainly not at this time, not without further research. I can assure you that we regard that as a very serious allegation, one that we take very seriously. Our hope is simply that we can continue this dialogue about our local obituaries."

"I don't see why not," Hubbell said. "I've certainly enjoyed it so far."

"Our hope is simply that our local obituaries will begin to reflect the multi-racial, multi-ethnic region we serve," Ms. Tuttle said. "And it is the firm belief of the executive council that with a little more initiative on your part, as well as a little community outreach, that goal is entirely achievable."

Hubbell could have gone the rest of his life without hearing Ms. Tuttle suggest that he show a little more initiative, but he realized that this was not the time to register his offense.

"I'll do my very best," he promised.

She smiled again.

"It's gratifying to hear you say that, Mr. Hubbell. And you can rest assured that we shall include your support for our thinking in our memorandum to Harold. Do you have any questions?"

"Oh, no," he said. "I think you've covered it all."

"Mr. Hubbell, just remember – people of color die, too."

AS HUBBELL WALKED back to Section Eight, Myron burst out of his chair and followed him back to his desk.

"So what did Pocahontas want?"

Hubbell pulled out his chair and sat down.

"Did you know," he asked Myron, "that in no less than eighty-seven percent of our obituaries last year, the deceased was white?"

"What are you talking about?"

"And did you know that of that eighty-seven percent, no less than seventy-three percent of the deceased were men?"

"She counted? She went back and counted them all? Are you kidding me?"

"The diversity committee's executive council has taken the liberty of auditing our obituaries over the past year, and Ms. Tuttle wanted to share their findings."

"Good Christ," Myron groaned.

"Don't worry, Myron. I'm sure you'll have a chance to offer your perspective on their findings. They're going to send a memo about our meeting to Hal, and I'm sure Hal will find the time to call you into his office to pass along his thinking."

"They're going to fuck me, aren't they?"

"Yes, they are, if they possibly can – you and me, both."

Myron closed his eyes and wagged his head.

"Well, here's another one," he said.

"Another what?"

"Conrad Jurgensen died."

"Are you serious?" Hubbell asked.

Myron handed Hubbell the manila folder filled with clips the librarians had pulled.

"A massive heart attack at some charity wine auction up in Napa – dead before he hit the ground, apparently."

Hubbell couldn't help but smile. Not only was Jurgensen a white male, he was rich, filthy rich, as they used to say, the owner of the largest chain of used car lots in the Bay Area, and if that wasn't enough to tighten Ms. Tuttle's colon, Jurgensen was also a registered Republican and a generous contributor to a broad spectrum of ultra-right-wing political causes, his current focus a campaign to make panhandling a felony. He was also, and perhaps mostly importantly, a friend of Thomas Fleming, the editor-in-chief, a standing member of Fleming's Wednesday afternoon foursome at the Olympic Club.

"How much do you think he's worth?" Myron asked.

"Friends of the editor-in-chief are always good for twelve to fifteen inches," Hubbell said. "I'll give Jurgensen eighteen, just to be safe."

"His stepson is going to call you with a comment from the family."

"Fine," Hubbell said.

HUBBELL OPENED the file folder and began reading through the clips the library had pulled. Jurgensen was a native of New Jersey and had grown up in Atlantic City. After the Korean War, he settled in San Francisco and took a job as a salesman at a used car dealership on Van Ness, and it was there that the gregarious Jurgensen realized he had found his true calling in life. Before he turned thirty, he had opened his own used car lot in Oakland, specializing in selling vehicles to buyers who had little or no money, retaining his own repossession team to seize those cars upon the first missed payment. It was a successful business model, even as it engendered a degree of ill will among those who believed they had been victimized by his predatory lending practices, and Jurgensen parlayed that first lot into a string of dealerships throughout the Bay Area, gaining in the process a measure of celebrity by appearing in a series of late-night television commercials, hawking his no-money-down deals, the consummate salesman in his hand-tailored suits, slicked-back hair, and winning smile.

He was a dashing figure off-camera, as well. Over the years, Jurgensen had gone through several wives, initially marrying his secretary at that first lot in Oakland and later the wife of a rival dealer in San Jose. But he struck gold seven years ago when he won the affections of Penelope Wagstaff, the oldest daughter of one of the wealthiest men in San Francisco, the owner of an insurance empire who thoroughly disapproved of Jurgensen but was, unfortunately, powerless to stop his daughter from eloping to Reno to marry him. Jurgensen and his new bride returned to the city to live in a mansion in Presidio Heights, and by virtue of his new wife's pedigree, Jurgensen managed to insinuate himself into the city's highest social circles, despite the New Jersey accent he could never quite shed and a penchant for the occasional lost weekend in Las Vegas.

After reading through the clips, Hubbell had just begun to work up a basic chronology of Jurgensen's life when the telephone rang. He reached over and picked up the receiver.

"Are you the poor bastard who writes the obituaries?"

"Yes, I'm the poor bastard."

"I'm calling about my stepfather – Conrad Jurgensen. I'm calling in a statement from my mother."

"Thanks for calling," Hubbell said. "I'm sure this is a very difficult time for you."

"Not really."

"At least for your mother, then."

"Not now, not anymore. The doctor was just here. She's fine now."

Hubbell was beginning to sense that the Jurgensen household was not overly disposed to sentiment.

"Shall I read the statement to you?"

"Please," Hubbell said.

"My mother wants to say, 'My husband's life was a modern-day Horatio Alger story. Born on the East Coast, Conrad was a man of humble origins who came to San Francisco to seek his fortune and succeeded beyond his wildest dreams. I will mourn his loss forever.'"

Hubbell wrote the statement down in his notebook.

"Did you get all that?"

"Yes, I got it," Hubbell said.

"So tell me, then – who the fuck is Horatio Alger?"

"He was a writer," Hubbell said.

"A writer?"

"He was a nineteenth-century novelist. He wrote novels that were essentially rags-to-riches stories."

"I've never even heard of him."

"He was very popular in the late 1800s, but his popularity has waned over the years."

"I can see why, if that's the kind of crap he was peddling."

"Not everyone is an admirer of his work," Hubbell conceded.

"Do you need anything else from me?"

"No," Hubbell said. "That should do it."

HUBBELL SPENT the rest of the afternoon working up the Jurgensen obituary, writing an initial draft and then writing it through from the lead to the walk-off, acutely aware that the obituary was of such high interest to the editor-in-chief that he might actually trouble himself to read it.

After polishing the obituary until it absolutely sang, he filed it to Myron. He was cleaning off his desk when Poopdeck walked over.

"The Senator just called," he said. "He wants us to meet him at the Tempest."

Hubbell knew that meant the Senator had news from the guild negotiating committee. He turned to Jennings and grabbed the arm of his chair and gave it a sharp shake. Jennings lurched awake, nearly falling out of his chair.

"Would you care to join us for a drink at the Tempest?"

Jennings gazed around the newsroom, as if seeing it for the first time, slowly regaining his bearings.

"Why, yes," he managed to say.

They shut down their computers and grabbed their coats and then started down the aisle leading through the newsroom. They exited the building through the Fifth Street guard station and walked down the sidewalk, then turned into the alley behind the loading dock, leaning into the gusting wind, sweeping up sheets of newsprint and pinning them to the chain-link fence.

As they entered the Tempest, they saw that the Senator was the establishment's sole patron, seated at his preferred table directly in front of the bar, sipping a martini, certainly not his first of the evening, and far from his last.

"Greetings, gentlemen," he said.

As they removed their coats and hats, Abby approached the table and took their orders – a glass of red wine for Hubbell and Jennings, a rum and coke for Poopdeck, and, of course, another martini for the Senator.

"So what the hell is Naomi Mitchell doing in Carleton Plank's old desk?" the Senator asked.

"She told me she's trying to get away from her editor," Hubbell said.

"I don't suppose we can fault her for that," the Senator said.

"She also said she's hoping to pick up a thing or two from her learned, if aging, colleagues, as in – us," Hubbell said.

The Senator nodded thoughtfully, no more immune to flattery than Hubbell.

"I've always liked Ms. Mitchell," he said. "I've always regarded her as one of our more promising younger reporters."

"As have I," Hubbell said.

"Of course, she's a woman," the Senator said.

"Yes, she is," Hubbell said.

"She's a redhead, is what she is," Poopdeck said.

Hubbell turned to Poopdeck, tugging at the tip of his beard.

"Redheads make me nervous," he said. "I don't know why."

Jennings looked up and ran his hand across his scalp, his eyes swimming beneath the lenses of his glasses.

"It's been quite some time since a woman sat with us."

"Margaret Dillard," Hubbell reminded them.

"Marge Dillard," the Senator said, summoning the name from the deepest recesses of his memory. "She was the last, wasn't she?"

"She was a pretty fair reporter, as I recall," Hubbell said. "She covered consumer affairs, didn't she?"

"Yes, she did," the Senator said.

"She was a freak about germs, is what she was," Poopdeck said. "Every fucking morning, the first thing she did was pull out a can of disinfectant and spray her phone and keyboard – her whole fucking desk."

"You can't be too careful," Hubbell said. "There are some pretty nasty bugs out there."

"That may very well be the case," the Senator said. "But it wasn't the germs that did Marge in, it was the brain tumor."

"That's quite true," Jennings said. "As the tumor grew, it compressed her optic nerves until she was functionally blind."

"You'd have to be blind to step into an open elevator shaft in the

PG&E building," Poopdeck said.

"Does anyone remember how far she fell?" Hubbell asked.

"Twelve floors, I believe," the Senator said.

"Ouch," Hubbell said.

"Heavyset gal like Marge, she must have made one hell of a mess," the Senator said.

They leaned back as Abby brought their drinks, placing them on the table in front of them. As she returned to the bar, Hubbell took a sip of wine, then looked across the table to the Senator.

"So tell us about the meeting," he said.

The Senator sipped at his martini, then set the glass on the table.

"Gentlemen, we've got a problem. It looks as if the company is going to try to eliminate seniority protections as part of the next round of layoffs."

"What are you talking about?" Hubbell asked.

"The company wants to target the layoffs," the Senator said. "They want to decide who stays and who goes."

"Good Christ," Poopdeck groaned.

"But we have a contract," Hubbell said. "And the contract specifically calls for layoffs to be conducted on the basis of seniority."

"Maybe not," the Senator said.

"What does that mean?" Hubbell asked.

"A contract can always be amended," the Senator said. "Provisions can always be waived."

"Not unless both parties agree," Hubbell said.

"That's right," the Senator said. "That's exactly right. And that's the problem."

That stopped Hubbell. He couldn't believe what he was hearing.

"You're telling us the guild might agree to waive the seniority protections in the contract?"

"The company wants to take fifty people out of the newsroom," the Senator said. "They're willing to offer buyouts to anyone who leaves the paper voluntarily. Anyone volunteering to leave will get a one-time severance payment of two weeks' pay for every year worked at the paper. So, if you've been here ten years, you'd get a severance check for twenty weeks' pay – and I don't need to tell you that that's going to look good to a lot of people. There are a lot of people in the newsroom who are worried about the viability of the paper, about the viability of their career, about the viability of the whole damned industry. And they're going to view those severance payments as damned generous."

"And the company thinks fifty people will raise their hands?" Hubbell asked.

"That's where it gets ugly," the Senator said. "If fewer than fifty people ask for a voluntary buyout, the company wants the right to impose involuntary buyouts on whomever they choose, regardless of their seniority."

"Those cocksuckers!" Poopdeck shouted.

"But the guild doesn't have to go along with this," Hubbell said. "The guild can insist that the company honor the contract, and the company would have to do so."

"That's true," the Senator said. "But is that what the membership wants to do?"

Hubbell sat back in his chair.

"The company has made it clear that if we do that, if the guild refuses to waive the seniority provisions in the contract, they will withdraw their buyout offer, and all those fifty people being laid off will get just two weeks of severance pay."

"I can't believe this," Hubbell said.

"We'll have to put the company's offer up to a vote of the membership," the Senator said.

"And you think it will pass?"

The Senator didn't hesitate.

"It won't even be close," he said.

"Jesus Christ."

"Think about it," the Senator said. "Imagine you've been working here for the past five years. You've got no meaningful seniority. You know you're going to get laid off. So you can vote to accept the company's offer and get ten weeks' pay when you leave, or you can vote to reject the offer and get two weeks' pay."

Poopdeck pounded the table, so hard the salt shaker toppled over.

"This is a fucking nightmare," Hubbell said.

"That's exactly what it is," the Senator said.

"No one cares about seniority anymore – nobody but us," Hubbell said.

"That's exactly right," the Senator said. "The company doesn't give a damn about us. All they care about are bylines. They want a newsroom filled with trained chimpanzees who can bang out five six-inch stories a day."

"We're fucked, aren't we?" Hubbell asked.

The Senator wasn't going to lie to them.

"Yes, we are, gentlemen. Yes, we are."

HUBBELL STARED out the window as the bus made its way through Chinatown. He couldn't believe the company was seeking to eliminate the seniority protections in the guild contract. It was nothing less than a duplicitous attempt to abolish rules of the newsroom that had been negotiated in good faith decades ago, preserving the jobs of reporters who had, in many cases, like Hubbell and his colleagues in Section Eight, devoted their entire professional careers to the Chronicle, their decades of hard work benefiting no one so much as the families that owned the paper. For years, the Senator had been the dean of the city's political reporters, the one reporter elected officials knew they had to talk to, regardless of the circumstances, regardless of the potential political fallout; Poopdeck, a seventh-generation Californian and a native San Franciscan, had written so extensively and so eloquently about the heritage of the city over the years that his work had been collected and republished in several anthologies; Jennings had literally risked his life with his front-line coverage of outbreaks of lethal diseases, notably the swine flu and AIDS epidemics. But none of that mattered now. Now, suddenly, Hubbell and his colleagues in Section Eight were expendable, old and in the way, their services no longer required. The company's attempt to undermine the contract's seniority provisions was unconscionable, as far as Hubbell was concerned, the severance payments nothing more than bribes, offered in the hope that he and his colleagues would go quietly and with a minimum of disruption.

When the bus reached Washington Square, he rose from his seat and grabbed the overhead rail and made his way down the aisle to the back door. After stepping down to the sidewalk, he stood back as the bus pulled away from the curb, then he limped down to Filbert Street and started up the hill, pausing to rest his sore foot several times before he reached his gate. After collecting his mail, he hobbled along the side of the Edwardian, surprised, when he looked up at his cottage, to see the light was on in the kitchen. He supposed he could have left it on when he departed for work that morning, but that didn't seem likely. As he passed through the garden, it seemed far more probable that someone else might have turned the light on, that someone else might even be in his cottage right now, waiting for him, and, of course, there was only one person that could possibly be.

As he grabbed the railing and began pulling himself up the stairs, the door of his cottage opened, and Ms. Gifford stepped out onto the landing, the light from the kitchen flooding out from behind her, a dark silhouette directly above him.

"Well, good evening, Graydon. Welcome home."

Hubbell had no idea what Ms. Gifford was doing in his cottage, but she was clearly untroubled by the fact that she had entered without his permission. He could only assume that she had found the key he kept under the doormat.

"Good evening, Lydia."

He began climbing the stairs, taking them slowly, one at a time, his legs trembling slightly from the walk up the hill.

"I didn't know when you would be home," she said. "I wanted to surprise you."

"Well, you certainly accomplished that," he said.

"I brought you something."

As Hubbell approached the landing, she retreated into the kitchen, standing in front of the stove in one of her tie-dyed sweatshirts, the cuffs of her khakis bunched up above her red, high-top tennis shoes, her long gray hair tied in a loose knot on top of her head, held in place by a single wooden chopstick.

He grabbed the doorjamb to steady himself.

"Can you smell it?" she asked.

He closed his eyes and raised his nose and took a sniff, but no, nothing.

"I'm sorry, but I don't."

"Oh, Graydon," she sighed. "It's soup! Lentil soup! It's another one of my specialties. It's got onions and green peppers and carrots and tomatoes – and lentils, of course. It's organic, very organic, if you ask me."

Hubbell wasn't entirely sure what a lentil was, but he didn't want to seem unappreciative, even to a woman who had entered his home unlawfully.

"That sounds wonderful," he said.

He put away his coat and hat. When he returned to the kitchen, he glanced over to the soup in the pot on the stove, dark and brown, bubbling like a mud spring. He sat down at the table and watched as Ms. Gifford ladled the thick soup into a large glass bowl and set it down in front of him.

"Go ahead and try it," she said. "I want to know what you think."

He picked up the spoon and dipped it into the soup and raised it to his mouth. It tasted only slightly better than it looked.

"It's delicious," he said.

Ms. Gifford smiled, then pulled out a chair and sat down at the table.

"I'm so glad you like it," she said.

"Aren't you going to join me?" he asked.

"Oh, no. I made it for you. It's to keep your strength up."

But then Ms. Gifford turned serious.

"Graydon, I want to tell you something."

Hubbell looked up from the soup as her right eye caromed off to the left, across the kitchen.

"I've been thinking about last night," she said. "And I don't want you to get the wrong idea."

"The wrong idea about what?" he asked.

"The wrong idea about dying," she said. "I don't want you to think I'm afraid of dying. The truth is – I'm not afraid of dying at all."

"I'm glad to hear that," Hubbell said.

"I'm a very spiritual person, if you want to know the truth."

"That doesn't surprise me."

"I believe that death is just a passage, a spiritual passage into another life, into the next life. You see, Graydon, I believe in reincarnation."

Of course she did.

"Oh, yes, I've been here before. I remember it quite clearly – I was a condor."

And, oddly enough, Hubbell could visualize Ms. Gifford as a condor, perched on a towering pinnacle of rock, high above the desert floor, spreading her huge ungainly wings and rolling into flight.

"Of course, that was many years ago, before the condors were nearly wiped out," she said. "There are very few condors left, you know."

"Yes, that's what I understand," Hubbell said.

"In my next life, I'd like to come back as a whale. A humpback whale – they're my favorites."

She shrugged.

"I know you don't get to choose, but I don't see the harm in hoping."

"Of course not."

"They make such beautiful music. I used to have an album with nothing but whale songs, and sometimes, late at night, I'd smoke a joint and put on the headphones and lie on the couch and listen to that album, and when I closed my eyes, I could visualize myself swimming with all the whales. It was like a vision."

Hubbell didn't have any trouble visualizing that, either, particularly Ms. Gifford smoking some of her marijuana.

"You seem to have given this considerable thought," he said.

"Oh, yes – yes, I have," she said.

She smiled, her right eye kicking up and looking past him.

"What about you, Graydon? What would you like to come back as?"

It was a fair question, and Hubbell should have seen it coming. But he had no answer for her. He had never envisioned himself as a member of the animal kingdom, in this life or any other.

"I don't really know," he said. "I'll have to give this a little more thought."

"I think that's a very good idea," she said. "I mean, what have you got to lose?"

"Yes, you're right, of course."

"You're not afraid of dying, are you, Graydon?"

The question straightened him up in his chair.

"Of course not," he hastened to say. "Absolutely not."

And that was true. That was the truth. Hubbell wasn't afraid of dying. He was sure he wasn't.

CHAPTER EIGHT

HUBBELL HOBBLED across Columbus, still favoring his aching foot as he entered Washington Square, passing through the ancient olive trees planted along the sidewalk, their small, gray-green leaves trembling in the morning breeze. As he started up the asphalt path that encircled the open bowl of grass, he spotted Maria's brothers sitting on a dark green bench in their baggy khakis, flannel shirts and tipped-back fedoras, oblivious, as always, to the sea of chortling pigeons at their feet.

Maria's older brother, Dominic, had worked for years as a union butcher and her younger brother, Vincent, as a journeyman carpenter, but both had been injured on the job and retired on permanent disabilities, Dominic chopping two fingers off his left hand and Vincent crushing several discs in his lower back when he fell off a three-story-high scaffold. They had grown soft and heavy over the years, citing the enduring effects of their on-the-job injuries as justification for the warm red jug wine they drank all day, the two splendid morons sunning themselves in Washington Square every morning, playing bocce ball behind the North Beach Public Library all afternoon, and holding court at the dinner table every evening, hurling the occasional plate when a point required emphasis.

It was Vincent who spotted Hubbell limping up the path.

"What the fuck happened to you?" he asked.

Hubbell reached down and slapped his thigh.

"It's brand new – the best leg money can buy. How did you know it was artificial?"

"Very funny," Vincent said. "Dom, our brother-in-law thinks he's a fucking comedian."

"A regular stand-up comic," Dominic said. "I hope I don't piss myself laughing."

"Would you gentlemen mind if I joined you?" Hubbell asked.

"Dom, our brother-in-law would like to join us."

"So I hear," Dominic said. "I wonder, does he know it's a free country?"

Vincent spread his arms.

"It's a free country – at least for now," he said.

"Why thank you, gentlemen."

Hubbell waded through the pigeons and sat down beside Vincent, setting his satchel on the bench between them.

"Dom, what do you suppose brought our brother-in-law down to Washington Square this morning?"

"A very good question, Vince. Why don't you ask him?"

"I came to tell you gentlemen that I've got cancer – terminal cancer," Hubbell said.

Vincent cocked his head, peering out from behind his large purpled nose.

"Did you hear that, Dom? Our brother-in-law says he's got terminal cancer."

Dominic leaned forward, looking past his brother, his swollen face a mass of broken veins.

"That sounds serious," he said. "Ask our brother-in-law if this terminal cancer is serious."

"It's called chronic myelogenous leukemia," Hubbell said.

"What the fuck is that?" Dominic asked.

"That must be Latin, Dom. That must be what they call it in Latin."

Dominic rocked back on the bench, then turned his head and blew a long cord of mucus out his left nostril, sending the pigeons into a feeding frenzy.

"I hate that fucking language," Dominic said, wiping his nose with the back of his hand.

"I thought you gentlemen ought to know," Hubbell said.

"Did you hear that, Dom? He thought we should know."

"And why would that be, Vince?"

"I thought you should know because I'm planning on being buried beside Maria," Hubbell told them.

"Did you hear that, Dom?"

"I am, technically, still a member of the family."

"He's getting technical now, Dom."

"I was hoping I could count on you gentlemen to make sure the gravediggers bury me in the right place."

"Did you hear that, Dom? Our brother-in-law wants our help."

"Now I see what this is all about," Dominic said. "Now I get it. Our brother-in-law has come to us, asking for help."

"I knew it was coming, Dom. I could feel it."

"There's always a catch," Dominic said. "Let that be a lesson to you, Vince."

"Make sure they bury me good and deep, will you?"

"Good and deep, did you hear that, Dom?"

"I heard him," Dominic said. "Our brother-in-law says he wants us to make sure he's buried good and deep."

"I wonder, does our brother-in-law want us to do anything else, once they plant his sorry ass in the ground?"

"No, that should do it," Hubbell said.

"He says that's it, Dom. He says that's all he needs from us."

"So he says, Vince. So he says right now."

Hubbell rose from the bench.

"Thank you, gentlemen. I knew I could count on you."

"Good riddance, that's what I say," Dominic said.

"You're right, Dom. You're exactly right. Good riddance, that's what I say, too."

Hubbell picked up his satchel, then reached up and tugged down the brim of his hat.

"I'll give your best to Maria."

AS HUBBELL STEPPED out of the elevator, he glanced down at his wristwatch and saw that it was not quite eleven o'clock, not quite an hour after he normally began his shift, but certainly not late – which was why, as he started down the corridor to the newsroom, he was surprised to see Myron bolt up from his desk and hurry toward him.

He stopped as Myron approached. Myron was not looking well, which is not to suggest that he ever looked well, but he was looking even worse than normal, his eyes squeezed tight, new blemishes erupting on his blanched skin, the tuft of hair at the crest of his forehead flattened upon his scalp.

"I've been trying to call you," he said. "But, of course, you refuse to carry your fucking cell phone."

And that was true. Hubbell and his colleagues in Section Eight had made it quite clear that they had no intention of carrying cell phones. It was bad enough that the company could effectively track their every thought on the personal computers they had reluctantly consented to use, from the moment they signed on the morning to the moment they turned the computer off in the evening. Now, the company wanted to be able to reach them at any hour of the day or night, no matter where they were, or what they were doing, or, frankly, what condition they were in. It was unreasonable, to say the least.

"We've got to talk," Myron said.

"About what?" Hubbell asked.

"Right now."

Myron slipped past Hubbell and pushed in through the door of the men's restroom. Hubbell followed him, placing his satchel on the shelf inside the door and then walking up to the mirror as Myron made his way down the row of stalls, checking to make sure they were alone.

"Are you feeling all right, Myron? You don't look well."

"We've got a problem with the Jurgensen obit."

"Don't tell me he's still alive."

"Have you read it?" Myron asked.

"I wrote it," Hubbell reminded him.

Myron shoved a copy of the Bay Area section at him.

"Read it," he said.

Hubbell took the section from Myron, folded back to the obituary page. And there was a photograph of Jurgensen, a publicity still taken at his dealership in Oakland. Beneath a long string of plastic pennants, he was standing in front of his office in a pinstriped suit, his right hand on the hood of a Camaro, smiling through a rack of perfect teeth.

"Do you want to tell me what the problem is, or am I supposed to guess?" Hubbell asked.

"Just read the fucking thing!"

So Hubbell began to read the obituary. The first paragraph seemed fine, stating the essential news that Conrad Jurgensen, owner of the largest chain of used car dealerships in the Bay Area, had died at the age of seventy-eight. The second paragraph also seemed fine, expanding upon the first paragraph, noting that Jurgensen, well known for his late-night television commercials, had been born in Atlantic City and moved west after World War II to parlay his boyhood love of the automobile into an automotive empire with used car lots in eleven Bay Area cities.

Hubbell looked up at Myron.

"This really is quite nicely done, isn't it?"

The third paragraph consisted solely of the hackneyed quote from Jurgensen's wife.

"My husband's life was a modern-day Horatio Alger story. Born on the East Coast..."

But that was not what Hubbell had written. His chest tightened. He could feel the blood rushing into his face.

"Jesus," he said.

Myron spun around and pounded the door of the first stall with his fist, sending it crashing back against the wall.

"Alger Hiss! You wrote that Conrad Jurgensen's life was a modern-day Alger Hiss story!"

"That does appear to be the case," Hubbell conceded.

Myron lunged toward the row of sinks, gripping the far right sink with both hands, leaning forward as if he was about to become violently ill.

"Did you have to libel Conrad Jurgensen?" he asked. "Did you have to libel one of the editor-in-chief's golfing partners?"

And that was Myron under pressure – falling to pieces at the slightest indication of a problem. Nor did he possess even a simpleton's grasp of the profession's relevant legal statutes, particularly that provision of the law beneath which more than one obituary writer had taken refuge over the years.

"Technically speaking, the dead can not be libeled," Hubbell informed him. "And even if the dead could be libeled, they would very likely have difficulty establishing any kind of meaningful damages, given the fact that they're already deceased."

But Myron wasn't listening.

"Alger fucking Hiss!" he shouted. "You called Conrad Jurgensen a Soviet spy!"

Myron wagged his head.

"I can't believe this is happening to me," he groaned.

"Yes, well, it appears that I made a mistake – a mistake that you failed to catch, I should point out."

Myron spun around to Hubbell.

"So this is my fault?"

"I'm merely pointing out that the editing process at least theoretically involves the detection of errors," Hubbell said. "The concept, as I have come to understand it over the course of fifty-three years in the newsroom, is to detect those errors before they are published."

"How was I supposed to know who Alger Hiss is?" he shouted. "I didn't major in history! I was a journalism major!"

"Well, there you have it," Hubbell said.

Myron pounded his fist against the wall above the urinals.

"I'm ruined," he cried. "I'm fucking ruined."

HUBBELL TOOK a deep breath, then pushed out of the restroom and started back to Section Eight. The newsroom was deadly quiet. Slumped down in their cubicles, his colleagues turned away as he walked up the aisle, then watched him from behind. He could feel their eyes on his back. They knew what had happened, of course. They all knew.

He placed his satchel on his desk, then walked over to the coat rack beside the window. After hanging up his coat, he took off his hat and placed it on his computer, then he pulled out his chair and sat down. Jennings turned around to him. Poopdeck rose and stood behind his computer. The Senator pushed up and lumbered over, bracing himself on the waist-high wall of his cubicle.

"I could have done the same thing," Jennings said.

"Any of us," Poopdeck said.

"A simple mistake – very easy to make," the Senator said. "It was almost inevitable."

"I'm surprised it hasn't happened before," Poopdeck said.

Hubbell raised his hand to stop them.

"Gentlemen, gentlemen – please," he said.

"Have you talked to Hal yet?" the Senator asked.

"No."

"Have you thought about what you're going to tell him?"

"What can I tell him?" Hubbell asked. "I'll tell him the truth."

The Senator shook his head.

"I wouldn't recommend it – not under these circumstances."

"Absolutely not," Poopdeck said.

"There's a time and a place for the truth," the Senator said. "And this, most assuredly, is neither the time nor the place."

Hubbell deeply appreciated the counsel from his colleagues, but they knew he was going to tell Harold the truth, just as he knew they would do exactly the same. They had all worked with Harold too long to willfully deceive him. Hubbell would no more lie to Harold than he would lie to them.

Then his telephone rang. He knew who it had to be.

"Good morning, Graydon."

"Good morning, Helen."

"Harold would like a moment with you."

"I'll be right there," Hubbell said.

He placed the receiver in its cradle and rose from his desk.

"Would you like me to go with you, as your duly elected guild representative?" the Senator asked.

"I don't think that will be necessary," Hubbell said.

"Are you sure?"

"I can handle this," Hubbell said.

"I'll be right here, if you need me."

"GO RIGHT IN," Helen said.

Hubbell leaned into Harold's office.

"Is now a good time?" he asked. "If not, I can come back in couple weeks."

Harold looked up, the Bay Area section spread out on his desk, the Jurgensen obituary circled in red. He pointed to the leather chairs arranged in front of his desk.

"Have a seat," he said.

Hubbell lowered himself into the chair on the left. He saw nothing to be gained by postponing the obvious.

"Listen, I apologize for screwing up the Jurgensen obit," he said.

"Would you like to tell me what happened?"

"Actually, I'd prefer to forget all about it."

"Why don't you tell me anyway."

Hubbell shrugged.

"Jurgensen's stepson called in the quote. He said Horatio Alger. I wrote down Alger Hiss."

"As simple as that?"

"As simple as that," Hubbell said.

Harold shook his head in disbelief.

"Jesus Christ."

"And Myron whiffed on it, of course."

"I think it's fair to say that Myron is not the source of the problem this morning."

"I can't say I got much help from the copy desk, either," Hubbell said.

But Harold wasn't listening.

"Alger Hiss?" he asked, as if he still couldn't believe it.

"I don't know what to tell you, Hal."

"Out of the blue?"

"Out of the blue."

"Jesus Christ."

"How did Fleming take it?" Hubbell asked him.

"I just hope he has another pair of trousers in his office," Harold said.

"I'll call Jurgensen's wife and offer my personal apology, if you think that might help."

"No, I don't think this is the time," Harold said.

He pushed the Bay Area section aside, then leaned back in his chair.

"So how are you feeling these days?" he asked.

"I feel fine for a seventy-six-year-old man."

"No symptoms of the cancer?"

"I get a little tired, now and again."

"I'm sure your doctor has warned you against pushing yourself."

"Yes, he has."

"But you still intend to keep working?" Harold asked.

"For now, yes."

Harold clasped his hands over his flat stomach.

"Have you given any thought to working part-time?"

"No," Hubbell said.

"That might be worth considering."

"Why?"

"It might be a way to preserve your energy."

"I didn't screw up the Jurgensen obit because I have cancer, if that's what you're suggesting," Hubbell said.

"If you say so."

"Is that what you think?"

"Honestly, I don't know what to think," Harold said. "I don't know what, if any, role your medical condition might have played in this fiasco. All I know is that it's my job to make sure it doesn't happen again."

"I understand," Hubbell said.

Harold shook his head.

"Jesus, Graydon."

"So where do we go from here?" Hubbell asked.

"Let's start by working up a correction for tomorrow's paper," Harold said.

HUBBELL HATED writing corrections. There was nothing he disliked more. He had always taken pride in the accuracy of his reporting, and over the course of his career, he had been compelled to write relatively few corrections, all of them quite minor. He understood that no one, least of all himself, is perfect. He understood that everyone makes the occasional mistake. Still, corrections were nothing less than humbling, if not humiliating – an admission of guilt, a public confession, and, in this case, a subtle suggestion that his career might be nearing the end.

He put off writing the correction for as long as he possibly could, ignoring repeated entreaties from Myron, but eventually, as the day wore on, he resigned himself to completing the odious task. Fortunately, there was not a lot to explain. As egregious as his mistake had been, there was nothing complex or nuanced about it, and he kept the correction as simple as possible, the guiding principle for any correction, noting merely that in yesterday's obituary for Conrad Jurgensen, the wife of the deceased had been misquoted. Her husband's life was "a modern-day Horatio Alger story," she told the Chronicle. And that was that. He read the correction over carefully, making sure, above all else, that he hadn't repeated his mistake, and then he filed it to Myron, relieved to be done with it and wanting to never hear Conrad Jurgensen's name again.

He wanted a drink. He wanted a glass of wine. He would buy a round of cocktails for his colleagues in Section Eight, a gesture, however modest, of appreciation for their unwavering support. And the time had come to tell them that he had been diagnosed with terminal cancer. They deserved to know that in all likelihood, he would be the next to go, that soon, too soon, there would be another empty desk in the back of the newsroom. It would be a difficult conversation, for his colleagues as much as for him, reminding them not only of their own frail mortality, but also, as occupants of Section Eight, as members of a species indigenous to the newsroom and to be found nowhere else, of the sad fact that they were moving inexorably toward extinction.

It was only last spring that they had lost Floyd Templeton, and they had taken his death hard. Templeton had been an exceptional reporter assigned to cover the public transportation beat. He possessed, of all things, a photographic memory, and, in service of his assignment, he had memorized the time and place of every stop on every line of the city's municipal bus and light rail schedule. It was an astounding mental feat, a tribute to the power of the human mind. Unfortunately, the gifted Templeton was also color-blind, unable to distinguish between green and red, and, in a moment of confusion, was run over, ironically, by a Muni bus while attempting to cross Market against the light. The accident had taken place not far from the Chronicle, which meant that one of the paper's photographers was able to get to the scene in time to capture an image of Templeton's feet protruding out from beneath the right rear wheel well of the bus, and in commemoration of his tragic death, a copy of the photograph was tacked up on the guild bulletin board in the corridor near the mailroom, complete with a handwritten caption that loudly proclaimed, "Next Stop Colma!" – an allusion, obviously, to the city of cemeteries on the Peninsula. It was nothing less than an extemporaneous expression of the dark humor that once flourished in the newsroom – before the younger generation arrived with their fondness for shallow irony – and no one would have enjoyed the caption more than Templeton himself, although, in retrospect, it was certainly regrettable that his distraught widow glimpsed the photograph when she came to the paper to collect her dead husband's personal effects.

"Gentlemen, would you care to join me for a cocktail at the Tempest?" Hubbell asked. "I would be honored if you'd permit me to buy the first round."

He didn't have to ask twice.

"It would be my pleasure," the Senator said.

"Aye," Poopdeck said.

Jennings nodded.

"Yes, I do believe I would like a glass of wine."

"Excellent," Hubbell said.

THEY PUSHED INSIDE the Tempest and followed the Senator to his preferred table. After removing his coat and draping it over the back of his chair, Hubbell walked up to the bar to order a round of drinks, only to observe that the bartender was already preparing them.

Abby delivered their drinks only moments later.

"Ah, mother's milk," the Senator said.

Hubbell raised his glass.

"Gentlemen, I thank you for your support today," he said. "I think it's fair to say that this was not my finest hour."

They raised their glasses to join him, then each took a blessed sip.

"But I'm afraid I have some bad news, above and beyond the problem with the Jurgensen obit," he said.

The Senator drained his martini, then raised the glass, signaling Abby that he would like another. The bartender had already poured it, of course, and she brought it over and set it down in front of him.

"Thank you, my dear," he said.

"I've got cancer," Hubbell said.

Their eyes fell on him.

"I've been diagnosed with a form of cancer called chronic myelogenous leukemia," he said.

He looked to Jennings.

"I'm sure you're familiar with CML," he said.

"I'm afraid I am," Jennings said. "May I ask what stage the cancer is in?"

"It's in the blast crisis stage," Hubbell said.

"Oh, my," Jennings said.

"What the fuck does that mean?" the Senator asked.

"It means they caught it late – too late," Hubbell said. "It means there's nothing they can do."

"You can't be serious," the Senator said.

Hubbell shrugged.

"My neighbor has me drinking a tea prescribed by her Chinese herbalist."

"Oh, for the love of Christ," Poopdeck said.

"I just started drinking it this week – but so far so good."

"The efficacy of herbal remedies, particularly those used for many years in the Orient, has been very difficult to establish," Jennings said.

"No shit," Poopdeck said.

"Researchers have had great difficulty replicating the beneficial effects in controlled studies."

"Now there's a fucking surprise," Poopdeck said.

"But that doesn't mean those positive results aren't real," Jennings said.

"What have I got to lose?" Hubbell asked.

"It's certainly worth keeping an open mind," Jennings said.

"I mean, why not – I'm dying, for Christ's sake."

The Senator took another sip of his martini.

"I don't suppose there's anything we can do," he said.

"Actually, there is," Hubbell said.

"Whatever you need – anything," the Senator said.

Hubbell took a sip of wine.

"Someone is going to have to take over the ghoul pool."

"You're absolutely right," the Senator said. "And let me assure you that in your absence, in your honor, we will do everything within our power to ensure the smooth operation of that hallowed institution."

Poopdeck pounded his fist on the table.

"I still want a rule banning management," he said.

And it occurred to Hubbell, at that moment, that Poopdeck might be just the one to assume the mantle of command.

"How would you like to run the ghoul pool?" Hubbell asked him.

"I second the motion," the Senator said.

"All those in favor, raise your right hand," Hubbell said.

He raised his hand. The Senator and Jennings promptly followed suit.

"Gentlemen, I can die in peace," Hubbell said.

AFTER CROSSING through the yard in the dark, Hubbell climbed the cottage stairs slowly, his hand gripping the railing as he pulled himself up one step at a time. It was late, nearly midnight. He had stayed at the Tempest too long, drinking with his esteemed colleagues, the Senator singing his union ballads and old folk standards, along with the occasional Negro spiritual; Poopdeck furiously playing pinball, grappling violently with the machine, pounding his fist on the glass when his ball disappeared; Jennings falling into a deep sleep, waking only when Abby set another glass of wine on the table in front of him. Hubbell hadn't intended to stay long, but he couldn't leave before his colleagues. He was, after all, the one who was dying, the guest of honor at his own pre-emptive wake. His colleagues were drinking to him, raising their glasses to the man he had once been. It was a fine farewell. He was glad to have been there.

At the landing at the top of the stairs, he dug his keys out of his pocket and let himself into the kitchen. He shrugged off his coat and hung it over the back of one of the chairs at the table, then crossed the kitchen and pulled open the door of the refrigerator. He reached in for the bowl of leftover lentil soup and carried it over to the counter. After spooning the heavy sludge into a saucepan, he put it on the stove and turned on the burner beneath it. He filled a second smaller pan with water and placed it on the stove to boil.

As he sat down at the table, he told himself that Ms. Gifford would be proud of him, finishing the soup she had made to keep his strength up, drinking a cup of the tea prescribed by her herbalist. She might be an imperfect tenant, but she was a fine neighbor, doing everything she could to keep him alive. It would be hard to ask a neighbor for more than that, and as Hubbell rose from his chair to stir the soup, it occurred to him that he needed to find a way to express his appreciation for all that Ms. Gifford had done for him. He needed a way to reciprocate, and the answer, as was so often the case, was right there in front of him – he would invite Ms. Gifford to dinner. It was a fine idea, and he knew he had to act now, before he found a reason not to, before he talked himself out of it.

He put the spoon down and walked over to the telephone and dialed Ms. Gifford's number, holding the receiver against his ear as he looked down to the back of her flat.

He saw the light come on in the kitchen.

"Hello?" she asked.

"Lydia?"

"Graydon, is that you?"

"I hope I'm not calling too late," he said.

"Are you all right?"

"I just got home, actually."

"It sounds like you had a long day."

"You could say that," he said. "But here I am now, in the kitchen, heating up your soup."

"I'm so glad you liked it."

Which was not what he said, of course, but he saw nothing to be gained by correcting her.

"It was very thoughtful of you to go to all the trouble of making it for me," he said.

"Oh, I didn't mind. It's really quite easy. I've made it so many times that I know the recipe by heart. Only I didn't quite get the lid of the blender on tight, and it flew off when I turned it on, and it took a little while to wipe up the mess, I mean, the cabinets and everything, but I didn't mind – I really didn't."

Hubbell reached up and massaged his temples with his fingertips, unable to prevent himself from envisioning the eruption in her kitchen.

"That's why I'm calling," he said. "I'm hoping you'll permit me to reciprocate."

"Reciprocate?"

"As an expression of my gratitude, I'd like to invite you to dinner."

"Graydon, are you serious?"

"I'm hoping you might be available tomorrow night."

"Oh, Graydon, I would love to come to dinner tomorrow night."

"Excellent," he said.

"And here, I thought something was wrong."

"No, nothing is wrong," he assured her.

"Instead, you're inviting me to dinner."

"Yes, that's right."

"I can't wait," she said.

"All right then," Hubbell said. "I'll see you tomorrow night."

"Goodnight, Graydon."

"Goodnight, Lydia."

Hubbell hung up the receiver. As he returned to the stove to stir the soup, he couldn't believe what he had just done. It had sounded like such a good idea. It had made so much sense. He could only shake his head. He was a fool, such a fool, and an old fool at that.

CHAPTER NINE

HUBBELL GLANCED DOWN at his side-view mirror, then guided the Mustang over to the side of Harrison Street and parked in front of Farentino Stoneworks, the name of the company in fading black letters above the door of the corrugated sheet metal warehouse. He climbed out of the car and crossed the sidewalk to the gate in a tall wrought-iron fence that enclosed a garden of statuary in front of the warehouse office – the weeping angels, ornate crosses and slender obelisks, the sculpted headstones and simple grave markers planted among the weeds that had taken root in a bed of compacted gravel. A sign taped to the door of the office warned that Trespassers Will Be Prosecuted. As Hubbell opened the gate and walked up to the door, he had to assume that didn't apply to prospective clients.

He knocked once, then reached down and let himself into the office. It was small and dark, the walls covered with mahogany paneling, the floor with a green shag carpet. A man in a gray sharkskin suit was sitting at a desk behind a short counter, drinking black coffee from a white Styrofoam cup. He scrambled to his feet as

Hubbell entered the office, a small black toupee clinging to the crown of his head, his face gaunt and as pale as ash, a thin moustache slanting across his upper lip, a cigarette pinched into the corner of his mouth.

He walked up to the counter, his right hand extended, a silver mesh bracelet dangling from his wrist.

"Tony Farentino," he said. "What can I do for you?"

Hubbell shook his hand.

"I'd like to talk to someone about ordering a headstone."

Farentino spread his arms.

"That would be me," he said. "You've come to the right place – satisfaction guaranteed."

Farentino crushed the cigarette in a shallow foil ashtray on the counter.

"Of course, we're extremely sorry to hear about your loss."

"Well, we haven't lost him quite yet," Hubbell said.

"A family member?"

"We're very close," Hubbell said.

Farentino picked up the Styrofoam cup and took a last sip of the coffee, wincing as he dropped the cup into a metal trashcan.

"Do you have a sense of what you're looking for?" he asked.

"A simple headstone – that's all," Hubbell said.

"This friend was a man of simple tastes?"

"I believe that would be fair to say."

"Why don't we step into the warehouse to see if we can find what you have in mind?"

Hubbell followed Farentino through the back door of the office and into the warehouse. In the light sifting down from the iron-framed skylights, they walked slowly through the thick slabs of granite lying on wooden pallets, the long rows of blank headstones arranged by gradients of size, the stacks of beveled grave markers. Across the warehouse, a large gray rat scurried through the dust that blanketed the concrete floor, disappearing behind the forklift parked beside the door to the storage yard behind the warehouse.

Farentino reached into his shirt pocket and withdrew a pack of cigarettes. He shook one out of the pack and took it in his teeth, then struck a match and lit it, flicking the spent match into the dust.

"I recommend granite," he said, waving his hand across the warehouse. "With a rating of six on the hardness scale, it's significantly more durable than marble, and we do want your friend's headstone to last, don't we?"

"That does seem to be the point," Hubbell said.

"Do you have a sense of the size of the headstone for your friend?" Farentino asked.

Hubbell reached down, his hand at the middle of his thigh, trying to recall how tall Maria's headstone was, wanting them to be the same size, equals even in the afterlife.

"Very nice," Farentino said.

He took a long drag on his cigarette, exhaling through his nose, then made his way slowly down the center aisle of the warehouse, stopping to run his hand across the smooth, gently rounded top of a blank headstone.

"Something like this?" he asked. "A standard double-die upright, thirty inches tall, twenty-four inches wide, two inches thick?"

"Yes, that looks about right," Hubbell said.

"A classic – very popular," Farentino said. "Of course, granite comes in many colors, as you can see."

"I'm sure he would prefer gray," Hubbell said.

"A face in the crowd, was he?"

"He was quite modest, actually," Hubbell said.

"We offer, naturally, a full range of etching and inscription services at what we like to think are very affordable prices."

Farentino took another drag on his cigarette, then waved the smoke out of his face.

"We can provide any number of decorative images for the face of the stone – crosses, roses, doves, however you'd like to doll it up."

"No, I don't think so," Hubbell said.

"Perhaps an inscription of an inspirational nature? Is your friend religious? We've got a whole binder full of inspirational material in the office."

"Perhaps I'll take a look later on," Hubbell said, though, of course, he had absolutely no intention of doing so.

Farentino took a last drag on his cigarette, then flicked the glowing butt into the rows of headstones.

"On the other hand, some of our clients have preferred a lighter touch," he said. "Does this friend of your have a sense of humor?"

He didn't wait for an answer.

"Maybe something like, 'I knew this would happen.'"

Farentino smiled through his yellow teeth.

"Or, 'You should see the other guy.'"

A laugh escaped Farentino, phlegm crackling deep in his lungs.

"Or how about, 'Don't get me started.'"

Farentino laughed again, but his laughter quickly devolved into a violent coughing fit. He leaned forward, hands on his knees, his whole body shuddering as he gasped for air. Finally, he managed to compose himself, taking a deep breath, his face as red as a boil, reaching up to make sure his toupee had remained in place.

"I'm not sure humor is what we're looking for," Hubbell said.

"Of course not," Farentino hastened to say. "It was just an option. I just wanted to make sure that you were aware of all your options."

Farentino shook another cigarette out of the pack and took it in his teeth.

"Perhaps a simple R.I.P.," he said.

"That sounds fine," Hubbell said.

"We can even inscribe it in Latin, if you'd prefer – Requiescat in Pace."

"Sure," Hubbell said.

Farentino pointed at Hubbell's chest.

"Classy – very classy," he said. "This friend of yours is a class act, if you want to know my opinion."

"So, how do we proceed from here?" Hubbell asked.

Farentino lit his cigarette, then used the tip of his index finger to dislodge a piece of tobacco from between his two front teeth. He spat it to the ground.

"There's not much we can do until this friend of yours does his part, if you know what I mean. We've got the stone in stock, but we can't begin the etching process until we have the date of your friend's death."

That made a certain grim sense.

"We'll go back to the office and write up a work order, and then when your friend bites the dust, you let me know, and we'll get started."

"That sounds fine," Hubbell said.

AFTER STOPPING at the market, Hubbell drove back to Filbert Street and parked the Mustang in the garage. As he carried the two bags of groceries back to his cottage, he was looking forward to preparing dinner for Ms. Gifford. He liked to cook, and he liked to think he was a capable cook, although it must be said that he didn't cook often, not lately, not anymore. It hardly seemed worth the effort to prepare a meal solely for himself.

He had learned to cook from Maria, of course, or at least from sitting at the table with a glass of wine, watching her, and he would use her recipe to make eggplant Parmesan for Ms. Gifford. As he crossed the kitchen and placed the bags on the counter, he knew that Maria would understand. In fact, it occurred to Hubbell that Maria might very well like Ms. Gifford, as a neighbor if not necessarily as a tenant. She would certainly appreciate all that Ms. Gifford had done for him recently, ever since she learned he was dying of cancer. Maria would surely understand why he felt obligated to reciprocate that kindness, why he had invited Ms. Gifford to dinner. He was doing the right thing, and he knew Maria would agree.

After taking a quick shower, he returned to the kitchen to begin preparing the eggplant Parmesan, placing her recipe card on the counter and following the instructions closely. He made the sauce first, and while it simmered, he cut up the eggplant and browned the thick slices in a skillet. After combining the ricotta, the grated Parmesan and two eggs in a large bowl, he assembled the dish in layers in a glass baking dish. And that was that. He wiped his hands on a dishtowel and stepped back to admire his work. It might not be a culinary masterpiece, but it was the best he could do.

He slipped the dish into the oven, not quite half an hour before Ms. Gifford was due to arrive, and soon the smell filled the kitchen. As he set the table, he heard Ms. Gifford climbing the stairs, right on time. He couldn't believe his ears.

He crossed the kitchen and opened the door and waited for her to reach the landing.

"Good evening, Lydia."

"Good evening, Graydon."

As she entered the kitchen, she closed her eyes and inhaled deeply, her lungs rising beneath her black turtleneck sweater, her long gray-blond hair drifting over her shoulders.

"What is that heavenly smell?"

"I hope you like eggplant Parmesan," he said.

"Oh, Graydon, I love eggplant Parmesan."

"It's not only vegetarian, it's fully organic."

"Graydon, you are so thoughtful."

"Would you care for a glass of vino?" he asked.

She smiled, her mouth drawn in red lipstick.

"That would be wonderful," she said.

Hubbell returned to the counter and took the bottle opener out of the drawer beside the refrigerator. After peeling the foil off a bottle of Pinot Noir, he twisted the worm into the cork and then pried it out of the neck of the bottle. He poured the wine into two glasses and handed one to Ms. Gifford.

"So, how was your day, Lydia?"

"I had a wonderful day," she said. "I went to my yoga class."

"I didn't know you were a practitioner," Hubbell said.

"Oh, yes," she said. "I've been a practitioner for many years now – almost two, actually, going on three or four."

"You must enjoy it."

"It's not as easy as it sounds," she said. "It turns out that I've got muscles I didn't even know about."

"That's very interesting," Hubbell said.

"But I'm very limber now – and I do mean very."

"It's important to be flexible," Hubbell said. "I've always said that."

"And it's very good for your breathing," she said.

"So I understand."

As he joined her at the table, she sat back in her chair and closed her eyes and took a deep breath. For a moment, Hubbell thought she might start chanting. Instead, she pressed her hands together in front of her chest, fingertip to fingertip as she slowly released the air in her lungs, passing through her pursed lips with a soft whistle.

Her eyes rolled open.

"Did you see that?" she asked.

"Yes, I did."

"That's exactly what I mean."

Hubbell took a sip of wine, wondering what, exactly, or even generally, she was talking about.

"You see, Graydon. It puts your whole body in proper alignment."

"Ah," he said, as if that explained it.

"It's very healing. With my body in perfect alignment, I feel like a whole new woman."

"Really?"

"Have you ever taken a yoga class?" she asked.

Hubbell had to smile.

"No, I've never taken a yoga class," he said.

But Ms. Gifford wasn't listening. She lifted her nose.

"Graydon, do you smell that?"

For a moment, Hubbell had no idea what she was talking about, then he leapt up from the table and pulled down the oven door. A cloud of smoke billowed out as he leaned down to look inside, the eggplant Parmesan bubbling furiously beneath a charred black crust. He grabbed the hot pads and reached in for the lip of the baking dish and pulled it out to the front of the rack, then he reached for the lip on the back of the dish. He managed to lift the dish off the rack, but the glass was too hot, burning his fingers through the hot pads. Before he could raise the dish to the top of the stove, he had to let go. The dish crashed onto the open door of the stove and then toppled onto the floor, the slices of eggplant slopping onto the linoleum as Hubbell danced back out of the way.

"Goddamn it!"

And then the kitchen fell into silence. As he stared down at the mess on the floor, he couldn't believe he had forgotten to set the timer or even note the time. He felt like an idiot, and not, he had to admit, without some justification.

He looked over to Ms. Gifford, her hands covering her mouth, her left eye wide with horror, her right eye having fled the premises.

"Oh, Graydon," she said.

Hubbell closed the oven door, then snapped the oven off in disgust. He walked over to the sink and opened the window, then he crossed the kitchen and opened the door, so the draft would draw the smoke out of the kitchen.

He returned to the counter and opened the upper drawer, reaching in for the Imperial Garden take-out menu and carrying it over to the telephone.

"How do you feel about Chinese food?" he asked her.

"I love Chinese food, Graydon – the hotter, the better."

HE KNELT DOWN and used a spatula to scoop the eggplant back into the baking dish, then he grabbed the hot pads and picked it up and placed it in the sink.

"Is there anything I can do to help?" she asked.

"No – thank you, but no."

On his hands and knees, he wiped up the mess. When the floor was clean, he grabbed the edge of the counter and pulled himself up to stand, then he washed his hands in the sink, turning back to Ms. Gifford as he dried them off.

"May I offer you a little more wine?"

"That would be very nice," she said.

He carried the bottle over to the table and refilled her glass, then he set the bottle on the table and sat down across from her.

"Graydon, may I ask you a personal question?"

"I suppose."

"You told me once that your wife died in a car accident."

"Yes, that is true."

"You told me it was a long time ago."

"She died in 1973."

Ms. Gifford shrugged, her right eye joining her left in looking down at her wine.

"That just seems so long ago," she said.

"Some days, it seems like it happened in another lifetime. Some days, it seems like it happened yesterday."

"I just thought you might have remarried at some point – that's all," she said.

"Is there something wrong with loving someone for life?"

"No, of course not," she said. "It just seems so sad. It just seems like such a waste."

"A waste of what?" he asked her.

"Of life, Graydon."

Hubbell allowed himself a smile. He had not anticipated being lectured on the meaning of life when he invited Ms. Gifford to dinner. Nor, for that matter, was Ms. Gifford in any position to characterize the last thirty-nine years of his life as a waste, in his humble opinion.

"Perhaps you'll tell me why you haven't remarried, Lydia."

"Oh, I'm ready, Graydon. Absolutely. All I need is the right man."

She batted her eyes at Hubbell. Fortunately, he heard the sound of footsteps coming up the stairs.

He stood up as the delivery boy appeared in the doorway, clutching a brown paper bag. Hubbell motioned for him to place the bag on the table, then reached for the bill stapled to the top of the bag. He withdrew his wallet and handed the delivery boy a twenty-dollar bill and a ten-dollar bill.

"Keep the change," he said.

Without a word, the delivery boy turned and left. After closing the door behind him, Hubbell began lifting the white cartons out of the bag, opening the flaps and folding them back so they could see what each of the cartons contained.

"Please, help yourself," he said.

As he folded up the bag, Ms. Gifford picked up a carton and began forking the steamed rice onto her plate. She wasn't shy, tucking her hair behind her ears as she reached for the carton of Kung Pao shrimp, tilting the carton on its side and raking the shrimp and peppers and peanuts onto the rice, the juice drizzling out the corner of the carton. Hubbell sat down across from her and reached for the carton of rice, scooping what remained of it onto his plate. As Ms. Gifford slipped a pair of wooden chopsticks out of the paper sleeve, Hubbell poured the rest of the shrimp onto his rice and set the carton aside.

He watched as Ms. Gifford used her chopsticks to deftly pick up one of the pieces of shrimp and raise it to her mouth. He had no intention of using his chopsticks. He hated chopsticks. Instead, he picked up a fork and stabbed a piece of shrimp. He took a bite, and, yes, it was hot, igniting in his mouth, a surge of heat climbing into his face.

"Jesus," he gasped.

He stood up and grabbed two glasses from the drying tray. He filled them with water and carried them over to the table.

"Here you are," he said.

But if the heat of the Kung Pao shrimp affected Ms. Gifford in any way, she gave no indication.

"Graydon, do you know what you need?"

"What would that be?"

"You need a life list."

He took another bite of the shrimp.

"Have you given any thought to all the things you want to do before you die?"

"Actually, I haven't," he said.

"Well, you should, don't you think?"

"I'm not sure I need a life list," he said.

"Don't be silly," she said. "Even I have a life list, and I have no intention of dying."

"I'm glad to hear that," Hubbell said.

"Oh, yes, I've been working on my life list for years, checking things off as I go. Next, I'm going to take some classes at the Academy of Art, as soon as I get the money anyway. I've always been artistically inclined, or so they say. In school, I was always drawing or doodling – I just couldn't help it."

"That doesn't surprise me," Hubbell said.

"Oh, yes – I'm a very talented doodler, or so they say."

"You're a woman of many talents."

"The first class I'm going to take is a figure drawing class with live nude models," she said. "You see, Graydon, I'm very comfortable with nudity. That's right. I believe the human body is beautiful, very beautiful, as a matter of fact, a work of art, in its own right, if you know what I mean."

Hubbell stabbed at another piece of shrimp and raised it to

his mouth, the heat once again rising into his face, although Ms. Gifford may have been at least partly responsible. He always became warm when Ms. Gifford talked about the human body, the female body, about nudity, about her breasts, even if she hadn't mentioned them specifically, although she might as well have, at least from his perspective.

"And, of course, I'd like to write a book," she said,

"Really?" he asked, relieved that she had moved on to the next item on her list.

"Oh, yes," she said. "I want to write down my philosophy of life, so to speak, all my theories and ideas and so forth and so forth."

"I'd certainly like to read that," Hubbell said.

"Why, thank you, Graydon. I've been taking notes for some time now. I have a whole shoebox full of notes. One of these days, I'm going to take that shoebox down and write out my whole philosophy."

"That seems like a very good idea," he said.

"Do you know what my philosophy is?"

"I don't believe you've ever shared that with me."

She straightened up in her chair, her shoulders drawn back. She smiled at him.

"If it feels good, do it," she said.

"Of course," Hubbell said. "It's hard to argue with that."

"I mean, why not?" she asked.

"You'll get no argument from me," he assured her.

"I mean, why the hell not?"

AS HUBBELL CLEARED the plates from the table, Ms. Gifford smiled up at him, her right eye wandering off to the left, as if feeling the effects of the wine.

"Graydon, would you mind if I smoked a joint?"

For a moment, he wasn't sure he had heard her correctly. He

wondered if she was joking. Then he realized she was serious.

"It's perfectly legal," she said. "It's medical marijuana. I bought it at one of the cannabis clubs."

She produced a slender marijuana cigarette, holding it up for him to see.

"I have a medical condition," she told him.

"I wasn't aware of that," he said.

"Oh, yes – anxiety. I can get very anxious."

Hubbell had to smile. And here, all this time, he thought Ms. Gifford was just getting high.

"I have a prescription from a doctor."

"It's good to know that your condition has been professionally diagnosed," Hubbell said.

"Oh, yes. He has a degree in medicine. It was just like a real doctor's examination."

He reached for the bottle of wine and saw that it was nearly empty.

"Perhaps I should open another bottle?"

But Ms. Gifford seemed not to have heard him. When he turned around, she was striking a match and lighting her marijuana cigarette. By not explicitly objecting, he had, apparently, given her his tacit approval. There was nothing he could do but watch as she sucked the smoke deep into her lungs, holding the smoke for as long as she could, then tipping her head back and exhaling, a thin stream of smoke pushing up at the ceiling. It made Hubbell nervous. He wondered if he was contracting her anxiety.

"Would you like to try it?" she asked.

"You can't be serious. I'm seventy-six years old."

Ms. Gifford shrugged.

"Suit yourself," she said.

As he tugged the cork out of a second bottle of wine, Ms. Gifford took another drag on her marijuana cigarette. He watched as she held the smoke in her lungs until she finally had to release it.

"Maybe you should put on some music," she said.

"Music?"

"What kind of music do you listen to, Graydon?"

It was a good question, but one he certainly hadn't anticipated.

"I haven't been listening to much music lately," he said.

"Oh, Graydon," she said, her voice sinking with disappointment. "What kind of music did you used to listen to?"

Hubbell had to think.

"I always liked Sinatra," he said.

"Sinatra! Of course!"

Ms. Gifford threw her head back and laughed. She laughed so hard she had to wrap her arms around her chest.

The humor eluded Hubbell.

"That's just so perfect, Graydon. I mean, who else would you listen to?"

"Perhaps I should apologize for being so obvious."

But Ms. Gifford reached out and placed her hand on his forearm.

"Oh, no – I'd love to hear some Sinatra," she said. "Why don't you put on your favorite Sinatra for us?"

"All right," Hubbell said, accepting the challenge. "I'll do just that."

He set the bottle of wine on the table, then he turned and walked into the living room. The stereo cabinet resided to the left of the fireplace. He knelt down in front of it and opened the cabinet door. His record collection was on the bottom shelf, so he turned his head sideways to read the names of the albums on the thin spines of their jackets. His Sinatra collection was on the far right. When he found the *Strangers in the Night* album, he pulled it out, and there on the cover was Sinatra in the recording studio – the chairman of the board in total command, young and cool as he stood before the music stand in his black tuxedo, his left hand raised as if to cue the orchestra, his right hand tracing the lyrics on the sheet of music as he lifted his voice to the descending microphone.

"My God, Graydon – that's a record."

Hubbell looked back over his right shoulder. Ms. Gifford had followed him into the living room and slumped down into the sofa.

"You have a record player."

"And your point, Lydia?"

"I feel like I'm in a time machine."

"Perhaps it's the marijuana," he said.

She smiled at that.

"Perhaps," she said.

Hubbell turned his attention back to the record player. He slipped the album out of the jacket and placed it on the turntable and turned it on. As the record began to spin, he lifted the turntable's arm and placed the needle on the shallow grooves at the edge of the record. Static crackled through the speakers as the needle chattered through the scratches, but then there was Nelson Riddle's orchestra playing that signature melody, the lilting strings and muted horns pouring through the static – and then that flawless voice.

He looked back at Ms. Gifford. Her eyes were closed. Her head was resting on the back of the sofa, her hands on the cushions on either side of her. She looked as if she had fallen asleep. Or perhaps she had passed out. He decided to listen. He had listened to this song, this album, a million times. He knew it by heart.

When the song ended, Ms. Gifford's eyes slowly opened. She smiled across the room.

"A little schmaltzy, but not bad," she said.

"Schmaltzy?"

"Oh, don't worry, Graydon. I like schmaltz."

"I'm glad to hear that," he said.

She stood up, requiring a moment to secure her balance, then she crossed the room to stand directly in front of him.

"Let's dance, Graydon, shall we?"

And just then, Riddle's orchestra began playing "The Summer Wind."

"You like to dance, don't you?"

"I haven't danced in years," he confessed.

She didn't seem to care. She stepped toward him. Before he fully realized what she was doing, she took his left hand and placed it on the ledge of her hip, then she clasped his right hand and clutched it between her breasts. Slowly, she began to move. He had no choice but to move with her, not dancing so much as simply turning in place in the middle of the living room, and then Ms. Gifford moved closer still, pressing the side of her head against his chest. As the music played, Hubbell realized that he wasn't dancing with Ms. Gifford so much as he was simply holding her, rocking slowly from side to side. He hadn't seen it coming. This certainly wasn't his intention. But if Ms. Gifford wanted to dance to his Sinatra, he was willing to indulge her. It was not, to be perfectly honest, altogether distasteful.

When the song ended, Ms. Gifford leaned back and looked up at him, her right eye joining her left, at least for the moment.

"You dance beautifully, Graydon."

"Why thank you, Lydia."

She leaned back into him, her head against his chest.

"I could dance all night," she said.

"Let's just take it a song at a time," he said.

THEY DANCED through all of Hubbell's best Sinatra. When the last song ended, when he heard the needle clicking on the record's interior grooves, he pulled away from Ms. Gifford and crossed the living room and switched off the turntable.

"That was very nice, Graydon."

"I'm glad my Sinatra met with your approval," he said.

She smiled at him.

"Oh, yes, I enjoyed the music, too."

Clever. Hubbell let the remark pass. Ms. Gifford was displaying her sense of humor, clearly under the influence of her marijuana.

"May I escort you back to your flat?" he asked.

"If you must," she said.

He gestured toward the door.

"I must," he said.

He followed her through the kitchen and out onto the landing, taking her by the back of the elbow as they descended the creaking stairs, offering her his arm as they crossed the patio. When they arrived at her back door, he reached down and opened it for her.

She turned to face him.

"Thank you for a lovely evening, Graydon."

"It was my pleasure."

He stepped to the side of the door so that she might enter her flat – but she didn't move. Instead, she closed her eyes and tilted her head back, pursing her plump lips, and, yes, Hubbell knew what Ms. Gifford was waiting for, he knew what she wanted. And that was fine. He didn't mind. He saw no reason not to kiss Ms. Gifford goodnight. If Ms. Gifford desired a kiss to bring the evening to a proper close, he, as her gracious host, was certainly willing to accommodate her.

And he would do so without delay, without hesitation, before his mouth grew any drier, his chest any tighter. He placed his hands on her shoulders, holding her still as he leaned down and lowered his mouth to hers, kissing her ever so lightly, ever so briefly. And that took care of that. He straightened back up, the kiss delivered, the kiss received.

As he released her shoulders, her eyes rolled open, her right eye somewhat reluctantly.

"That's it?" she asked.

Hubbell took a step back, stung by the question.

"That wasn't much of a kiss," she said.

"Yes, well, it's late, quite late," he said in defense of himself. "I suppose I'm a little tired."

"Maybe you ought to take another shot at it."

A nervous laugh escaped him.

"You might enjoy it," she said. "I'm quite the kisser, Graydon, or so I've been told."

"Yes, I'm sure that's true," he said. "I'm sure that's quite true."

"There's nothing like a good kiss, not in my book, anyway."

Hubbell didn't dispute her. He certainly didn't want to argue.

"But that's all right," she said.

She reached out and ran a fingertip down his forearm, forgiving him.

"I'm sure you'll do better next time."

Hubbell had no idea what Ms. Gifford was talking about. Next time? Once again, she had lost him.

"Yes, well, we'll see about that," he said.

She smiled up at him again.

"Goodnight, Graydon."

"Goodnight, Lydia."

She slipped past him, entering her flat. After closing the door behind her, waiting a moment for her to secure the deadbolt, he turned and started back to his cottage, relieved the evening was finally over, but still smarting, frankly, from Ms. Gifford's critique of his kiss. He was sorry to have disappointed her. He was sorry his kiss had failed to meet her expectations. But what did she expect? It was only a goodnight kiss, nothing more, nothing less. It was purely perfunctory, a mere formality. That was all it was. That was all it was intended to be.

Surely Ms. Gifford understood that. And surely, he suddenly found himself hoping, Maria understood that, too. But there was no way to know what she might have been thinking as she looked down on them from above, as she watched him kiss Ms. Gifford. He could feel his face burning with shame and embarrassment. As he crossed the patio, he felt as if Maria had caught him doing something wrong. And perhaps she had.

Perhaps it had been a mistake to invite Ms. Gifford to dinner. Perhaps it had been a mistake to play her his best Sinatra. Perhaps it had been a mistake to kiss Ms. Gifford goodnight. He realized that he may very well have given Maria the wrong impression. He may very well have given Ms. Gifford the wrong impression, too. He should have known better. He did know better. A kiss was never just a kiss. A kiss was only the beginning. A kiss was always the beginning.

CHAPTER TEN

HUBBELL PUSHED through the door of the men's room and made his way down the row of unoccupied stalls. The door to the last stall was closed. When he stooped down and peered beneath it, he observed a pair of dark brown trousers piled up on a pair of dark brown shoes.

He stood up.

"Senator, is that you?"

"Yes."

"It's me – Graydon."

"I know."

Hubbell stepped back.

"Do you have a minute?" he asked.

"Apparently so," the Senator said.

"Katrina Reisner wants me to swing by her office. I was hoping you could be there, as my guild representative."

"Right now?"

"Well, she just called."

"I'm a little busy."

"How much longer do you think you'll need?" Hubbell asked.

"It's hard to say."

Hubbell understood.

"I'll wait for you back at my desk, and when you're finished here, we'll go meet with her."

"That would be fine," the Senator said.

HUBBELL HAD TO ASSUME that Ms. Reisner had received the estimates for repairing the cars he had damaged in the parking lot, which was why he wanted the Senator to accompany him to the meeting in her office. He wanted the Senator there to establish the foundation for negotiating an extended repayment schedule, stretched out over as many months as possible, and it had also occurred to Hubbell that he might try to delay the date of the first payment for as long as he could, reasoning, obviously, that the further he pushed that date back, the greater the likelihood he would die before writing even a single check to the paper. It was certainly worth a try.

Sitting at his desk, he waited for the Senator to conclude his business in the men's room, requiring not quite an hour before Hubbell saw him striding down the corridor and through the newsroom, each step long and purposeful, pumping his heavy arms, trailing his long black hair.

When he reached Section Eight, he raised his hand and slapped Hubbell a high-five.

"Are we ready?"

"I think so," Hubbell said.

"Then let's do it."

Hubbell followed the Senator back through the newsroom, past the mailroom and through the vacated Business and Sports departments to Ms. Reisner's office. They paused for a moment to collect themselves in the hallway outside her office, the Senator hiking up his trousers and Hubbell straightening his tie, then Hubbell reached down and opened the door.

"Hello, Katrina," he said.

"Hello, Mr. Hubbell."

Seated in front of her computer, Ms. Reisner had selected a green-and-blue flannel shirt to wear to the office that morning, the sleeves rolled up, baring her thick wrists and blunt fingers, her fingernails painted a lustrous black, a fine compliment to the full range of flannel shirts in her wardrobe, as well as, Hubbell had to assume, a color that women of her ilk must find fetching. Her shaved head was now covered with a mat of stiff blond hair, and if she had recently engaged in any physical altercations in the bars she was believed to frequent, she appeared to have emerged unscathed.

Hubbell stepped to the side, allowing the Senator to enter Ms. Reisner's office.

"Hello, Katrina," the Senator said.

She gestured toward the chairs in front of her desk.

"Please, gentlemen – have a seat."

The Senator passed before Ms. Reisner's desk and dropped down heavily into the chair directly in front of her, his stomach lapping over the chair's thin wooden arms. Hubbell sat in the chair to his right.

"So," the Senator said. "Graydon tells me that you called and asked to meet with him."

"That is correct," Ms. Reisner said.

The Senator offered Ms. Reisner a broad smile.

"Well, here we are," he said. "What can we do for you?"

"Do either of you gentlemen happen to know Howard Freeburg?" she asked.

"The name is vaguely familiar," the Senator said.

"No," Hubbell said.

"Mr. Freeburg is an executive in the circulation department. He owns one of the vehicles Mr. Hubbell collided with the other day, specifically the vehicle Mr. Hubbell ran into while backing out of the parking space reserved for the city desk cars. As I'm sure you can imagine, Mr. Freeburg was not pleased when he walked out to the parking lot and discovered the damage to his car."

"That's certainly understandable," the Senator said.

"Unfortunately, Mr. Freeburg's first reaction was to call his insurance agent," Ms. Reisner said.

Hubbell's stomach dipped.

"It was our understanding that the insurance companies were not going to be involved in this incident," the Senator said.

"Yes, that was what I had hoped," Ms. Reisner said. "Unfortunately, Mr. Freeburg contacted his agent before I could speak to him."

"But you did assure Mr. Freeburg that Graydon intended to pay for the damages to his car, didn't you?" the Senator asked.

"Not, unfortunately, before Mr. Freeburg's insurance agent contacted our insurance agent," Ms. Reisner said. "And then, of course, our insurance agent called me."

Hubbell could only shake his head.

"And what did our agent have to say?" the Senator asked.

"As you might expect, she wanted to know what happened."

Ms. Reisner leaned back in her chair and folded her arms over her chest.

"Gentlemen, I had no choice. I had to tell her the truth. I told her exactly what happened."

The Senator looked over at Hubbell, then turned back Ms. Reisner.

"And what was her response?" he asked.

"I think it's fair to say that she found it all a little hard to believe – as I still do, to be perfectly honest."

"Did you inform our agent that Graydon has agreed to personally cover the cost of the damages?" the Senator asked.

"Yes, I did," Ms. Reisner said. "But she made the point that our carrier is still legally responsible for those damages, regardless of any informal arrangement we might negotiate – hence, her concern."

"That may be technically true," the Senator said. "But what does it matter? Who gives a damn, if I might speak freely?"

"She also expressed her very specific concern about our carrier's exposure to future damages, particularly with Mr. Hubbell behind the wheel."

"What does that mean?" Hubbell asked.

Ms. Reisner didn't blink.

"It means our carrier is extremely concerned about your ability to safely operate a motor vehicle," she said.

"One minor incident – and she thinks I can't drive?"

"You see the trend," she said.

"That's not a trend," the Senator protested. "One minor incident does not constitute a trend."

"Be that as it may, henceforth, the official policy of the San Francisco Chronicle, developed in consultation with our insurance carrier, shall be that Mr. Hubbell will no longer be authorized to drive any vehicles owned by this company."

"What?" Hubbell burst.

"That's an outrage!" the Senator shouted.

He pushed up out of his chair, rising so quickly that he nearly lost his trousers, which were unzipped, unfortunately, not an altogether uncommon occurrence for the Senator, whose rotund physique made visible inspection of his zipper difficult, if not impossible.

"You can't do that!"

"Of course we can," Ms. Reisner coolly informed him. "The company owns the vehicles. The company has every right to decide who operates them."

"This shall not stand!" the Senator shouted.

"Of course it will," Ms. Reisner said.

"We will take this preposterous new policy to our legal counsel!"

"That's fine," Ms. Reisner said. "You go get your lawyer, and I'll get our lawyer, and then we'll all sit down and watch the videotape. How does that sound?"

But the Senator had had enough. He wheeled around and stormed out of Ms. Reisner's office. As Hubbell pushed up to follow him, Ms. Reisner wagged her index finger at him.

"Mr. Hubbell, let me be perfectly clear. If, for some idiotic reason, you decide to check out one of the city desk cars in defiance of our new policy, we'll fire your sorry ass on the spot. Do I make myself perfectly clear?"

ON THE WAY back to the newsroom, Hubbell stopped in the alcove off the mailroom for a cup of coffee. The pot was nearly empty. There was no way to know how long the coffee had been sitting on the hot plate. But Hubbell didn't care how bitter the coffee might be. Nor did he care if anyone saw him pouring a cup without dropping his fifty cents into the slot on the top of the coin box, not today, not now that the company had prohibited him from driving the city desk cars. It was ridiculous, absurd, humiliating. As he returned the empty coffee pot to the hot plate, he was sure that word of the new company policy was already spreading through the newsroom, no doubt to the delight of Ms. Reisner.

He carried the cup of coffee back to his desk, seething about the suggestion that he might be a liability behind the wheel. He took great pride in his driving record, amassed over no less than six decades. Until the unfortunate incident in the parking lot, he had never been involved in an accident of any kind. The only blemish on his record was a minor citation he had received last summer when he turned the Mustang into a parking lot on Polk Street, cutting across the bicycle lane and inadvertently causing a bike messenger to crash into the rear of a parked car, and he might not have received that citation if the bike messenger hadn't been such a bleeder, arousing the concern of the meter maid, who had chanced upon the scene and gave Hubbell the citation as if to compensate the bike messenger for his injuries.

For the past several years, Hubbell had been the only reporter in Section Eight still authorized to drive the city desk cars. For that matter, he was the only reporter in Section Eight who still possessed a valid driver's license. Jennings was legally blind and hadn't driven in years; Poopdeck's license had expired, and he hadn't been able to pass the written examination to get it renewed, failing the test no less than three times, his scores growing progressively worse with each attempt; and the Senator had lost his license last year, when, after several martinis, he decided to drive down to his ex-wife's condominium complex in Daly City, there to exercise his right to joint custody of their basset hound, only to accidentally clip three posts supporting the roof of the carport behind her condominium, causing it to collapse onto a row of six neatly parked cars, totaling all of them.

As Hubbell sat down at his desk, he had absolutely no intention of allowing the company to publicly humiliate him by prohibiting him from driving the city desk cars. He'd file a formal grievance through the guild. He'd bring in Liberatore and sue. He'd call his congressman. They couldn't do this to him.

Only then did he notice the message across the top of his computer screen: Harold wanted to see him. He had no idea what Harold wanted, although he supposed it was possible that Ms. Reisner had called to inform him that he was no longer authorized to check out the city desk cars. For all Hubbell knew, Ms. Reisner was planning to announce the new policy over the building's public address system.

He took a sip of the coffee, still so hot it scalded the tip of his tongue, then he set the cup down and stood up and walked back through the newsroom to Harold's office. He looked in through the door. Harold was seated at his desk, the knot of his red-and-blue-striped tie pulled down from the stiff collar of his light blue shirt, a few strands of his pewter-gray hair falling onto his forehead as he read what appeared to be a memo clipped to a thick sheaf of computer printouts.

"You wanted to see me?"

Harold motioned for Hubbell to enter his office.

"Come on in," he said.

Hubbell crossed his office and sank down into one of the black leather chairs arranged in front of Harold's desk, far more accommodating than the hard wooden chairs in Ms. Reisner's office.

"So what did you ever do to piss off Abigail Tuttle?" Harold asked him.

"Am I to assume you have received her memorandum about our obituaries?"

Harold waved it at him.

"It's six fucking pages long, single-spaced, complete with annotated copies of every obituary you've written over the past year."

"And I assume you've read it?"

"Did I have any choice?" Harold asked. "And now I have to meet with her and the diversity committee's executive council, or whatever the hell they call themselves."

"God help you," Hubbell said.

Harold tossed Ms. Tuttle's memo and the attached obituaries onto his desk. It landed with a thump.

"So is it true?" he asked.

"Is what true?" Hubbell asked.

"Is it true that eighty-seven percent of our obituaries are about white people?"

Hubbell shrugged.

"So she says."

"And of that eighty-seven percent, seventy-three percent are men?"

"That's better than I would have guessed, to be perfectly honest," Hubbell said.

"In other words, she makes a legitimate point."

"She's not altogether wrong," Hubbell conceded.

Harold shook his head.

"She's fucking killing me," he said.

Hubbell sympathized – to a point.

"There's nothing worse than an idiot in possession of the facts," he said.

"I need you to help me out here," Harold said.

"I hate to disappoint you, but I don't decide who dies."

"I need to be able to tell Ms. Tuttle that you and I talked and that you've assured me that these numbers are going to go down."

"Ms. Tuttle seems to think that all that will take is a little more initiative on my part," Hubbell said.

Harold couldn't resist a smile.

"Yes, I saw that," he said. "I believe she also recommended a little community outreach."

"I'll leave the community outreach to Myron," Hubbell said.

"That's fair enough," Harold said.

Hubbell crossed his right leg over his left, clasping his hands on his knee.

"So what the hell are you going to do about her?"

"I'm more worried about what she's going to do about me," Harold said.

It was an exaggeration, to be sure, but his point was well-taken.

"It won't be long before we're all working for her," he said.

"So true," Hubbell said. "So true."

He gripped the arms of his chair, as if to stand up.

"Do you need me for anything else?"

"Yeah, before you leave…"

Hubbell watched as Harold reached back for his wallet.

"Give me Mickey Rooney, will you?"

"Are you serious?" Hubbell asked him.

"Absolutely."

"He's a midget – those little fuckers live forever."

But Harold wasn't convinced. He withdrew a dollar bill from his wallet and pushed it across his desk to Hubbell.

"Have you seen him lately?" he asked.

"No, I don't believe I have."

"He looks bad, I mean really bad – he can't last long."

"It's your money," Hubbell said.

HUBBELL REACHED DOWN and unlocked the bottom drawer of his desk, then withdrew the yellow legal pad in which he recorded the ghoul pool wagers and the envelope in which he kept the cash. After slipping the dollar from Harold into the envelope, he flipped back through the legal pad until he came to the current list and dutifully recorded Harold's wager on Mr. Rooney. The selection brought the total value of the pool up to eighty-eight dollars, a handsome figure, certainly, but a far cry from the value of the pool when McCaleb ran it, before the first waves of layoffs and buyouts, those pools easily exceeding several hundred dollars, nearly enough, the Senator had once observed, not entirely in jest, to split with a hired assassin.

After returning the legal pad and the envelope to the drawer, Hubbell turned to his computer to check for any news about Jerry Lewis, conducting a rudimentary search of the Internet, an endeavor he always found vaguely terrifying, afraid he might find himself trapped in some remote inescapable corner of cyberspace, the screen of his computer besieged with pornographic images, or even worse, whatever that might be. But he found nothing new, nothing about Lewis's current state of health, one way or the other. He couldn't believe that it was entirely possible, if not likely, that he was going to pass away before the Nutty Professor, and that, he told himself, was an injustice of the first degree.

It was then that Ms. Mitchell rose from her desk and crossed the aisle to stand beside Hubbell's cubicle, her freckled hands on the top of the cubicle wall, a black turtleneck enclosing her slender neck, her hair falling across her right eye.

"How would you like to let me buy you lunch?" she asked.

Hubbell wasn't sure he heard her clearly. Among his failing senses, his hearing was not what it used to be.

"You want to buy me lunch?"

"You do eat lunch, don't you?"

"Of course," he said. "Of course I eat lunch."

"I say we walk down to Tu'lan."

"And why do you want to do that?"

"Like I told you – I want to pick your brain, what's left of it, anyway."

Hubbell recognized, of course, her thinly veiled reference to the Jurgensen obituary, and, assuming the subject had been both broached and dispatched, he saw no reason to decline her offer. If she wasn't afraid to be seen with him, he wasn't afraid to be seen with her. And a free lunch was, after all, a free lunch.

"If you insist," he said. "But just this once."

As he rose from his chair, Ms. Mitchell drew a cross upon her heart.

"I swear I'll never offer to buy you lunch again."

HUBBELL PUSHED through the heavy glass door, then stood to the side and held it open for Ms. Mitchell to step out onto the sidewalk behind him. As the door swung closed, he reached up and tugged down the brim of his hat, and then they started down Mission Street, buffeted by the wind as they walked past the deserted warehouses and padlocked storefronts, stepping over the drunks and junkies sprawled out on sheets of soiled cardboard beneath the steel grates and opaqued windows. When they reached the pornographic video arcade at the corner, they turned right and made their way down Sixth Street, negotiating a path through the crowds congregating in front of the loan offices and liquor stores, the pawn shops and boarding houses, observing with some confidence that not all of those gathered on the sidewalk were active members of the working class and that some might, in fact, be members of the criminal element.

Fortunately, they made it to Tu'lan without incident, ducking beneath the green canvas awning above the restaurant door. As Hubbell removed his hat, Ms. Mitchell looked up at him and smiled.

"It's always an adventure, isn't it?"

"Indeed, it is, Ms. Mitchell. Indeed, it is."

They spotted two unoccupied seats near the end of the counter and started back to them, slipping past the tables shoved up against the wall. As Hubbell sat on the seat on the left, he realized that it had been months since he had last eaten at Tu'lan, months since the cockroach fell off the ceiling and down the back of Poopdeck's shirt, precipitating an incident that could only be described as unfortunate. But he knew exactly what he wanted, exactly what he always ordered at Tu'lan – the imperial rolls with strips of barbecued pork over a mound of steamed rice.

While Ms. Mitchell deliberated over the paper menu, Hubbell watched the cook as he labored over the stove, sweating through his threadbare flowered shirt, his slick black hair falling across the thick frames of his glasses. Finally, Ms. Mitchell ordered the bean cake with bamboo shoots and mushrooms.

"So?" she asked.

She turned to face him, then reached up and tucked her hair behind her ears.

"Did you read my story this morning?"

"As a matter of fact, I did," Hubbell said.

"And what did you think?"

"I thought it was very competent – quite competent, in fact."

"That's not much in the way of a compliment," she said.

"Of course, it is. And I mean it," Hubbell said. "You're a very capable reporter."

"I'd like to become a little more than competent," she said. "I'd like to become a little more than capable."

"There's nothing wrong with a little ambition."

"I'd like to become a good reporter, as a matter of fact – a damned good reporter."

"And I'm sure you will," Hubbell said.

"Not if they won't let me off the night shift," she said. "Not if every story I write is about drug pukes killing drug pukes and gangbangers killing gangbangers."

"The stories may not change, but you will, over time," Hubbell said.

"And how will I change?"

Hubbell smiled.

"You'll get older – and wiser," he said.

Ms. Mitchell cocked her head to the left and crossed her eyes, then stuck a finger in her ear.

"Really?" she asked through her nose.

Hubbell was pleased to see that Ms. Mitchell was an aficionado of physical comedy. She might very well be a fan of the Nutty Professor himself.

"I recommend getting older highly," he said. "It certainly beats the alternative."

"Oh, that's very wise," she said.

Hubbell reached out and took a sip of water, returning the glass to the ring it had perspired onto the counter.

"I like to think I'm a little wiser now than I was when I was first sent down to the Hall of Justice," he said.

She smiled up at him.

"On the other hand, how wise do you have to be to write obituaries?"

"Wiser than you might think, Ms. Mitchell."

"Naomi," she said. "Do you think you could call me Naomi, at least while we're having lunch, at least while I'm buying you lunch?"

It seemed like a reasonable request, a small price to pay.

"Of course," Hubbell said. "Of course, Naomi."

They leaned back as the cook placed their plates on the counter in front of them. Hubbell reached for the cup of sweet-hot sauce, the intoxicating elixir composed of ground peanuts, carrot shavings and flakes of red pepper, then drizzled it over his imperial roll and barbecued pork. After setting the cup down, he picked up his fork and stabbed one of the sections of imperial roll and raised it to his mouth, closing his eyes as he chewed it slowly, remembering how much he loved Vietnamese food and vowing to return to Tu'lan more often, even if his colleagues in Section Eight were no longer willing to accompany him. Perhaps he would return with Ms. Mitchell, or Naomi, he should say. Perhaps one day he would offer to buy Naomi lunch.

She nibbled at a piece of the bean cake, then turned to him, her chopsticks in her right hand.

"So," she said. "What brilliant advice would you give to a young reporter such as myself?"

Hubbell stabbed another section of the imperial roll. He had to think. No one asked for his advice anymore. No one had solicited his opinion in years. Aside from Ms. Mitchell, his younger colleagues thought they knew everything. The arrogant little bastards certainly believed they knew more than Hubbell and his colleagues in Section Eight.

"Did anyone ever give you any advice, when you were a young reporter?" she asked.

"Now, that's a different question," he said.

He permitted himself a smile.

"One night, when I was working the late shift, right after I'd been promoted from copyboy, I was pulled aside by the legendary Bernie Goodell, the finest rewrite man I've ever known. Bernie told me there were three rules adhered to by every good guild reporter. The first was: Never work a minute of overtime without putting it on your timecard – if you do, the sons of bitches will start expecting it from all of us. The second rule: Put in for every penny of expenses – the sons of bitches are hoping you won't, which is why they make it such a pain in the ass to fill out an expense report. And the third: Never volunteer for anything, no matter how bad you want it – the sons of bitches will think they're doing you a favor, and they'll make you regret it for the rest of your career."

Ms. Mitchell smiled, tucking her hair back behind her ear.

"Mr. Goodell was a rather cynical fellow, wasn't he?"

"A good union man," Hubbell said. "It was good advice then – and it's good advice now."

She picked up another piece of the bean cake and lifted to her mouth, taking it in her teeth.

"So, if you were to pull me aside, the way Mr. Goodell pulled you aside, what would you tell me?" she asked.

Hubbell stabbed a piece of the barbecued pork. He chewed it thoughtfully, swallowing a knot of gristle. After all these years in the newsroom, he wasn't entirely sure what wisdom he had to impart. But perhaps the best advice was the simplest advice, the most obvious.

"I suppose I would encourage you to make sure you have a backup plan," he said.

She only looked at him.

"You never know when it's all going to blow up on you," he said.

"My job?" she asked.

"Your job, the paper, the whole damned industry."

A shallow laugh escaped her.

"That's pretty depressing," she said.

Hubbell shrugged.

"It's the best I can do," he said.

She looked at him for a moment, then turned her attention back to her bean cake, a smile slipping out the corner of her mouth.

"That's all right," she said. "I forgive you."

AFTER RETURNING to the newsroom, Hubbell hung up his coat and sat down at his desk. As he reached for his keyboard, he saw Myron walking back to Section Eight. He was tempted to pick up the telephone and wave Myron off, as if he had just received an important phone call, but the sad fact is that Myron would only return.

"Jeremy Suskind died," he said.

It was a name Hubbell hadn't heard in years – the name of one of the leaders of the Free Speech Movement at U.C. Berkeley in the 1960s.

"They caught him?"

"He died in a car accident up in Montana," Myron said.

"What the hell was Jeremy Suskind doing in Montana?"

Myron handed Hubbell the folder of clippings the library had pulled.

"I have no idea," he said. "But you can ask his mother. She called it in. I gave her your number."

"All right," Hubbell said.

"Harold wants it for tomorrow."

"I'll do what I can."

As Myron turned to leave, Hubbell opened the folder – and there was Suskind on the front page of the Chronicle, the iconic photograph of him standing on the roof of a police car, angry and defiant, his fist clenched and thrust up through the swirling tear gas. Suskind had been one of the leaders of the increasingly strident demonstrations against the university's policy prohibiting political speech on campus, a gifted if somewhat profane orator, who called upon the demonstrators to take over Sproul Hall and later, as the war in Vietnam intensified, exhorted the masses to revolt against the nation's right-wing military-industrial complex. But in the early 1970s, as the de facto leader of an underground organization implicated in an attempt to blow up the police department's Central Station in North Beach, Suskind vanished. Over the years, Suskind was reported to have been seen on numerous occasions, including any number of sightings in the Bay Area, but none of those reports was ever confirmed, at least as far as Hubbell knew, and Suskind remained a fugitive.

He was reading through the articles pulled by the library when his telephone rang.

"Mr. Hubbell?" a woman asked.

"Yes," he said. "This is Graydon Hubbell."

"My name is Diana Suskind. I was told that you're the one I need to talk to about my son Jeremy."

"Hello, Ms. Suskind. I've been expecting your call."

She began to cry. After a moment, he gently tried to help her.

"I understand your son Jeremy passed away."

But she cried only harder. There was nothing he could do but wait until she composed herself.

"We're all very sorry about your loss and extend our heartfelt condolences," he said. "Do you think you could tell me what happened?"

"He was in an accident," she managed to say. "He was in a car accident out in Montana."

"Can you tell me where in Montana the accident took place?"

"It was near the town of Kalispell."

"And the accident happened yesterday?"

She had to think.

"Yes, yesterday. They called me last night."

"Who called you?"

"The sheriff's deputy called me. He told me Jeremy lost control of his car and drove off the road and rolled down into a ditch. He told me Jeremy died before they could get him to the hospital."

And then she began sobbing. Again, there was nothing Hubbell could do but wait for her to collect herself.

"Do you think you could tell me what Jeremy was doing up in Montana?" he asked.

"He was living there," she gathered herself to say. "He was living on one of those communes near Flathead Lake."

"How long had Jeremy been living there?"

"I don't know, not exactly – for several years. I never understood why. He lived in a teepee."

"A teepee?"

"He was such a sweet boy," she said. "He was so bright. He was such a wonderful pianist."

"I didn't know Jeremy was musically inclined."

"He had beautiful hands – such beautiful hands. He gave his first recital when he was just eleven years old. He had a scholarship to the Conservatory of Music at Bard, but Jeremy wanted to go to Berkeley. I tried to talk him out of it. His father, God rest his soul, tried to talk him out of it. But Jeremy wouldn't listen."

She began to cry again.

"And then he fell in with those communists. They took over his mind with their mind control, and now my Jeremy is dead."

"I'm very sorry," Hubbell said.

He saw no point in pressing her further. He had enough for the obituary.

"Again, we're all very sorry for your loss. Thank you again for calling. We'll try to run an obituary for Jeremy in tomorrow's paper."

THE LIBRARY MANAGED to locate a number of Suskind's former associates from the heady days of the Free Speech Movement, but those Hubbell spoke with had relatively little to say about Suskind, their memories largely sanitized by the passage of time, the demonstrations they had attended and the acts of civil disobedience they had engaged in now no more than the harmless indiscretions of their youth. They all remembered Suskind as a passionate and charismatic speaker, but no one had seen or heard from him in years. They were uniformly surprised to learn that he had been living on a commune in Montana and were, of course, deeply saddened to hear that he had died in a car accident. But they had provided little for Hubbell to use in Suskind's obituary, other than to recommend that he contact a man named Ellis Fielding, who they believed was Suskind's closest comrade all those years ago.

At Hubbell's request, the library tracked down a telephone number for Fielding at the University of Michigan, where he was currently a professor of economics. Hubbell dialed the number for Fielding's office on campus and leaned back in his chair. The telephone rang several times before the professor answered.

"This is Dr. Fielding."

"Yes, Dr. Fielding – my name is Graydon Hubbell. I'm calling from the San Francisco Chronicle."

"Is this some kind of a joke?"

"I'm afraid not," Hubbell said.

"Then what do you want?"

"I'm afraid I have some bad news," Hubbell said.

"Now, there's a surprise – bad news from a corporate media conglomerate profiteering on the misery of the masses."

Hubbell sensed that Dr. Fielding was predisposed to hold the fourth estate in low regard. Over the years, Hubbell had found that this was not an uncommon view among academics, particularly those emboldened by tenure.

"I'm afraid Jeremy Suskind is dead," he said.

"What the fuck are you talking about?"

"He died yesterday in a single-car accident up in Montana," Hubbell said.

"Montana?"

"He had been living in a commune near Kalispell, apparently."

"You can't be serious."

"I'm afraid I am."

"So what has this got to do with me?" Fielding asked.

"I'm working up an obituary for Mr. Suskind, and I was hoping you could tell me a little about him. I understand that you knew Mr. Suskind very well."

"I see," the professor said. "The corporate flunky needs my help."

"That's one way to look at it," Hubbell said. "Or, you might view this as an opportunity to embellish the legacy of one of your former comrades, and, of course, by association, your own legacy as well."

It was an opportunity Hubbell knew the professor couldn't resist. And the professor didn't let him down.

"Yes, Jeremy and I were comrades," Fielding hastened to say. "We shared an ideology, a political philosophy, a vision for the world. We were committed to fomenting change, and we were willing to put our bodies on the line."

"Perhaps you could elaborate," Hubbell said.

Of course, he could.

"We were arrested in the summer of 1964 in Meridian, Mississippi, for having the temerity to help our black brothers and sisters register to vote. We were arrested that December for occupying Sproul Hall, when the tyrants in the U.C. administration tried to deny us our fundamental First Amendment right to free speech. We were arrested the following summer for trying to block the troop trains heading to the Oakland Army Base, for trying to stop the nation's imperialist aggression in Southeast Asia."

"That's an impressive resume," Hubbell said.

"Does the media puppet think he's funny?" Fielding asked.

Hubbell did, actually, but he knew better than to say so.

"Do you know why Mr. Suskind may have been involved in an attempt to blow up the Central Station?"

"That's not very difficult to understand, is it? It's quite simple, really. Jeremy hated the police, a point of view I happen to share, candidly. We hated the swine not just for who they were but for what they stood for – brutal mercenaries defending a morally bankrupt military-industrial complex. The police in San Francisco should feel honored that Jeremy selected them as a target."

"I'm sure they do," Hubbell said. "And then after Mr. Suskind disappeared, you enrolled in graduate school?"

"That is correct," Fielding said. "I elected to bring about change from within the system, from within the belly of the beast, as it were."

"And how, exactly, do you do that?"

"I teach economics – Marxist economics, to be precise."

"Now there's an ideology that really caught on," Hubbell said.

"I wouldn't expect the corporate tool to understand."

"Oh, I think I do," Hubbell said.

HUBBELL SPENT the rest of the afternoon working on the Suskind obituary, meticulously checking and rechecking every fact or statement against the clippings from the library and the notes he had taken during his interviews with Suskind's mother and former associates, including the obnoxious Dr. Fielding, reading the obituary down and then reading it down again, polishing every sentence, every word, until the obituary absolutely sang.

As he sent the Suskind obituary to Myron, he liked to think that it was one of the finest obituaries he had written in some time. The fact is, time had been kind to Suskind. While it was true the authorities believed Suskind was involved in the plot to blow up the Central Station, it was important to remember that he had never been convicted of anything more serious than disturbing the peace, and as a civil rights activist working in the Deep South, a leading voice during the Free Speech Movement, and an early opponent of the war in Vietnam, Suskind, ultimately, was on the right side of history, his political views shared by the overwhelming majority of Bay Area residents, if not necessarily the conservative readers of the Chronicle. That Suskind would spend nearly four decades on the run, driven underground largely because of his political beliefs, only made him a more sympathetic figure.

And, for once, Hubbell decided to wait for Myron to finish editing the obituary, not for the benefit of his editorial observations, but to make absolutely certain he didn't unilaterally screw it up. He was waiting for Myron to finish when he saw Harold walking up the aisle leading through the newsroom. It was an unusual sight in that Harold rarely ventured into the open expanse of the newsroom anymore, hoping to avoid, if at all possible, uncontrolled encounters with his reporters, preferring the rigid confines and relative privacy of his office to deny their desperate pleas and inane proposals, not to mention their insupportable requests for pay raises, made without the slightest recognition of the fact that the paper was in a financial death spiral. It also appeared as if Harold was walking back to Section Eight, which was even more uncommon. In recent years, Harold seemed particularly reluctant to venture all the way back to Hubbell and his colleagues, as if his presence there might imply that he still regarded it to be a legitimate province of the newsroom, its occupants productive members of the paper's dwindling staff.

After nodding at the Senator and Poopdeck, and ignoring the snoring Jennings, Harold stood in front of Hubbell's cubicle.

"That's not a bad obituary," he said.

Hubbell leaned back in his chair.

"I thank you for the compliment," he said.

"Do we have this alone?"

"As far as I know."

Harold turned to Myron.

"Have you seen anything on the wires?"

Myron shook his head.

"I've been checking all afternoon," he said.

"The wires didn't pick anything up from any of the local papers?" Harold asked. "There must be a paper in Kalispell."

"I checked their website, but I didn't see anything about the accident," Myron said.

"They might not know who Suskind is," Hubbell said. "They might think he's just another hippie shitting in the woods."

"Did you get a sense that any of the people you interviewed had talked to anyone else?" Harold asked.

"No one had heard a thing," Hubbell said. "They were shocked when I told them Suskind was dead."

That was enough for Harold. He turned to Myron.

"Let's take it out front," he said.

"You want the Suskind obituary for Page One?" Myron asked.

"Why not?" Harold asked. "Put a news lead on it, and we'll run it at the bottom of the page."

"I can work a new top and have it back to you in fifteen minutes," Hubbell said.

"Let's do it," Harold said.

HUBBELL CLIMBED UP onto the bus and made his way down the aisle, spotting an empty seat against the window directly behind the back door. He slipped through the passengers standing in the aisle and eased himself into the seat. As he leaned back to catch his breath, he was still utterly delighted that Harold had decided to run the Suskind obituary on Page One. It was an inspired call, to say the least. Although the Suskind obituary did have a certain news value, and there was no doubt that the obituary would be widely read, if for no other reason than it resolved the mystery of Suskind's disappearance more than forty years ago, Harold rarely took obituaries out front, no matter how prominent or newsworthy the dead might be. He was far more inclined to run a small mug shot of the deceased above a brief reference to the obituary in the Bay Area section. As Hubbell gazed out the window of the bus, he had to believe that by taking the Suskind obituary for the front page, as well as by walking back to Section Eight, Harold was sending a message to the newsroom on his behalf, making it clear that he still trusted him, his egregious mistake in the obituary for Conrad Jurgensen notwithstanding. It was an extraordinarily generous gesture from an old friend, who knew that Hubbell's remaining days in the newsroom were few, and Hubbell was deeply appreciative.

It was certainly cause for celebration, and when the bus arrived at Washington Square, Hubbell stepped down onto the sidewalk and started back up Columbus. He crossed Union Street and entered Coit Liquors, walking directly to the coolers in the back of the store, passing along the tall glass doors until he came to the sparkling wines. He grabbed a bottle of champagne and carried it up to the cash register at the counter near the door. As he pulled out his wallet, he tried to remember the last time his work had appeared on Page One. For that matter, he tried to remember the last time he had a reason to buy a bottle of champagne. He drew a blank, unfortunately, on both accounts.

With the bottle cradled in his left arm, Hubbell walked down Columbus and then turned up Filbert. The evening was still warm, even as the sky faded from blue to black, and he could feel himself beginning to perspire as he climbed the hill. But he felt good, favoring his right foot only slightly, and made it up to the Edwardian relatively easily, requiring only a moment to collect himself before opening the gate and walking along the side of the two flats below his cottage.

When he reached the garden, he crossed the patio and peered in through the glass panels in Ms. Gifford's back door. Inside, she was watering the potted begonias on the windowsill above her sink. He knocked lightly on the door. When she turned and saw it was him, she set the brass watering can on the counter and walked over to open the door.

"Would you care to join me for a glass of champagne?" he asked.

She smiled broadly, dimpling her round cheeks.

"Are you serious?"

He lifted the bottle out of the bag.

"Yes, I am."

"A glass of champagne sounds wonderful, Graydon."

They crossed the patio, passing beneath the rose-covered trellis arched over the steps leading to the upper yard, then climbed the stairs to his cottage. He opened the door and stepped inside, cracking the window above the sink to let the evening air move into the kitchen.

"What are we celebrating?" she asked.

As she sat down at the table, he began twisting off the wires that secured the cork in the bottle of champagne.

"Let's just say I had a good day," he said. "Let's just say I had a hell of a good day."

He gripped the bottle of champagne with both hands, straining to dislodge the cork with his thumbs. Finally it popped, the cork shooting up to the ceiling, then ricocheting across the kitchen, nearly hitting Ms. Gifford, who shrieked as the cork sailed past her. Suddenly, a torrent of white foam surged out of the bottle. Hubbell raised the bottle to his mouth, trying to gulp the foam down. Still, it poured out of the sides of his mouth and streamed down his chin, splashing onto his shirt and tie before finally subsiding.

He turned to Ms. Gifford.

"Are you all right?" he asked her.

"That was quite exciting," she said.

"I'm afraid I'm out of practice."

He reached up and opened the cabinet above the counter. He didn't have any flutes for the champagne. His wine glasses would have to suffice. He had a feeling that would be all right with Ms. Gifford. He had a feeling that it would be all right with Ms. Gifford if they drank the champagne out of mason jars.

He poured the champagne into the glasses, letting the foam die down before he carried them over to the table.

"We're celebrating because one of my obituaries will be running on the front page of tomorrow's paper," he said.

"Oh, that's wonderful, Graydon."

He extended his glass to Ms. Gifford. They clinked their glasses together.

"Who died?" she asked.

Hubbell took a sip of champagne.

"Jeremy Suskind," he told her.

"I'm afraid I'm not familiar with Mr. Suskind."

"He was one of the leaders of the Free Speech Movement."

"The Free Speech Movement?"

Hubbell started to explain, but then stopped himself. Ms. Gifford was not a student of history. He saw no reason to burden her with the political turmoil of the 1960s.

"It doesn't matter, not now, not anymore," he said. "All that matters is that he's dead."

"I love celebrating," Ms. Gifford said. "And I love champagne. It's right up there with tequila, in my humble opinion."

"Would you like a little more?" Hubbell asked.

She smiled at him, her right eye angling down at the bottle of champagne, as if it wanted to celebrate, too.

"Perhaps, just a little," she said. "Perhaps just one more glass."

"By all means," Hubbell said.

HUBBELL PICKED UP the bottle and poured what remained of the champagne into his glass, using both hands to shake out the last drop. Ms. Gifford was smoking one of her marijuana cigarettes, holding the smoke in her lungs for as long as she could, then tilting her head back and exhaling toward the ceiling. Hubbell drank the last of the champagne. As he set his glass back down, he saw that Ms. Gifford was squinting at him from across the table, or at least trying to squint at him with just the one obedient eye.

"Graydon, may I ask you a question?"

"Of course."

"I mean a very frank question. As you know, I can be very frank."

"Yes, I'm well aware of that," he said.

She fingered the stem of her empty glass.

"Are you trying to seduce me?"

Hubbell sat back in his chair.

"Of course not," he said. "Absolutely not."

"I just want to be sure," she said. "I just want to make sure we understand each other here. The last thing I want is some kind of misunderstanding."

"I can assure you that I most certainly am not trying to seduce you," he said. "I wouldn't even know where to begin."

"I would think it could begin anywhere," she said.

"You mean here in the kitchen?"

"I would think it could begin with a bottle of champagne."

That puzzled Hubbell.

"Or in your bedroom," she said. "Of course, I've never even seen your bedroom."

"There's really not much to see," he said. "There's just the bed and a bureau and a chair."

"That's really all you need, don't you think?"

"That's all I've ever needed," Hubbell said.

"Would you mind if I took a look?"

"Of course not," Hubbell said.

"Or perhaps you'd like to show it to me?"

She grinned at him again. It had to be the marijuana. She tended to grin after she smoked one of her marijuana cigarettes.

He saw no reason not to show Ms. Gifford his bedroom. He certainly didn't have anything to hide.

"Would you like me to show you my bedroom?" he asked.

"How kind of you to offer," she said.

He rose from the table. She slipped her arm through his.

"Shall we?" she asked.

He led her down the hallway to the door of his bedroom. They stopped there in the dim light, before them the dark form of his bed with its brass head rail and posts.

"Oh, my lord, Graydon – you make your bed!"

She turned to him.

"Do you make it every morning?"

"Of course," he said.

She laughed and released his arm and entered his bedroom to inspect the bed. She ran her open hand over the blanket, stretched taut across the mattress.

"And you've done a very fine job," she said.

"Thank you," he said.

"Can I sit on it, or are you afraid I'll mess it up?"

"Would you like to sit on it?"

"Why don't we," she said.

He entered the bedroom as Ms. Gifford sat on the edge of the mattress, the bedsprings groaning beneath her. She gave it a good bounce.

"This is very nice," she said.

"I'm glad you like it."

He sat down beside her. She slipped her arm through his.

"Should we lie down?" she asked.

"That's a very good question," he said.

"We can always sit back up," she said.

"Yes – that's true."

"Would you like to go first?"

Hubbell had no idea what the protocol might be in this kind of situation, but if Ms. Gifford wanted him to lie down, he would comply with her wish.

"All right," he said.

He leaned back and swung his legs up and stretched out on his back. In the dark room, he stared up at the ceiling.

"Graydon, don't you think you should take your shoes off?"

She was absolutely right. He pushed up onto his elbows.

"Yes, of course," he said.

But she placed her hand on his chest.

"I'll take them off for you," she said.

As he looked up at the ceiling, he could feel her untying the laces of his right shoe. He could feel her hand beneath his heel, slipping the shoe off his foot, protecting his wounded toe. The shoe landed with a thud on the hardwood floor.

But when she began to roll down his sock, he sat back up.

"No, please," he said. "My feet will get cold."

Ms. Gifford laughed.

"The last thing I want is a man with cold feet."

"My circulation – it's not what it used to be."

"That's all right, Graydon, really."

"I used to have excellent circulation," he said. "I rarely got cold feet when I was younger."

"Of course," she said.

She removed his left shoe, then she stretched out alongside him, and they lay on the mattress in silence. Her hand found his. He closed his eyes again.

"This is very nice, don't you think?" she asked.

"Yes, it is – very nice," he said.

When he opened his eyes, he saw that Ms. Gifford had propped herself up on an elbow, her cheek resting in the palm of her hand. She was looking down at him, her face in shadow.

"Shall I give you a back rub?" she asked. "How long has it been since you had a good back rub?"

He had no idea.

"Don't tell me," she said. "I don't want to know. Just take off your shirt and tie."

Again, he did as Ms. Gifford instructed. He saw no immediate harm in it. If it got bad, he could always ask her to stop. He sat up and tugged apart the knot in his tie, then he unbuttoned his shirt and took it off. After pulling his undershirt over his head, he balled up his clothes and hurled them toward the chair beside his bureau.

"Now lie down," she said.

He stretched out on his stomach, his arms along his sides, his face buried in the pillow. Ms. Gifford positioned herself beside him and reached up to his shoulders and began to knead the cords of muscle at the base of his neck.

"Good lord, Graydon – you're as stiff as a corpse. Try to relax, will you?"

"I am relaxed," he told her, his voice muffled by the pillow. "This is as relaxed as I get."

But properly scolded, he took a deep breath and let it out slowly. He could feel himself sinking into the mattress as Ms. Gifford's hands traveled across his back and over his shoulders, down to the base of his spine. He felt as if he were dissolving beneath her fingertips. He had no idea how long she massaged his back. It could have been hours. It could have been days.

Finally, she leaned down and whispered in his ear.

"Now, it's my turn," she said.

But he couldn't move – not for a moment. He was groggy and disoriented, as if emerging from a trance. It was all he could do to roll onto his back and look up at her.

"That was wonderful," he said.

"Now fair is fair," she said.

Hubbell managed to swing his legs over the edge of the mattress, then he pushed up to sit, requiring a moment to collect himself.

"Would you mind if I took off my shirt?" Ms. Gifford asked.

A good question, one he hadn't considered.

"You want to take your shirt off?"

"Yes, I thought I would – unless, of course, you'd prefer that I didn't."

"No, I wouldn't object," he said. "I'm sure I wouldn't."

"Would you like to help me unbutton it?"

That was another good question, another question he hadn't found occasion to consider.

"Start with the top button, please."

Hubbell nodded. He nodded a second time. If Ms. Gifford

wanted him to help unbutton her shirt, he would do his best. He stared at the small white button beneath her open collar, then reached down and tried to slip the button back through its narrow slit. It wasn't as easy as it looked, frankly.

"Why don't you keep going, now that you've gotten the hang of it."

"Yes, of course," he said.

He reached over to Ms. Gifford again and began working his way down the buttons, the front of her denim shirt slowly falling open, revealing her heavy bosom and the large white cups of her brassiere.

"Very nicely done, Graydon."

She pulled her arms out of the long sleeves and handed the shirt to him.

"Would you mind putting this on the chair?" she asked.

"Of course not."

He rose from the bed and carried the shirt across the room and draped it neatly over the back of the chair. When he turned around, Ms. Gifford reached up and released the clasp between the cups of her brassiere, her breasts slumping down as she slipped off the thin shoulder straps. His chest shuddered as she held it out to him.

"Would you mind putting this on the chair, too?" she asked.

"Certainly," he said.

As he reached for the brassiere, he tried not to stare at her breasts, but he was not altogether successful. He could feel his heart threatening to burst in his chest. It was a relief, actually, to turn away and carry the brassiere over to the chair. But then he had to turn back to her. He took a deep breath, then turned and tried to look past her, beyond her, into the darkness across the bedroom.

"What do you think?" she asked him.

"What do I think?"

"What do you think about my boobs, you old fool? Do you like them?"

"I like them very much," he managed to say.

She looked down at her breasts, cupping them in her hands.

"I've always thought I had great boobs."

"I can't imagine you've had many complaints."

"Not one – not a single complaint in my whole life."

She patted the mattress beside her.

"Come sit beside me," she said.

"Of course."

He joined her on the edge of the bed, blood pumping through his ancient veins.

"Would you like to touch them?" she asked.

"Oh, yes," he said. "I would like very much to touch them."

"Go ahead, then, Graydon. You have my permission."

"But not yet," he said.

He pointed at the pillow.

"It's your turn," he said.

Ms. Gifford smiled.

"As you wish, Graydon."

She stretched out on the mattress, and he moved over to sit alongside her, then he reached up and began to massage her bare shoulders. She issued a long sigh.

"That feels heavenly," she said.

Hubbell was glad to hear it. He took a deep breath, then he did to Ms. Gifford what she had done to him, working his fingers up to the back of her neck, across both shoulders and down her spine, working the muscles fanning out from each vertebrae, down to the soft rise of her rump.

"Would you do this for the rest of my life?" she asked.

But his hands quickly began to tire, his wrists to ache. He had to sit back and rest for a moment. He fully intended to resume, but Ms. Gifford rolled onto her back and stared up at him.

"Why don't you lie down beside me," she said.

"Are you sure you don't want me to rub your back a little longer?"

"I would like for you to lie down next to me."

Again, he did as instructed, stretching out alongside Ms. Gifford, lying on his back, staring up at the ceiling again. She placed her hand on his stomach. He covered it with his.

"I think I know where we're headed here," he said.

"Is that all right?" she asked.

He couldn't help but worry that he was making a terrible mistake, inviting unspeakable humiliation.

"I'm not sure I can do this," he said.

"Sure, you can. Of course, you can."

"It's been a long time."

"It's been a long time for me, too," she said.

"I mean a very long time," he said.

She raised herself up and looked down at him, then she kissed him lightly on the forehead.

"Let me see what I can do," she said. "Let me see if I can work a little magic."

CHAPTER ELEVEN

HUBBELL SAT back in the pew, the last pew on the right, beneath the arching columns that supported the cathedral ceiling, the high stained glass windows filled with the early morning light, votive candles flickering in the shrines along the wall. Aside from two old women, dressed all in black as they knelt before the gilded marble altar, Hubbell was alone in the church. The first Mass wasn't scheduled to begin for another hour. He still had some time.

He hadn't been inside Sts. Peter and Paul for nearly forty years now, not since the funeral Mass for Maria. He could still see her oak casket in the aisle in front of the altar, draped in calla lilies and white carnations. He could still hear the muffled sobbing, the wrenching eulogies, the priest's empty words of consolation. He would never forget the long procession to the cemetery. He would never forget standing above her open grave, the wind ruffling the canvas canopy as he mouthed his final farewell.

But that, of course, was not why he had come to Sts. Peter and Paul. He had come here because this was also where he and Maria were married. This was where they exchanged their vows. This was where he pledged to honor that commitment for the rest of his life. And he had done so faithfully for nearly four decades – until last night. He leaned forward, his forearms resting on his thighs, his hands clasped. He was profoundly sorry that he had betrayed Maria. He would never forgive himself for violating the trust that had bound them together for so many years. He had no excuses. He had betrayed her willingly, freely. He had no one to blame but himself.

And yet, it was not that simple. As guilty as he felt about what he had done last night, he was also deeply grateful for what had been done to him. Ms. Gifford, it must be said, was quite the magician. He closed his eyes and could see her as he had left her in his bedroom, sprawled out across the mattress, her arms and legs splayed out in all directions, the blanket kicked to the floor and the sheet barely covering her waist, revealing all that flesh, and, sweet Jesus, those great white breasts.

Yes, he was stricken with remorse for having betrayed Maria. He would have to live with that sorrow and regret for the rest of his life. But as he opened his eyes and leaned back in the pew, he could not bring himself to wish last night hadn't happened. Last night had been nothing less than a revelation, an awakening, and he had absolutely no intention of denying himself the unexpected pleasures of Ms. Gifford's company in the days that remained to him.

He picked up his fedora and rose to leave. Perhaps that was wrong. Perhaps he was making another terrible mistake. He didn't care. He simply didn't care.

HUBBELL WALKED along the bakery's glass display case, peering down at the trays of decadent pastries, deluged with fruit and filled with jellies and creams, thick wedges of cake and layered squares of tiramisu, cannoli dusted with powdered sugar and cookies dipped in dark chocolate. Hubbell had been coming to Stella's Pastries for more than fifty years, which is to say he knew exactly what he wanted and where to find it. He had no intention of denying his most elemental desires, not now, not anymore. In a narrow sense, he felt oddly liberated by the knowledge that he was dying, at least to the extent that he was determined to indulge himself as often as possible in the days that remained to him.

At the far end of the display case, he stopped and pressed the tip of his index finger to the glass, pointing down at the sacripantina, the rum-soaked vanilla sponge cake filled with a layer of a light custard called zabaione, residing neatly on a white paper doily.

"I'll take a slice of the sacripantina," he told the woman in the dark blue apron behind the glass case.

Liberatore, standing beside Hubbell in a gray suit and red bow tie, looked up at him through bloodshot eyes.

"Sacripantina – at eight o'clock in the morning?" he asked, as if it were obscene.

"And an espresso," Hubbell told her.

Liberatore shook his head.

"Just an espresso for me," he said.

With their orders placed, they walked over to the white, marble-top table in the front window of the bakery. Hubbell pulled out one of the chairs and sat down, placing his satchel on the floor as Liberatore eased himself into the chair across from him.

"I've made a few decisions based on our discussion last week," Hubbell told him.

"I'm glad to hear that," Liberatore said.

"I'd like to ask you to serve as executor of my estate."

"If that's what you need me to do, of course I'll do it," Liberatore said.

Hubbell leaned back as the woman from behind the display case placed their espressos on the table in front of them.

"I've also decided on the beneficiary of my estate," he said. "My sole beneficiary will be a woman named Lydia Gifford."

"I don't believe I know Ms. Gifford," Liberatore said.

"She's a neighbor. She's going to help me with my medical directives – at least some of them, at least I hope she will."

"That doesn't sound like a very firm commitment."

"Firm commitments are not her style," Hubbell said.

"And you know Ms. Gifford well?"

"She's been renting from me for about three years now."

Liberatore arched an eyebrow.

"She's a tenant?"

"That's right."

"A tenant," Liberatore said, as if to be sure.

Hubbell watched as the woman from behind the case set his sacripantina down in front of him.

"May I ask what Ms. Gifford does for a living?" Liberatore asked.

"She was a teacher for a while, but apparently that didn't work out," Hubbell said.

"What does she do now?"

"Nothing, as far as I can tell."

Hubbell cut a piece of the sacripantina and raised it to his mouth. He closed his lips around it and pulled it off the fork, allowing it to luxuriate on his tongue for a moment before he reluctantly swallowed it.

"She's terrible with money – I can tell you that," he said. "We'll need to set up some kind of trust that sends her a check every month."

Liberatore sipped at his espresso, then returned the cup to its saucer.

"So, I may assume that Ms. Gifford doesn't have much money of her own?"

"No, not so far as I can tell," Hubbell said.

As he cut another piece of the sacripantina, he could feel Liberatore watching him.

"You want to leave your entire estate to one of your tenants

– a woman you've known for just three years with no discernible income or assets?"

"That's right."

"Are you serious?"

"Yes, I am."

Liberatore rocked back in his chair.

"As your legal counsel, I would strongly advise you to take a little more time to think this through."

"I don't need any more time," Hubbell said.

"Do you have any idea what those flats and your cottage are worth?"

"That's not the point."

"Are you sure this woman isn't just after your money?"

Hubbell wanted to laugh.

"Lydia isn't interested in my money," he said.

"You're sure of that? You're absolutely sure of that?"

"Trust me, Pietro – she couldn't care less."

Liberatore wagged his head.

"You've lost your mind," he said.

"I don't even intend to tell her about this," Hubbell said. "I don't want her to know about this until I'm gone. Then you can tell her."

"You've lost your fucking mind," Liberatore said.

"Maybe so, Pietro. Maybe so."

HUBBELL CAUGHT the 30 Stockton heading downtown. He appreciated Liberatore's concern about his decision to leave his estate to Ms. Gifford. That was Liberatore's job, and Hubbell would have been disappointed if Liberatore hadn't voiced his reservations. And perhaps he was right – Hubbell might very well have lost his mind. But he didn't care. The idea to leave the two flats and his cottage to Ms. Gifford had come to him in the middle of the night, after she fell asleep, as he lay in bed beside her, staring up at the ceiling and wondering what would become of her when he departed for the ever-after. He had no idea where she would go, or how she would come up with the money for another flat or apartment, and it had occurred to him then to find a way for her to remain in the lower flat indefinitely. It seemed so simple. It made so much sense. He saw no downside, other than the fact that he wouldn't be around to witness Ms. Gifford's reaction when Liberatore informed her that the property was hers. Hubbell liked surprises. He always had, just so long as they happened to someone else.

He got off the bus at Union Square and walked down to Macy's, slipping past the flower stand and the espresso vendor on the sidewalk in front of the department store's west entrance. After passing through the open doors, he made his way past the display tables stacked high with packaged shirts and ties to the escalator leading to the upper floors. He paused at the foot of the escalator, watching the stairs materializing at his feet, trying to measure their speed, observing with no little trepidation that they seemed to be moving somewhat faster than the last time he had come to Macy's, a possibility that unsettled him nearly as much as the knowledge that he had certainly gotten slower.

After checking to make sure his shoelaces were tied, he took a deep breath and raised his right foot and then hopped forward, reaching out to grip the handrail as he landed safely on the bottom step. The successful execution of that perilous first hop should have given him a degree of confidence, but already he was worried about getting off. As the escalator carried him up to the second floor, he looked ahead to the steps disappearing at the top of the flight and raised his right foot once again, waiting for the precise moment and then leaping ahead to land on the linoleum floor. He staggered forward and nearly fell, but he managed, somehow, to maintain his balance. He straightened up. One flight down – he had just two more flights to go.

After taking another deep breath, he hopped onto the flight

leading up to the third floor, negotiating it successfully as well, then he positioned himself to mount the flight that would deliver him to the fourth floor. With his satchel in his left hand, he hopped onto the step taking form in front of him, steadying himself with his right hand on the rail, feeling the subtle vibration of the escalator through the thin soles of his shoes. As he approached the top of the flight, he watched the stairs as they sank down and vanished, preparing to leap off, counting out the timing once again, waiting until the very last moment to minimize the distance, afraid to fall short if he leapt too soon. But suddenly he panicked, fearing that he might have waited too long. He lunged forward, extending his right leg as he cleared the last step, airborne for only a moment before his foot landed on the floor. But his leg buckled beneath him, and he stumbled onto his hands and knees, skidding onto his chest as his satchel slid across the aisle in front of him.

Stunned, he lay there, trying to comprehend what had just happened. Only after a moment did he place his hands on the floor and push up to sit. As he rose to his feet, he felt a hand upon the back of his right arm, just above his elbow, steadying him.

"Good heavens – are you all right?"

Hubbell turned to the man who had come to his assistance, dapper and middle-aged in a dark gray pinstriped suit, his hair slicked back and parted down the middle of his scalp.

"Yes, I'm fine," Hubbell said, although he wasn't entirely sure that was true.

"You took a rather nasty spill there."

Hubbell peered down at his nametag, pinned to his lapel – a Macy's employee by the name of George Baptiste.

"Yes, well, thank you for your help," he said.

"Is there anything I can do for you?" Baptiste asked. "Would you happen to be interested in our selection of footwear?"

"I am, actually, looking for a new pair of shoes."

"Excellent," Baptiste said. "May I ask what kind of footwear you might be interested in?"

"I need a pair of shoes to wear in the casket."

That puzzled Baptiste for a moment, but like all shoe dogs, he was quick on his feet. He raised his right hand and drilled a fingertip into his cheek, then he pointed the finger at Hubbell.

"I think I know just what you're looking for," he said.

He spun around on a heel, then cast a glance back over his left shoulder.

"Please, right this way," he said.

Hubbell picked up his satchel and followed Baptiste through the display tables and across the soft carpet to a wall covered with shelves lined with glossy black dress shoes. Baptiste stood off to the side, presenting the shoes with a florid wave of the hand and a deferential bow.

"Voilà," he said.

Hubbell stepped up to the shelves, but he had no idea what he was looking for. He was more than a little relieved when Baptiste took down one of the black leather oxfords and showed it to him, holding it in his hands as if he had polished it himself.

"Perhaps this might interest you – a classic tuxedo oxford made of fine Italian leather, with, as you can see, a smooth cap toe and a classic welt construction."

"It looks very nice," Hubbell said.

"Would you care to try it on?"

Hubbell sat down in one of the chairs arranged in front of the shelves, then watched as Baptiste brought over one of the fitting stools and positioned it in front of him. As Baptiste sat on the padded stool, Hubbell lifted his right foot and placed it on the angled footrest. He watched as Baptiste unlaced his shoe and pulled it off and set it aside.

"My big toe is a little sore," Hubbell said.

"We'll be very careful," Baptiste assured him.

He gently placed Hubbell's foot on the calibrated scale.

"Ten and a half," he said. "I'll be right back."

As Hubbell leaned back in his chair, he looked down at the blue-and-gray argyle sock on his right foot. It had taken several minutes that morning to search through his bureau drawer to find a pair of socks without holes in the toes or heels, and, even then, the pair he had finally selected had lost their elasticity and drooped down to his ankles. At least he had discovered a pair of black socks suitable for wearing to the afterlife, which, in and of itself, seemed like nothing less than divine providence.

When Baptiste returned, he sat on the fitting stool and opened the shoebox, lifting the lid to reveal the new oxfords wrapped in white tissue paper. He took out the right shoe and laced it up, then he placed it on the footrest so Hubbell could slip his foot into it, guiding his heel into place with a stainless steel shoehorn. After pressing on the toe to determine the shoe fit properly, Baptiste gave the laces a firm tug, then tied a simple bow.

"How does that feel?"

Hubbell gripped the arms of the chair and rose to stand. He was surprised, frankly, how good the new shoe felt.

"Would you like to put the other shoe on?" Baptiste asked.

"Yes, I believe I would," he said.

He sat down and leaned back as Baptiste removed his left shoe and then eased his foot into the new oxford. After he tied the laces, Hubbell stood up and stepped around the fitting stool and walked over to the shoe mirror, canted at an angle on the floor. As he looked down at the mirror, he hiked up his trousers to reveal the new shoes, sleek and elegant beneath his knobbed ankles. They might very well have been the finest shoes he had ever worn. They were certainly in compliance with his new determination to indulge himself at every opportunity. He had no idea why he had worn his old shoes for so long, why he hadn't purchased a new pair years ago. He had no idea what he had been waiting for, why it had taken him so long to care.

He released his trouser legs, allowing the cuffs to drop down onto the shoes, then turned to Baptiste.

"I'll take them," he said.

IN HIS NEW SHOES, Hubbell walked up Market Street, through the crowds emerging from the underground BART and Muni stations, the broad brick sidewalk fronted by the soaring windows of the city's grand retail emporiums. After waiting for the streetcar to pass, he crossed Market and walked up Fifth Street, anxious to see that morning's front page, eager to see the play the Suskind obituary had received. It was all he could do to resist the temptation to stop at one of the Chronicle's newsboxes and buy a copy.

He pushed into the lobby. After flashing his identification card at Leonard, he took the elevator up to the third floor and walked down the corridor to the newsroom. He walked directly over to the Page One desk and picked up a copy of the paper from the stack on the file cabinet – and there was the Suskind obituary, prominently occupying the first two columns at the bottom of the front page, beneath the archival photograph of Suskind standing on the roof of the police car as the tear gas swirled around him. Hubbell couldn't help but smile. He had all but forgotten how good it felt to see his byline on Page One.

He folded the paper in half and tucked it under his arm and then made his way back to Section Eight, where his esteemed colleagues were waiting for him.

"Well done," the Senator said, raising his hand to slap Hubbell a high-five.

"Goddamned right," Poopdeck said, rising to stand beside the Senator.

Jennings looked up as Hubbell placed the newspaper on his desk.

"I thought your obituary for Jeremy Suskind was exceptionally well-written," he said.

Hubbell removed his coat and hung it on the rack beside the

window.

"I thank you, gentlemen, for your very kind words."

"You've done us proud," the Senator said.

"Well, it was Harold's decision to take it out front."

"And a damned fine decision it was," the Senator said.

Hubbell placed his hat on his computer, then sat down in his chair. He lifted his satchel into his lap and pulled it open, then carefully slipped in the copy of the paper to take home that evening. He knew all too well that the Suskind obituary might be the last of his work to appear on the front page, and he wanted a copy to commemorate the occasion, perhaps even to show to Ms. Gifford, so that she might see, if not fully appreciate, the value of his work, the value of his career, for that matter.

As he set the satchel on the floor at the foot of his desk, his telephone rang. He reached over and picked up the receiver.

"Good morning, Graydon. Harold is hoping that you might have a moment for him."

"Of course," Hubbell said. "I'll be right there."

As he rose from his chair, he was glad that Harold wanted to see him. He had intended to drop by his office at some point to thank him not just for running the Suskind obituary on Page One but for the broader message his decision to do so had sent to the whole of the newsroom. He was glad the opportunity had presented itself before they were both overtaken by the events of the day.

"Go on in," Helen said.

He opened the door and stepped into Harold's office, where he was startled to see Lieutenant Thomas Neagle, a tall lanky cop in a powder blue sports coat, sitting beside Stanford Rawlings, the paper's grotesquely overweight in-house legal counsel.

"Come in, Graydon," Harold said. "I believe you know Lieutenant Neagle."

"Yes, of course, I do," Hubbell said.

He crossed the office and extended his hand to Neagle, his long blond hair falling to his shoulders, his coarse blond moustache curling around the corners of his mouth. Hubbell had known Neagle ever since he joined the department in the early 1970s. Neagle was initially assigned to the Mission Station, and it was there that he quickly displayed a fondness for subduing criminal suspects, as well as the occasional unlucky bystander, with his long-handled flashlight, preferring its powers of persuasion over his much lighter nightstick. On no less than six occasions, Neagle was the subject of citizen complaints charging him with the use of excessive force, and Hubbell had felt obligated to write about those complaints when they were taken up by the Police Commission and Neagle received a nominal suspension. It's fair to say that Neagle didn't appreciate the story, or at least that was the sentiment he expressed when he shoved Hubbell up against the wall at the Hall of Justice, proving yet again that among the city's finest, the thicker the skull, the thinner the skin. In the years since his suspension, Neagle had been promoted to the narcotics squad, where he had served without distinction, other than having been implicated, but never formally charged, in connection with a series of thefts in the department's evidence room that, ultimately, resulted in prosecutors dropping the charges against dozens of alleged drug dealers.

"Hello, Tommy."

"Hello, Graydon."

"And, of course, you know Stan."

Unfortunately, that was also true. Rawlings had been the paper's in-house attorney for nearly a decade now, a position acquired solely by virtue of his marriage to the editor-in-chief's sister. He was widely despised in the newsroom for his surpassing cowardice, absolutely terrified by the prospect of having to defend the Chronicle in a court of law, and so, by default, his legal strategy consisted almost exclusively of launching pre-emptive strikes against any stories even remotely controversial, much less potentially litigious, searching for any conceivable reason to eviscerate, if not spike, those stories before they made it into print.

"Hello, Stan," Hubbell said.

He joined Neagle and Rawlings in the chairs arranged in front of Harold's desk.

"Would anyone like a cup of coffee?" Harold asked.

When no one took him up on his offer, he turned to Helen.

"Thank you, Helen. That will be all."

As she left the office, closing the door behind her, Harold turned back to them.

"So," he began, "I got a call this morning from Lieutenant Neagle here, who raised a few questions about our obituary for Jeremy Suskind, and I thought it might be best for all of us to sit down together and listen to his concerns."

Hubbell's chest tightened. He didn't like the sound of that at all.

"Well, as you know," Neagle said, "we've been looking for Suskind for damned near forty years now, ever since he and his comrades tried to blow up Central Station."

He smiled, his long teeth descending beneath his moustache.

"When you kill a cop, or try to kill a cop, or even think about killing a cop – we tend to take it personally."

"Of course," Harold said.

"And we've thought we had a line on Suskind more than once," Neagle said. "We thought we had a line on him up in Mendocino County, where he was growing high-grade marijuana. At one point, we tracked him to a ranch down in the desert near Joshua Tree, where he was dealing peyote and mescaline. We later received a tip that he had moved to Santa Monica and was apparently involved in the wholesale distribution of ecstasy."

Hubbell wanted to laugh. He couldn't believe what he was hearing.

"You're telling us that Jeremy Suskind was a drug dealer?"

"That's right," Neagle said. "That's exactly right. And our last tip put him back here in the city, where we believe he's been engaged in the manufacture and sale of LSD and other pharmaceutical hallucinogens."

Hubbell shook his head and looked to Harold.

"I hadn't heard any of this," he said.

"So you can imagine how surprised we were when we picked up the paper this morning and saw that Suskind had died in a car accident up in Montana," Neagle said.

"Suskind's death surprised everyone," Hubbell said.

"I'm sure it did," Neagle said. "But it didn't make any sense. I mean, what the hell was Jeremy Suskind doing up in Montana?"

Hubbell made no attempt to answer.

"So I picked up the telephone and called the Flathead County Sheriff's Department and asked them about Suskind – and they had no idea what I was talking about."

"They didn't know anything about the accident?" Hubbell asked.

"Nothing," Neagle said.

"That can't be right," Hubbell said.

"I don't know why they would lie to me."

"Could Suskind have been living under another name?"

Neagle pointed his finger at Hubbell.

"I had the very same thought," he said. "In fact, Suskind has used any number of aliases over the years."

He turned to Harold.

"Unfortunately, just two fatal car accidents have occurred in Flathead County during the past several weeks, and in both accidents, the victims were locals."

"There has to be a mistake," Hubbell said. "Suskind's mother told me that one of the sheriff's deputies called and told her about the accident."

"Which is why I decided to give Suskind's mother a call myself," Neagle said.

"And what did she tell you?" Hubbell asked.

"She didn't know anything about an accident involving her son in Montana," Neagle said.

Hubbell's stomach sank.

"You can't be serious," he said.

"She also told me that she'd never talked to anyone from the San Francisco Chronicle."

"For the love of Christ," Rawlings groaned.

"I hate to say it, gentlemen, but I think you've been had," Neagle said. "It looks to me like Suskind and his comrades set you up. This has to be some kind of attempt to throw us off his trail."

A rush of heat rose up into Hubbell's face. He could feel the perspiration beading on his forehead.

"I can't believe this," was all he could say.

"Suskind's a crafty little prick – I'll give him that," Neagle said.

"So let me get this straight, just to make sure I'm not missing anything," Rawlings said. "We have a story on our front page this morning about the death of one of the leaders of the Free Speech Movement, and we now have no reason whatsoever to believe he's actually dead? In fact, rather than dead, we have every reason to believe he may very well be a major drug trafficker."

"That does appear to be the case," Neagle said.

Rawlings turned to Hubbell, who tried to defend himself, even as he knew it was futile.

"A woman called, identifying herself as Diane Suskind – I had no reason to believe she might be someone else. When she told me her son had died in a car accident, I had no reason to suspect she wasn't telling me the truth."

"But she wasn't, was she?" Rawlings said.

Hubbell looked to Harold.

"This can't be happening," he said.

Neagle rose from his chair and straightened the broad lapels of his coat, then started toward the door.

"Well, I'll leave you gentlemen to sort all this out," he said.

Harold stood and walked out from behind his desk to let Neagle out of his office. He opened the door, then shook Neagle's hand.

"Thanks for bringing this to our attention, Lieutenant."

Neagle turned and smiled down at Hubbell.

"Believe me, it was my pleasure."

As Neagle left, Harold closed the door behind him. Hubbell watched as he returned to his desk.

"Is Fleming in this morning?" Harold asked Rawlings.

"I haven't seen him," Rawlings said.

"We need to let him know we have a problem," Harold said.

"I'm sure he's at the Olympic Club," Rawlings said.

"We can wait until he finishes his round," Harold said. "That gives us a little time."

Rawlings struggled up to stand.

"All right," he said. "Let me know when you decide how you think we should proceed."

"I will," Harold said.

AS HAROLD STEPPED OUT of his office for a moment, Hubbell reached for his handkerchief and mopped the perspiration from his forehead and upper lip. He couldn't believe that Suskind hadn't died, that the accident had never taken place, that he had been duped by the woman who called in claiming to be Suskind's mother. It was all an act, a hoax. She had played him for a fool. But that, unfortunately, was no defense. He had no defense. He should have called the sheriff's department in Kalispell to confirm that Suskind had died in an accident. It didn't matter that no one could have seen this coming, that aside from the occasional disparaging remark or salacious rumor, no one had ever willfully deceived him while he was writing obituaries, that he had always worked in good faith, in a spirit of trust. All that mattered now was that he had gotten it wrong, terribly wrong, totally wrong.

He had no idea what he was going to write in the correction, for the simple reason that it wasn't at all clear what anyone actually knew to be true. They knew, unfortunately, that Suskind hadn't died in a car accident, but the fact that he hadn't been killed last week in Montana didn't even mean that the son of a bitch was alive. He might very well have returned to the city, as Neagle had suggested. He might very well be trafficking in LSD and other hallucinogens. But the police didn't know any of that for a fact. The only thing any of them knew for certain was that they didn't know much of anything for certain.

Hubbell watched as Harold returned to his office and closed the door.

"I'll try to work up a correction," Hubbell said. "But I'm not exactly sure what it's going to say."

Harold shook his head.

"No, I'll have Myron work up the correction."

Hubbell had no idea what that meant.

"You want to give it to Myron?"

Harold leaned forward, his forearms on his desk.

"Fleming is going to want me to fire you, Graydon. Hell, he wanted me to fire you last week, after you screwed up the Jurgensen obituary."

"You've got to be kidding me."

"But I talked him out of it. I told him he couldn't just fire someone for an inadvertent mistake, no matter how badly he might want to, no matter how egregious the mistake might have been. I told him the guild would fight him, and eventually, as much as it pained him, he conceded the point."

Harold leaned back in his chair.

"But I can't save you this time, not after this – and neither can the guild."

"So what does that mean?" Hubbell asked.

"My recommendation is that you take an indefinite medical leave, effective immediately, before we have to tell Fleming about this and he goes berserk."

"You can't be serious."

"That's the best I can do," Harold said.

Hubbell could only stare at him. He had no idea what to say.

"You're dying, Graydon. You're dying of cancer. I should have forced you to take a medical leave the day you told me about your diagnosis. I shouldn't have listened to you. I shouldn't have let you keep working. None of this would have happened."

It was only then that Hubbell began to fully understand what Harold was telling him.

"You're telling me it's over?"

"It ends for everyone," Harold told him. "It's going to end for all of us, including me, sooner or later."

Hubbell was utterly stunned. He had no idea what to say.

"Jesus, Hal."

"I told Helen to contact human resources and get the paperwork started."

Hubbell nodded. He offered no resistance. There was nothing to say. He couldn't blame Harold. He didn't blame him.

"All right," he said.

"I'm sorry, Graydon."

Hubbell pushed up to stand.

"So am I," he said.

AFTER LEAVING Harold's office, Hubbell walked back down the corridor to the newsroom. He stopped beside the fax machine and looked out across the cubicles occupied by his colleagues. He listened hard, but all he could hear were the halting conversations and clacking keyboards, the occasional burst of profanity above the low murmur of the televisions and computers. He took a deep breath and started up the aisle leading back to Section Eight, profoundly relieved that he didn't hear mention of his name. He could only assume the newsroom didn't know about the Suskind obituary yet – they didn't know yet that his career was effectively over. But it was only a matter of time. As he walked back to his desk, he knew it wouldn't be long before word got out.

The Senator was standing beside Poopdeck's desk. He turned to Hubbell when he noticed him approaching.

"More kudos from our fearless leader, I trust?"

"Not exactly," Hubbell said.

As he dropped into his chair, the Senator lumbered over to stand beside his computer.

"Then what did Hal want, if not to praise your superb work?"

Hubbell looked up at the Senator. As Poopdeck rose from his desk to join them, Jennings turned around in his chair.

"Gentlemen, I'm afraid this is my last day at the Chronicle," Hubbell told them.

"What?" the Senator asked.

"I'm taking an indefinite medical leave, effective immediately."

"What the fuck are you talking about?" Poopdeck asked.

Hubbell let his shoulders slump. He allowed himself a deep breath.

"There was a problem with the Suskind obituary."

"What kind of problem?" the Senator asked.

"It seems the son of a bitch didn't die last week."

"Suskind survived the wreck?" the Senator asked.

"There was no wreck. Suskind didn't survive anything. It never happened."

"What the fuck are you talking about?" Poopdeck asked.

"I was duped. It was a hoax, presumably to throw the police off Suskind's trail," Hubbell told them.

"What?" Poopdeck gasped.

The Senator stepped back, as if recoiling from an explosion.

"Oh, my," Jennings said.

In the corner of his eye, Hubbell glimpsed Ms. Mitchell looking on from her desk across the aisle, her mouth open, eyes wide. He couldn't believe she was there to witness his humiliation.

"But why the medical leave?" the Senator asked. "I don't understand."

"It was take an indefinite medical leave or get fired."

"Fired? For what? They can't fire you," the Senator declared. "This is not your fault. You're the victim of this hoax – not the perpetrator."

"The medical leave was Harold's suggestion, actually."

"We'll fight this!" the Senator declared. "They can't do this! This shall not stand!"

But Hubbell shook his head. He reached out and turned off his computer, watching as the screen drew back into darkness.

"That won't be necessary," Hubbell said. "It's done. It's over. The paperwork is being drawn up right now."

He reached down and picked up his satchel. With his colleagues looking on, he opened the satchel and withdrew the copy of that morning's paper. He tossed it into the trash, wanting nothing more than to be done with it.

"You can't let them do this to you," the Senator said.

But Hubbell had already pushed up from his chair. He walked over to the coat rack beside the window. He slipped his coat off the wooden hanger and slid his arms down the sleeves.

"I hate to leave you, gentlemen, but I'd like to get out of here before everyone in the newsroom finds out what happened."

HUBBELL MADE HIS WAY down Market Street, eyes downcast as he slipped through the crowd. At the bus stop on Third Street, he caught the 45 Lyon and dropped into the seat directly behind the driver. He couldn't believe his career at the Chronicle was over. He couldn't believe how suddenly the end had come. Only last night, he was on top of the world. Now, he wanted nothing but to disappear. He closed his eyes and reached up to massage his aching forehead. He needed to think. He needed to think it all through. He needed a drink.

He got off the bus at Columbus and started up Green Street. As matter of practice, Hubbell rarely drank in bars, much less in the afternoon, but when he did, he drank at Gino and Carlo's, one of the oldest bars in North Beach. He pushed in through the door, stepping into the murky blue light and the haze of cigarette smoke, slipping past the illuminated jukebox, past the patrons seated along the bar, hunched over their cocktails. He spotted an unoccupied stool near the end of the bar. As he hiked up his right hip and slid onto the padded seat, the bartender walked down to him.

"Give me a bourbon on the rocks," Hubbell told him.

The bartender turned and walked back to the sink behind the bar and grabbed one of the glasses from the drying tray. Hubbell watched as he filled the glass with ice, then reached for the Early Times in the long row of bottles arranged against the wall. He knew the bartender knew who he was, even if not necessarily by name. The bartender knew he hadn't come for conversation or camaraderie. He knew he came to Gino and Carlo's only when he needed refuge, a place to hide, if not from the inevitable, then at least for a while.

The bartender placed the glass on a white paper napkin directly in front of him.

"Thanks," Hubbell said.

He raised the glass and took a sip. As he returned the glass to the napkin, he glanced down the bar at the other patrons. He didn't recognize any of them. He had no idea who they were or why they sought sanctuary at Gino and Carlo's. The only patron he had ever known was the Professor. They had all known the Professor, as well as his sidekick Shorty, of course.

The Professor had been in his late sixties with dazzling blue eyes and long gray hair pulled back into a ponytail as thick as a dock rope. He had been a housepainter by trade, permanently disabled by recurring balance problems caused, in his view, by years of exposure to toxic paint fumes. They called him the Professor because he was a voracious reader who spent his mornings in the North Beach Library, his afternoons at Caffe Trieste, poring over the books he had checked out, and his evenings at Gino and Carlo's, holding forth from his stool beside the door. Over the years, Hubbell had had the pleasure of listening to the Professor dissect Hannibal's bold decision to cross the Alps in the dead of winter to attack Rome from the north, insist that William Carlos Williams' *In the American Grain* is the finest novel in the canon of American literature, and warn about the bizarre phenomenon of spontaneous human combustion, in which an untold number of men and women had inexplicably burst into flame. And it was just last fall that the Professor had delivered an impassioned lecture about the Second Law of Thermodynamics.

It is fair to say that few of the patrons at Gino and Carlo's that night, including Hubbell, were familiar with any of the laws of thermodynamics, much less the second law. But as the Professor explained, the laws of thermodynamics merely describe the behavior of heat. The second law holds, at least in part, that while a hot object left alone will eventually cool, a cool object will not spontaneously grow hot. Nothing could be more simple than that. Hubbell and the other patrons knew it to be empirically true. A cup of hot coffee will gradually grow cold, but a cup of cold coffee will never grow hot.

And by the same principle, the Professor explained, the Second Law of Thermodynamics may be applied to broader systems of order. An ordered state, the Professor told them, inexorably degenerates into a state of chaos from which it will never recover.

As Hubbell sipped at his bourbon, he could still see the Professor standing at the far end of the bar, raising his empty glass.

"Imagine, gentlemen, if you will, an empty jar. Imagine the bottom half of the jar filled with salt. Imagine the top half filled with pepper. The grains of salt and the flakes of pepper are in a state of perfect equilibrium, are they not?"

"Goddamned right they are," mumbled Shorty, a stump of a man who favored a black beret and rose-tinted glasses.

"Then give the jar a sharp shake and look at the salt and pepper now! Do you see what has happened? Chaos! The salt and pepper are thoroughly mixed together! And no matter how long you continue to shake the jar, the salt and pepper will never return to that perfect state of equilibrium! Do you follow me? Do you see what I am getting at?"

"Goddamn right I do," Shorty said.

"Look around you, gentlemen! You see it everywhere! Hope collapses into despair! Dreams devolve into madness! Love plunges into sorrow! Do you understand what I am saying?"

"Hell, yes, I do!" Shorty shouted.

"What kind of fool would believe the human condition is exempt from the laws that govern the universe?"

Shorty leapt down from his stool and punched the air with his fist.

"Not this fool!"

Not Hubbell, either. He knew exactly what the Professor was saying that night. He knew exactly what the Professor meant. The Professor's extemporaneous lecture about the second law was one of his finest, in Hubbell's view, delivered only a few short weeks before he passed away, dropping dead of a cerebral aneurysm in Molinari's delicatessen. Hubbell liked to think that he had written one of his finest obituaries for the Professor, recalling him as a man of unbounded curiosity and uncommon wisdom, who shared his eccentric knowledge with all those who had the good fortune to meet him. He would never forget the Professor. He would never forget his lecture about the second law. The Professor was right. Hubbell knew it then, and he knew it now. As he took another sip of bourbon, he could feel his life coming apart, and he knew, beyond any doubt, that there was no way to pull it back together.

He raised his empty glass to get the bartender's attention.

"Hit me again," he said.

SHORTLY BEFORE MIDNIGHT, Hubbell rose from his stool and staggered out of Gino and Carlo's, feeling the effects of the afternoon and evening he had spent there, sequestered in intense deliberation at the end of the bar, contemplating his future, mulling over his options, the options for any seventy-six-year-old white, male, former newspaper reporter, for that matter, and by the time he started down the sidewalk, he had narrowed his future prospects to joining the space program or campaigning for the U.S. Senate.

He ambled down the sidewalk, trailing his fingers along the sides of the cars parked along the curb as if to maintain both his course and his balance, turning right at Stockton and making his way down to Washington Square. As he stood at the corner and looked up at the twin spires of Sts. Peter and Paul, bathed in cool white light as they rose above the trees that ringed the square, he decided to walk directly across the square, rather than around it, a tactical decision that would not only shorten his route home but mitigate the possibility of injury should he stumble.

And it was precisely to avoid stumbling that he spread his arms as he started across the moist grass, swooping down upon the statue of Benjamin Franklin in the very center of the square, mounted on a concrete pedestal amid a glade of slender poplars, only to emerge from the square near the children's playground. He waited for the streetlight to change, then he crossed Columbus and started up Filbert, his progress unsteady, to say the least, the slope of the hill, even on those lower blocks, requiring an unusual effort, and by foregoing a straight path up the sidewalk in favor of a gently weaving approach, his progress was slow, measured driveway by driveway.

It seemed to take a lifetime to reach Jones Street, at the foot of the last steep block below the gate leading back to his cottage. He leaned against the wall of the building at the corner. As he caught his breath, he couldn't help but wonder if he could make it all the way up to the gate. But he had no choice. He couldn't just stand there. There was certainly no turning back. So he took a deep breath and started up the sidewalk, his heavy legs wobbling beneath him, gasping for every breath. The climb had never seemed so steep, the distance never so great, and he thought for a moment he was going to collapse onto his hands and knees. In desperation, he lunged for the ficus tree planted in front of his neighbors' front door, wrapping his arms around its thick white trunk, hugging it to his chest until he managed to position his feet beneath him. Only as he straightened up did he feel the convulsion in his stomach.

He doubled over as the bourbon surged up out of him and splashed down the trunk of the tree. He coughed and spat and slowly straightened back up. Oddly enough, he felt much better as he wiped his mouth on the sleeve of his coat. He glanced up and down the block to see if anyone had observed the unseemly spectacle of his taking ill, realizing only then that he had lost his hat. When he looked down, he saw it at his feet. With one hand on the ficus to brace himself, he bent down and picked it up. After placing it on his head and tugging down the brim, he pronounced himself fit and resumed his progress up the hill, deeply grateful that he didn't have far to go.

He managed to make it to his gate, pausing there to fumble through his pockets for his keys. After letting himself in through the gate, he walked slowly along the side of the two flats, making his way carefully in the darkness, brushing the building with his left shoulder, shuffling his feet across the concrete. He stopped when he reached the garden, relieved to have finally made it home but needing a moment to gather his strength before climbing the stairs leading up to his cottage.

In the soft blue glow of Ms. Gifford's television, spilling through the back door of her flat, Hubbell decided to rest for a moment in one of the canvas chairs arranged around the table on the patio. As he walked across the brick, he reached for the edge of the table, inadvertently bumping it with his right thigh, dropping his satchel as he gripped the nearest chair's wooden armrests and slumped down into the canvas seat. A wave of nausea washed over him, but it passed quickly. He took a gulp of air.

It was then that the door of Ms. Gifford's flat opened. In a loose, white, long-sleeve shirt, she leaned out onto the patio.

"Graydon? Is that you?"

"Good evening, Lydia."

She stood on the threshold.

"I heard a noise," she said. "I thought it might be a raccoon."

That amused Hubbell. He was not often mistaken for a raccoon.

"No, it's just me," he said.

"What are you doing out there?"

"I'm just resting."

"Have you been there long?"

"Oh, no – only for a moment," he said. "It's very nice, actually."

She stepped out onto the patio and looked up at the moon. Hubbell looked up with her, but it made him nauseated, and he preferred, if the truth be known, looking at Ms. Gifford's bare legs, descending from beneath the tail of her shirt.

She looked back down at Hubbell.

"You smell like you've been drinking," she said.

"Yes, that's quite true."

"You smell like you've been puking, too."

"Oh, yes," he said.

"You poor thing."

"I hope it doesn't bother you."

"Oh, Graydon – please. I'm a Deadhead. Puke doesn't bother me – not in the least."

"I haven't puked in years. It just gushed right out of me."

"You must have gotten some on your shoes."

"They're brand new. I bought them this morning. I'm planning on wearing them in the casket."

"You might want to wipe them off first."

"Oh, yes," he said. "That's a very good idea."

"Would you like to do that now?" she asked him. "Would you like me to help you up the stairs so we can clean off your new shoes?"

"I'd be most appreciative," he said.

HUBBELL ROSE unsteadily to his feet, then reached down and picked up his satchel. He took Ms. Gifford's extended arm. Together, they made their way up the steps between the two levels of the yard, then across the upper patio to the stairs leading up to his cottage. Using the railing to pull himself up, he led the way up the stairs, as exhausted as he was intoxicated. It was all he could do to lift his feet from stair to stair, Ms. Gifford positioned directly behind him, her hand at the small of his back, encouraging his progress and preventing him from falling backward. When they reached the landing at the top of the stairs, Hubbell leaned over the railing and vomited again, the remaining contents of his stomach splashing onto the patio below.

He turned to Ms. Gifford.

"I hope I missed the raccoons," he said.

"I'm sure they'll be fine."

After leaning him against the wall of the cottage, she retrieved the key from beneath the doormat and unlocked the door, reaching in to turn on the light before leading Hubbell inside and sitting him down in one of the chairs at the table. As he sat there, leaning forward slightly so she could remove his coat, he knew he couldn't have made it up the stairs without her.

"Oh, Graydon – you got some puke on your hat, too."

He felt not an ounce of shame.

"I puked on myself from head to toe," he told her.

He watched as she knelt on the floor to remove his shoes.

"These are very nice shoes," she said. "But they've had a rough day."

He sat back as she rose and carried the shoes over to the counter beside the sink.

"So have I," he declared.

"I'll clean these off after I get you into bed," she told him.

"You're going to put me to bed?"

"I think that would be a good idea, don't you?"

Hubbell shrugged. He didn't have any ideas – good or bad.

"Whatever you say," he said.

He raised his right arm, and she helped him up to stand, then wrapped her arm around his waist and led him out of the kitchen and down the hallway to his bedroom. She sat him on the edge of the bed, and he immediately flopped onto his back. But she reached down and grabbed his hands and pulled him back up to sit, then began unbuttoning his shirt.

"Today was my last day at the Chronicle," Hubbell told her.

She stopped.

"Is that true, Graydon? I had no idea."

"I worked there fifty-three years."

She resumed unbuttoning his shirt and slid the sleeves down his arms, then tossed the shirt onto the chair beside the bureau.

"That's such a long time," she said. "I can't even imagine."

He flopped back onto the mattress.

"Only I wrote an obituary for a man who isn't dead."

It took a moment for Ms. Gifford to realize that that was a problem.

"Oh, Graydon."

She unbuckled his belt and unfastened his trousers and pulled them down his legs, over his ankles and feet.

"It's a hell of a thing to lose your career – just like that," he said, trying without success to snap his fingers.

She draped his trousers over the back of the chair.

"You worked too hard, for too long, if you ask me."

He tried to raise his head but quickly abandoned the effort and stared up at the cracks in the plaster ceiling.

"I'm going to miss my job," he told her.

"I'm sure you will."

"I'm going to miss my byline most of all."

She tossed his socks at the chair.

"There were times when I used to think my byline was all I had."

She sat down on the mattress beside him.

"Just think of yourself as free," she told him.

He looked up at her. He tried to think.

"Free?"

"Yes, free – as free as a bird."

"What kind of bird?"

"Any kind you want," she said.

"How about a blackbird? I've always liked blackbirds."

"Sure, Graydon. Just imagine you're as free as a blackbird."

Hubbell nodded. He liked that.

"Very well, Lydia. That's exactly what I'll do."

CHAPTER TWELVE

HUBBELL OPENED his eyes slowly, as if afraid of what he might see. His head pounded. A deep growl rose from his evacuated stomach. He could smell the alcohol seeping from his pores. He rolled onto his left side and lowered his feet to the floor, sitting up carefully, gripping the edge of the mattress to steady himself as the room reeled around him. He took a deep breath and slowly stood up, reaching for the closet door, pausing there briefly before slipping on his robe and walking barefoot down the hall to the kitchen. He made a pot of coffee, then opened the cabinet above the counter and took down the bottle of aspirin. He shook the last seven capsules into the palm of his hand and popped them into his mouth, then washed them down with a gulp of water. He didn't care the recommended dosage called for just two capsules. Recommended dosages meant nothing to him, not anymore. When he needed relief, he wanted it right away.

He had no appetite. All he had eaten yesterday was the slice of sacripantina, so he dropped two slices of stale sourdough bread into the toaster, then cut a grapefruit in half and placed the smaller of the two halves on a plate. When the toast was ready, he forked the charred slices onto the plate and then sat down at the table and forced himself to eat, shedding crumbs down the front of his robe with each bite of the blackened toast, wincing as he ate the bitter wedges of grapefruit. He dreaded the prospect of returning to the Chronicle. Everyone in the newsroom surely knew by now what had happened with the Suskind obituary. Everyone knew that his career was over. Everyone knew that he was dying of cancer. But he had no choice – he needed to sign and formally submit the paperwork for his medical leave.

When he finished the toast and grapefruit, he placed the dishes in the sink, then walked back down the hall to the bathroom. After taking a shower, he put on a pair of dark wool trousers, a white long-sleeve shirt and a deep blue tie. As he knotted his tie, he studied his reflection in the mirror on the bureau, hoping the clean, neatly pressed clothes would lift his spirits, if not mask his physiological distress. But he was not that fortunate. He looked old and frail, stooped slightly forward, his shoulders sagging down. He looked older, frankly, than he ever had, older, certainly, than yesterday. He looked as if he were aging by the hour.

He turned away from the mirror and returned to the kitchen, where he slipped on his new shoes, wiped clean by Ms. Gifford, God bless her, then grabbed a dark gray coat and an old gray fedora from the closet, his tweed coat and brown fedora still bearing evidence of yesterday's folly. With the coat draped over his left arm, he let himself out of the cottage and made his way down to the garage, hoping he could persuade the Mustang to deliver him to the Chronicle one last time.

He opened the car door and grabbed the edge of the roof and eased his aching body into the seat behind the wheel, then he pulled the door shut, tugging it firmly to overcome the groaning hinges. But as the door closed, the window slipped off its track and crashed down inside the door. He tried to crank it back up, but to no avail. Hubbell could only shake his head. The Mustang wasn't in any better shape than he was.

THE PARKING GARAGE across from the Chronicle was nearly full, but Hubbell guided the Mustang down the ramp and found a space in the basement. He reached down and killed the engine, then he leaned forward, closing his eyes and resting his pounding forehead on the steering wheel. He still couldn't believe that his career had imploded so suddenly. He still couldn't believe he was leaving the Chronicle under such humiliating circumstances.

He climbed out of the Mustang and walked across the garage to the stairs leading up to the sidewalk. After waiting for the light to change, he crossed the street and pushed into the Chronicle. He flashed his identification card at Leonard, then took the elevator up to the third floor and ducked into the men's room. After placing his satchel on the shelf inside the door, he stepped up to the mirror above the row of sinks, reminding himself that the end of his career, no matter how ignominious, was no reason to abandon the sartorial tradition that he had upheld for the past fifty-three years. He straightened the lapels of his coat and adjusted the brim of his hat, then he took a deep breath, summoning his nerve and what remained of his pride, then pushed out of the bathroom and started down the corridor to the newsroom.

As he passed the fax machine and walked up the aisle leading back to Section Eight, a pall of silence abruptly descended upon the newsroom. He was not surprised. He expected no less. As he passed along the waist-high file cabinets, he could feel the heat of the eyes on his back. But he conceded nothing, his head held high and his shoulders drawn back, looking straight ahead, refusing to be defeated by the sordid circumstances of his departure. He didn't care what any of his younger colleagues thought – not about him, not about anything. He had never cared what they thought. There was certainly no reason to start caring now.

Finally, he arrived at his desk. As he removed his coat and hat, he found it hard to believe that this would be his last day in the newsroom, but already he felt like a visitor, a stranger, soon to join the list of all those who had departed before him. He gazed out at all the empty desks once occupied by colleagues who had long since passed away, the sight of the vacant desks depressing him nearly as much as the knowledge that tomorrow his desk would be empty, too. And with the buyouts and layoffs looming, it wouldn't be long before his esteemed colleagues were compelled to abandon their desks as well. As hard as it was to believe, much less accept, Hubbell knew it was only a matter of time before Section Eight simply ceased to exist.

He pulled out his chair and sat down. He had no intention of cleaning out his desk, much less his cubicle. He would leave that for the building manager and the simpletons who worked for him. They could throw out the cardboard boxes containing the files from all of the obituaries he had written. He didn't care what they did with the dictionaries, style manuals and reference books he had accumulated over the years. The detritus that filled the drawers of his desk meant nothing to him now. All Hubbell wanted was the bundle of letters in his upper left drawer, sent to him by readers – family members and friends grieving the loss of loved ones, thanking him for the kind words he had written on the occasion of their passing. He opened the drawer and withdrew the letters, feeling their solemn weight in his hand, fanning the corners of the ragged envelopes with the pad of his thumb. He had saved every letter. They were one of his most cherished possessions. They were nothing less than the truest measure of his work.

It was then that Hubbell heard Myron approaching, the oddly subdued clapping of his wingtips on the linoleum. When he looked up, Myron was standing beside his computer, peering down at him through his wire-rimmed glasses, blemishes erupting on his sallow cheeks, the tuft of hair at the crest of his forehead wilting onto his brow.

"Hello, Myron."

"Hello, Graydon."

"Is there something I can do for you?"

"I hear you're taking a medical leave."

"That is correct."

"I hear you've got cancer."

"That is also correct," he said.

"When I asked the other day, you told me you were fine."

"Yes, I did."

"But that wasn't true."

"No, it wasn't."

Myron had to think.

"Why didn't you just tell me?"

"I didn't want you to know," Hubbell said without hesitation.

That didn't seem to satisfy Myron.

"You lied to me."

"Only because you asked, Myron. If you hadn't asked, I wouldn't have lied to you."

Myron allowed himself an existential smile, revealing his small teeth.

"So it was my fault?" he asked.

"Exactly."

Myron shook his head, then walked over to the window. He parted the blinds with his fingers and peered down at the street.

"They're sending me back to the copy desk," he said.

He turned back to Hubbell.

"It's like they blame me for the Suskind obituary," he said. "I mean, why else would they do that to me?"

"There's always the possibility that they're doing it because you're a lousy editor."

"I knew this would make you happy."

"I expect the news will be warmly received by my colleagues, as well."

"You never did like me, did you?"

"No, I never did."

"None of you did, ever."

"I think that's fair to say."

"Was it something I did?" he wanted to know. "Was there something I should have done?"

"No, Myron – there was nothing you could have done. You were our editor. It's as simple as that. We weren't going to like you no matter what you did."

Myron shoved his hands into the pockets of his trousers, as if he didn't know what else to do with them.

"So today is your last day?"

"Yesterday was my last day, officially," Hubbell said. "I'm just here to put through the paperwork for my leave."

Myron nodded.

"Well, so long, I guess."

And for a moment, Hubbell nearly pitied Myron, his tenure as an assistant city editor abruptly terminated, his return to the copy desk as humbling as it was imminent. But to Hubbell's immense relief, that moment quickly passed.

"So long, Myron," he said.

ON HIS WAY to sign the papers for his medical leave, Hubbell ducked into the alcove off the mailroom for a cup of coffee. Several of his younger colleagues were gathered in the alcove, drinking their first diet colas of the day, deep in conversation as they stood in front of the counter. They looked vaguely familiar, even if Hubbell had no idea what their names were, much less their assignments in the newsroom. Nonetheless, he greeted them warmly, as if they had been working together for years.

"And how is everyone doing today?" he asked.

They backed away as if he were radioactive, uttering not a sound as they dispersed and fled back down the hallway to the newsroom.

"Excellent," he said as he reached for the pot of coffee. "That's wonderful."

He filled his mug with coffee, declining, as always, to slip his quarters into the coin box, then he turned and started back through the vacant Business and Sports departments to meet with Bethany Milhouse, the newsroom's director of human resources, a specialist in corporate downsizing, hired several years ago primarily to oversee the initial wave of buyouts and layoffs in the newsroom, an assignment she undertook with such zeal and enthusiasm that she quickly became known as "Bethany the Executioner."

As he stood outside Ms. Milhouse's door, Hubbell couldn't help but feel apprehensive about meeting with her. As director of human resources, Ms. Millhouse was also responsible for conducting the newsroom's mandatory annual sexual harassment seminar. The seminar featured, among other things, a brief film in which a troupe of actors performed a series of skits suggesting that it was inappropriate for newsroom employees to decorate their cubicles with posters or calendars depicting women, or men, for that matter, in various stages of undress; tell jokes that described, no matter how colorfully, human genitalia in any of their many applications; or for male employees to ask their female colleagues for their undergarments, no matter how flattering they intended the request to be. Unfortunately, last month, during the seminar Hubbell attended with his colleagues from Section Eight, Poopdeck objected to the film as a full frontal assault on his First Amendment right to freedom of expression, becoming so agitated during the post-film discussion that Hubbell and the Senator had to forcibly lead him out of the conference room. Hubbell could only hope that Ms. Millhouse didn't hold his association with Poopdeck against him.

He knocked lightly, then reached down and opened the door. Sitting at her desk in the back of her office, Ms. Milhouse turned toward the door as Hubbell opened it, a small woman with short blond hair that curled beneath the rim of her jaw, her eyes blue, her heart-shaped mouth drawn in red lipstick, the ruffled collar of her white blouse rising along the side of her neck.

"I believe we have an appointment to discuss my medical leave," Hubbell said.

"Please, Mr. Hubbell – come in," she said.

As he entered her office, closing the door behind him, Ms. Milhouse rose from her desk, smoothing down her red skirt, then picking up a blue folder and gesturing toward the small round table in the corner of her office.

"Why don't we sit at the table," she said. "That might be more comfortable."

"Certainly," Hubbell said.

He stood beside the table as Ms. Milhouse walked out from behind her desk, her nylons swishing between her thighs as she crossed the office. Hubbell waited until she was seated at the table before he sat down across from her, a small bowl of hard candies placed in the center of the table, there, no doubt, to sweeten the bad news she so cheerfully delivered to those whose careers she had been hired to terminate.

"So, Mr. Hubbell – I understand you're leaving us."

"Yes, I'm afraid that's true," he said.

"All good things must come to end, I suppose."

"So I hear," Hubbell said.

"You are, after all, seventy-six years old."

"Yes," Hubbell said. "Yes, I am."

"You could have retired years ago."

"Well, I enjoyed my job, by and large."

"But you didn't expect to work here forever, did you?"

"No, of course not."

She smiled brightly at Hubbell, pleased that he had conceded the point.

"Harold tells me that you have cancer," she said.

"Yes, that is also true."

"I'm sorry to hear that."

"I thank you for your concern," Hubbell said.

"I must say, though, that you don't look like you're sick. You look perfectly healthy to me, as healthy as a man your age is capable of looking, I suppose."

"What can I say?" Hubbell asked. "Looks can be deceiving."

"Yes, so true, so very true."

She opened the blue folder.

"Which is why, obviously, we will need official verification of your medical condition from your primary care physician, or your oncologist, if you prefer."

"You don't believe me?"

"Of course, I believe you," Ms. Milhouse said. "But surely you see my point, as it pertains to all the employees in the newsroom."

"No, I'm afraid I don't."

"The system is rife with abuse, Mr. Hubbell. As much as I might want to take everyone at their word, that would be irresponsible, wouldn't you say? If I trusted you, I'd have to trust everyone – and then where would we be?"

Hubbell's head hurt. He needed more aspirin.

"You see the problem, don't you?"

"Of course," he said, though of course he didn't.

He watched as Ms. Milhouse thumbed through the documents in the folder.

"I believe your paperwork is in order," she said. "I believe I have marked every place that requires your signature or your initials. And I've included the verification form you'll need to give to your physician."

She closed the folder and slid it across the table to him.

"Obviously, we won't be able to process your application for a medical leave until we receive the verification form and the signed documents."

"I'll get them back to you as soon as I can," Hubbell said.

HAROLD EXTENDED his left arm, gesturing toward the black leather sofa, positioned beneath a gallery of some of the most dramatic Chronicle front pages over the years, mounted on the wall of his office in thin black frames.

"I'm glad I caught you before you left," he said. "I'd offer to buy you a drink, but if Fleming found out, he'd fire me for consorting with the enemy."

"I gather he didn't respond well when you told him about the Suskind obituary?"

"It's his crazy view that publishing obituaries for people who aren't necessarily dead could undermine our credibility."

Harold smiled.

"But, he calmed down when I told him you're dying."

Hubbell sat on the sofa, the leather groaning beneath him as he leaned forward and placed his mug on the glass coffee table, setting it down beside one of the handsome commemorative volumes the paper had published on the centennial anniversary of the great earthquake and fire that ravaged the city in 1906. It was a splendid tome containing scores of extraordinary photographs culled from the newspaper's extensive archives, the culmination of a year-long project hailed as a brilliant idea and launched with the highest expectations, but its publication, alas, had proven only that the Chronicle was just as capable of losing money publishing books as it was producing a daily newspaper.

"I didn't see a correction this morning," Hubbell said.

Harold sat down in the dark gray club chair on the opposite side of the table, the knot of his maroon tie pulled down beneath his unbuttoned collar, his silver hair combed straight back off his forehead.

"The correction is in Rawlings' hands now," he said. "He's been consulting with the Hearst lawyers in New York. I think it's fair to call this a unique situation."

"I'm sorry the Hearst lawyers had to get involved," Hubbell said. "I'm sorry this ran all the way up to New York."

But Harold waved him off.

"The truth is, Graydon, you're getting out of this business just in time."

"If you say so," Hubbell said.

"Honestly, I don't know how much longer this place has," Harold said. "I don't know how much longer we can go on losing so damned much money."

"Surely, the vaunted Hearst brain trust has a strategy for stemming the losses," Hubbell said.

"As you may have noticed, developing a strategy to stanch the bleeding is not the same as developing a strategy for the paper's long-term financial viability," Harold said.

"When do you expect to announce the next round of buyouts?"

"I believe the company is still working that out with the guild, but it shouldn't be too long," Harold said. "Perhaps as early as next week."

"I worry about my colleagues back in Section Eight," Hubbell said. "I worry about what they'll do if they lose their jobs."

"I worry about them, too," Harold said. "Of course, I also worry about you."

Hubbell shrugged off his concern.

"It's not like I've got a lot of time left to worry about," he said.

"All the more reason to use it wisely," Harold said. "All the more reason to enjoy it fully."

"This is all I ever wanted to do," Hubbell said. "All I ever wanted to be was a reporter."

"We were lucky, Graydon. We've been luckier than either of us had any right to expect."

Hubbell couldn't argue with that.

"I remember my first day," he said. "I remember the first time I walked into the newsroom. Everything seemed so urgent, so important."

"Yes, I know exactly what you mean," Harold said.

Hubbell leaned back, extending his arms across the cushions.

"Whatever happened to the big stories – I mean the really big stories?" Hubbell asked. "We had the Moscone and Milk assassinations, the Jonestown massacre, the Zodiac killings..."

"Not to mention the kidnapping of our favorite newspaper heiress," Harold reminded him.

"We haven't had a truly big story in years."

"No, not like those," Harold conceded.

"That's what the Chronicle needs now," Hubbell said. "What this place needs is a good serial killer."

"You'll get no argument from me," Harold said.

"Maybe that's what I'll do, now that I have the time," Hubbell said. "Maybe I'll become the serial killer the Chronicle needs to return to profitability."

"I'm sure the Hearst Corporation would be deeply grateful," Harold said.

"It's the least I can do – after all the company's done for me lately."

Harold allowed himself an amused smile.

"I think you'd make a splendid serial killer," he said.

"Well, it's settled, then."

Hubbell leaned forward and pushed up to stand. Harold rose with him.

"I suppose I might as well get started," Hubbell said. "I suppose I should start stalking my first victim."

Harold thrust out his hand.

"I look forward to following you in your new career."

"It's been grand," Hubbell said.

"Yes, it has," Harold said.

AS HUBBELL WALKED back to Section Eight, he saw that his colleagues were seated at their desks – Jennings dead asleep, the Senator and Poopdeck staring at the screens of their computers and giving every appearance, at least to the untrained eye, that they, like their younger colleagues, were working. Hubbell knew better, of course. He knew the odds were long that either the Senator or Poopdeck were committing what might be even loosely defined as an act of journalism, the Senator far more likely to be checking the personal accounts he had established with several offshore gaming syndicates, Poopdeck more likely to be searching the Internet for videos of nude female mud wrestlers.

It was the Senator who spotted Hubbell approaching.

"Do my eyes deceive me, or do I see the inimitable Graydon Hubbell, returning, dare I hope, to do battle with the clowns who run this place?"

"I'm afraid not," Hubbell said.

"A disappointment, to be sure, but be advised that I stand at the ready to provide my services as a duly elected officer of the guild," the Senator said.

"And should I have need of those services, I shall not hesitate to ask," Hubbell assured him.

As he walked over to his desk, Hubbell realized the time had come for the smooth and orderly transfer of authority for the ghoul pool. He leaned down and unlocked his bottom drawer and withdrew the legal pad upon which he recorded the ghoul pool wagers and the envelope containing the cash. After closing the drawer, he carried them over to Poopdeck's cubicle, observing, as he approached, that Poopdeck had eaten lunch that afternoon at John's Grill, one of his favored venues. Hubbell could see that, as always, Poopdeck had ordered the crab and shrimp salad. Traces of the creamy dressing were congealing in the wiry tendrils of his beard, and as Hubbell stood before Poopdeck, he caught a curious smell and had to wonder if one of the wily crustaceans might have dropped off his fork and fallen into his shirt pocket, there to reside indefinitely, or at least until he speared it with the tip of his pen. It had happened more than once.

"Well, here you are," Hubbell said. "I hereby deliver to you the ghoul pool ledger and prize money. I trust you will guard them with your life."

"You have my word," Poopdeck said.

"As commissioner emeritus, I ask only that you keep me apprised of developments, as they warrant."

"Of course."

"And I hasten to point out that I am not leaving the paper. I am merely taking a medical leave of absence, which, in my view, extends my eligibility to participate in the pool – unless, of course, in your new capacity as commissioner of the pool, you see otherwise."

"You are most certainly eligible to participate," Poopdeck assured him.

"I've still got money on Jerry Lewis."

"And in commemoration of your years of service to the pool, I hope the son of a bitch dies tomorrow."

Behind Poopdeck, the Senator gripped the top of the wall of his cubicle and pulled himself up to stand, grunting as he tucked the long tails of his shirt into his trousers, one of the buttons having burst while straining to contain his robust paunch, revealing a mat of tightly coiled belly hair. He cinched his belt around his waist, clasping the buckle but neglecting, as was too often the case, to raise his zipper.

"Gentlemen, dare I suggest that we repair to the Tempest for a round of libations in honor our esteemed colleague's departure?"

But Hubbell wasn't interested.

"I thank you for your kind offer, but I'm afraid this is not an occasion I wish to commemorate."

"I do understand," the Senator said, his long black hair tangled upon his shoulders. "But I find it a grievous injustice that a journalist of your caliber should conclude his storied career without so much as a moment of proper reflection and appreciation."

"Given the circumstances of my departure, I would prefer to leave with a minimum of drama," Hubbell said.

"That makes it no less of an outrage," the Senator said, his anger darkening.

"It's a bitch, is what it is," Poopdeck said. "It's a bitch royale."

"This is a dark day," the Senator declared. "This shall go down as one of the darkest days in the history of the Chronicle."

He turned around and looked across the newsroom to the glass offices of the senior editors.

"For shame!" he thundered, shaking his clenched fist. "For shame!"

Hubbell could sense that his request for a quiet departure was running into conflict with the Senator's lust for confrontation and natural gift for oratory, so he turned and walked back to his cubicle. He sat down at his desk. Beside him, Jennings was still asleep, of course, his slumber untroubled by the Senator's spirited exhortations. Jennings had been sleeping incrementally longer every day, it seemed to Hubbell, and he was reluctant to disturb him. But the time had come.

He reached over to the arm of his chair and gave it a gentle shake. Jennings emitted a series of sharp porcine snorts but didn't wake, so Hubbell shook his chair once more, this time slightly harder. Jennings sputtered awake, convulsively rocking forward in his chair, kicking his feet as if sprinting through the air, the soles of his shoes six inches above the floor. But he managed to compose himself and leaned back and stared up at the water-stained acoustic ceiling tiles, his eyes wide, breathing heavily.

"I'm sorry to disturb you," Hubbell said.

As Hubbell released the arm of the chair, Jennings turned to him, still drifting through the haze of sleep, a trail of saliva leaking out the corner of his mouth and down his stubbled chin, and it was then that Hubbell realized that Jennings' disorientation was deeper than merely being roused awake. He realized that Jennings didn't recognize him.

"It's me – Graydon," he said.

And even then, a long moment passed before Jennings fully comprehended who Hubbell was.

"Of course," Jennings finally said.

"I'm about to leave," Hubbell told him.

Jennings nodded, running his hand across the top of his head.

"Yes, of course," he said.

"I wanted to say good-bye."

"Yes, well it's a shame you're leaving," Jennings said.

"It's my time – that's all," Hubbell said. "It's just my time."

He extended his hand.

"You take care of yourself," he said.

"Yes, you do the same," Jennings said.

Hubbell squeezed Jennings's hand, holding it for a long moment, then stood up and walked over to the coat rack beside the window. After slipping on his coat, he put on his hat, running his thumb and forefinger around the edge of the brim, then he reached down and picked up his satchel and placed it in the seat of his chair. He opened the satchel and looked inside, making sure the bundle of letters was there, then he snapped it shut, fully realizing, at that very moment, that he was about to walk out of the newsroom for the last time. It seemed unreal, an out-of-body experience, as if it were happening to someone else.

He took a deep breath, then he picked up his satchel and walked over to the Senator and Poopdeck, standing beside the Senator's desk.

"So is this it?" the Senator asked.

"I'm afraid so," Hubbell said.

He stepped up to the Senator and shook his hand, then he turned to Poopdeck and shook his hand, too.

"Gentlemen, it's been an honor and a privilege."

"Yes, it has," the Senator said.

"Goddamn right," Poopdeck said.

And that was it. The time had come. His time had come. Without another word, Hubbell turned to leave – noticing only then that Ms. Mitchell was standing in the aisle, leaning back against the wall of her cubicle, her arms crossed over her maroon turtleneck sweater, her green eyes rimmed with tears. He couldn't leave, obviously, without saying good-bye to her.

He walked over and stood before her.

"I'm so sorry," she said.

But the last thing Hubbell wanted was Ms. Mitchell's pity. And to the extent that the ghastly events of yesterday had, at the very least, confirmed the wisdom of his advice to her, he hoped they might part on a positive note.

"You're dying," she said. "I can't believe you're dying."

So much for the positive note.

"It happens to the best of us," he said.

She slipped her arms around his neck and leaned into him. With his satchel in his left hand, he placed his right hand at the small of her back and held her until she finally began to pull away.

"I'm going to be watching you," he said. "I'm going to be reading your stories, and I want to start seeing your byline on Page One."

A tear streaked down her freckled cheek. She rubbed it away with the heel of her hand.

"Good-bye, Mr. Hubbell."

"Good-bye, Naomi."

And that was all Hubbell could take. He turned and started down the aisle through the newsroom, every step as heavy as if he were walking in sand. It seemed a lifetime before he finally reached the corridor leading to the elevators. He stopped there and turned back to take one last look at the newsroom – and there were his colleagues, standing beside each other back in Section Eight, the Senator, Poopdeck, and Jennings, three of the finest journalists he had ever worked with, three of the finest men he had ever known, and Ms. Mitchell, too, watching him depart, all of them applauding him, even if the clapping of their hands could barely be heard above the din of the newsroom, bidding him farewell in the newsroom's time-honored tradition. They had no idea how much that meant to him.

He reached up and doffed his hat, signaling his eternal gratitude, then he turned and started for the elevators.

HUBBELL PARKED the Mustang in the garage below the two flats, then walked back through the garden and up the stairs to his cottage. After putting away his coat and hat, he returned to the kitchen and poured himself a glass of water, taking a long drink before leaning back against the counter to catch his breath. It had been a difficult day, to say the least. But the day he had dreaded for so long had come and gone. His career was over, but that was fine. That was all right. He was proud to have been a newspaper reporter. He was proud to have been a journalist. He had always believed that journalism was a noble profession, a calling as much as an occupation, and he wanted to believe that the work he had done over the course of his career had served not only the readers of the Chronicle but, in a larger sense, the interests of the broader public, the interests, no less, of a free and democratic society. True, his career might not have concluded as he would have preferred. After fifty-three years, he might very well have chosen to leave the newsroom under more pleasant circumstances. But as he carried the glass of water over to the table, he felt nothing less than a profound sense of relief. Ms.

Gifford was right, absolutely right. For better or worse, he was a free man now, even if not necessarily for long.

As he leaned forward, his elbows on the table, holding the cool glass of water to his forehead, he heard Ms. Gifford's back door open. A moment later, he heard her climbing the stairs to his cottage, and then she was standing on the landing in a pair of white coveralls, her hair flowing out from beneath a blue bandanna, her hands behind her back.

"You won't believe what I just found," she told him.

He had no idea what she was talking about, but that was hardly unusual.

"A jar of the tomato sauce!"

She brought it out from behind her back and showed it to him, as if he might not have believed her otherwise, her right eye fixed upon the jar, as if to claim full credit for its discovery.

"Congratulations," he said.

"Isn't it always like that – you go looking for one thing and find another?"

He was willing to take her word for it.

"This always happens to me," she said. "This is why I never worry when I lose something – because I know I'm going to find something else."

"What were you looking for when you found the tomato sauce?" he asked.

She had to think. When that didn't work, she shrugged it off.

"I can't even remember," she said.

"It doesn't matter," Hubbell said.

She dropped down into the chair across from him.

"Shall I make us some pasta tonight?"

But the offer, however generous, was more than Hubbell could accommodate.

"I'm sorry," Hubbell said. "Can I take a rain check? I'm afraid I don't have much of an appetite this evening."

She reached across the table and placed her hand on his forearm.

"Of course," she said.

"Perhaps tomorrow night?" he suggested.

"How are you feeling?" she asked.

"I'm feeling all right, at least to the extent that I'm sitting upright."

She smiled at him.

"I'm glad to hear that," she said.

"I appreciate your assistance last night," he said. "I hope I wasn't too much of a bother."

"You were pretty wasted," she said.

"I think it's fair to say that I drank a little more than might be considered prudent for a man my age, for a man in my condition."

"Have you had your tea yet?" she asked.

He was afraid she was going to ask about the tea, and he was tempted to tell her that he had. But he couldn't persuade himself to mislead her, even if he knew what her response would be.

"No, I'm afraid I haven't," he said.

"Would you like me to put some water on to boil?" she asked.

"I don't know that that will be necessary," he said.

"Oh, Graydon."

"Honestly, I'm not sure it's making much of a difference."

"You can't be sure of that," she said. "How would you know?"

"I have an appointment with my doctor tomorrow morning," he said.

"You're going back to the doctor who said there was nothing he could do? Why? I don't understand."

He didn't want to explain it to her, not yet. He wished he hadn't brought it up.

"I don't expect him to cure my cancer," Hubbell said. "I don't expect him to do anything, actually."

"So you're just going to give up?" she asked.

Hubbell leaned back in his chair. He hadn't intended to upset Ms. Gifford. He knew how strongly she believed in the curative powers of the tea prescribed by her Chinese herbalist, and he hadn't intended to dispute his wisdom, or hers, for that matter. He raised both hands, realizing that there was nothing to be gained by resisting. If for no other reason than to please Ms. Gifford, he would resume his daily consumption of two cups of tea.

"You're right, Lydia. Of course, you are. If you'd be so kind as so put some water on to boil, I'd be most appreciative."

Her mouth formed an angled smile.

"It would be my pleasure," she said.

He watched as she rose from the table and took a saucepan from the drying rack on the counter beside the sink. She filled the saucepan with water and placed it on the stove, bending down to adjust the ring of flames before she returned to the table.

"Graydon, I've been thinking about the other night – the night you asked me to help make sure your medical directives were carried out. And I want you to know that I'll do whatever you want me to do, whatever you need me to do."

"That's very kind of you, Lydia."

"But only so long as you don't give up, only so long as you don't quit on me."

That seemed like a fair deal.

"I won't quit on you," he said.

"Even if the tea gives you just one more day, wouldn't that be worth it?"

Hubbell couldn't argue with that.

"Of course," he said. "Of course it would."

AS HUBBELL SAT at the table and stared out at the lights on the bay, he was relieved to know that Ms. Gifford had agreed to see that his medical directives would be carried out as his cancer progressed, although it must be said that he had believed all along that she would consent to help him, even as she protested that she wouldn't.

And yet, as she left, she seemed strangely subdued, perhaps even sad, as if she finally understood that the time that remained to Hubbell would not be measured in months but in weeks, if he was lucky, and eventually, if not sooner, in days. That was his life's new equation, and she seemed to finally understand that the tea prescribed by her herbalist was not likely to significantly alter that fundamental calculus.

He knew he had to eat, which is not to say he had much of an appetite, but he cut up an apple and sliced some cheese, placing them on a plate and carrying them into the living room. He set the plate on the coffee table, then sank down into the sofa and turned on the radio to listen to the ballgame. But he found it difficult to sustain his attention from pitch to pitch, so he stretched out on the sofa and closed his eyes, as if that might help him concentrate. Instead, of course, he drifted asleep.

He didn't wake up until well after the game had ended. But he didn't mind. It didn't matter. Tomorrow, the Giants were playing an afternoon game, and it just so happened that he had tomorrow off and would be free to tune in. It felt good to have a plan, however modest it might be.

He rose from the sofa and took a shower and slipped into bed, and he might very well have fallen asleep if he hadn't heard the sound of his cottage door opening. He raised himself onto his elbows, momentarily alarmed, but quickly realized that it had to be Ms. Gifford, that it could only be Ms. Gifford.

He listened to her walk down the hallway, and then she was standing in his bedroom doorway in her white, long-sleeve dress shirt, visible in the moonlight sifting in through the curtain in the window.

"Graydon?"

"Yes, Lydia."

"Are you awake?"

"Yes, I am."

"I thought maybe you could use some company."

"Of course," he said. "Would you like to lie down for a moment?"

"If it's not a bother," she said.

"No, of course not," he told her.

He laid back on the mattress and watched as she unbuttoned her shirt and hung it over the back of the chair beside his bureau, then he raised the sheet and blanket so she could slide in beside him. She draped her arm across his chest and rested the side of her head on his shoulder. As he slipped his arm around her, he could smell the earthy musk of her hair.

"I don't want you to think I was lonely, or anything like that," she said.

"Of course not," he said.

"I rarely get lonely, not lonesome, per se. I have my yoga class every week, and I'm going to be taking my figure drawing class as soon as I get the money, and my music and my gardening keep me very busy."

"Of course," Hubbell said.

"The time just disappears," she said. "I don't know where it goes."

"It does fly by, doesn't it," Hubbell said.

She ran her hand across his chest, her fingertips brushing the side of his neck.

"I was watching a movie," she said. "It was very sad."

"What movie was that?" he asked.

"Oh, I don't know," she said. "I never pay attention to titles. I only forget them, so what's the point?"

Hubbell recognized that as another of Ms. Gifford's rhetorical questions, requiring no answer.

"All the men wore hats – like you," she said. "They reminded me of you."

She lifted her head and looked down at him, her right eye lying in shadow.

"I've always had a weakness for men who wear hats."

"I wasn't aware of that," Hubbell said.

"Oh, yes – it's the first thing that attracted me to you."

Hubbell couldn't resist a smile.

"I had no idea."

She returned her head to his shoulder.

"That's how I'm going to remember you, Graydon. I'll always remember you wearing a hat."

Hubbell stroked her hair.

"Remember me anyway you want, Lydia. Anyway you want is fine with me."

CHAPTER THIRTEEN

CHAINED TO THE LAMPPOST in front of the medical center, the Chronicle newsbox teetered on three legs, its yellow paint chipped and streaked with rust, cracks running through the glass in the door. Hubbell dug into his pocket and pulled out a handful of coins. After feeding three quarters into the coin slot, he reached down to collect his copy of the newspaper. But the door refused to release. He pounded the coin box with the heel of his hand, as if that might free the recalcitrant latch, then gave the door another tug. Still, the door refused to swing open.

Hubbell was hardly surprised. Over the years, it had been his experience that the Chronicle's newsboxes rarely functioned properly, and, candidly, he was not always in possession of precisely the right change when he wanted a copy of the paper – which is to say the dilemma was not new to him. After waiting for a nurse in blue scrubs to walk past, he placed both hands on the door handle, then rose up onto his toes and pressed down hard, using his weight to torque the hinges and spring the latch and then pull the door open.

It was a technique he had learned long ago and, as always, it worked to perfection. As he reached in and took a copy of the Chronicle from the stack inside the newsbox, he wondered why he had bothered to pay for the newspaper in the first place.

With the paper tucked under his arm, he entered the medical center for his appointment with Dr. Martin, taking his place in the line in front of the receptionist's window. He waited patiently. He was in no hurry, newly released from the obligations of gainful employment, a man of leisure and comfort now, as free as a blackbird.

When his turn came, he stepped up to the window. The receptionist looked up and smiled at him.

"Good morning, Mr. Hubbell. Please, have a seat. Dr. Martin will see you shortly."

Hubbell crossed the waiting room and sat in one of the chairs along the opposite wall, making himself comfortable, crossing his right leg over his left as he unfolded the paper, glancing down at the front page before he turned back to the Sports section. But something was wrong. The front page looked decidedly familiar. Hubbell squinted down at the page to examine it more closely. Of course, the front page looked familiar – the paper was three days old.

HUBBELL STOOD in the window of the examination room and gazed out through the salt-streaked glass, across the flat, tar-and-gravel roofs below, still fuming about the seventy-five cents he had paid for a three-day-old copy of the Chronicle. He was tempted to return to the newsbox with the Mustang's tire iron and pry open the coin box, not just to get his money back but to compensate himself for the inconvenience and aggravation. At a minimum, he intended to contact the paper's circulation department to demand an immediate refund, as well as share a thought or two in the context of customer satisfaction. And, he vowed, with Maria as his witness, that he would never purchase another copy of the Chronicle as long as he lived.

He turned around when he heard Dr. Martin open the door and step into the room.

"Good morning, Graydon."

In his white lab coat, the doctor closed the door and crossed the room to shake Hubbell's hand.

"How have you been?" he asked.

An empty laugh escaped Hubbell.

"It's been an interesting few days," he said.

"Is that right?"

"I've been having a little trouble maintaining my sense of humor, to be perfectly honest."

The doctor gestured toward the examination table.

"Why don't you have a seat," he said.

As Hubbell sat on the table, Dr. Martin walked over to the sink and turned on the water to wash his hands.

"How have you been feeling – physically?" he asked.

"I've been feeling fine."

"Any fatigue?"

"I've been feeling fatigued for the past twenty years."

Dr. Martin glanced over to Hubbell.

"Perhaps I should have asked if you've been feeling unusually fatigued."

"I've been drinking an herbal tea, recommended by a Chinese herbalist."

"Really."

"I figured what the hell."

"Sure," Dr. Martin said, turning off the water and drying his hands with a paper towel. "What the hell."

He tossed the paper towel into the trash.

"Any tenderness in your abdomen or lymph glands?"

"No," Hubbell said.

"Do you mind if I check?"

"If you must."

Dr. Martin smiled.

"I'll need you to remove your coat and shirt," he said.

Hubbell slipped down from the table and took off his coat and his shirt and tie, hanging them on the hook on the back of the door. When he returned to the examination table, Dr. Martin began gently probing his upper body.

"Any soreness there?" the doctor asked, pressing Hubbell's liver.

Hubbell stared across the room at the posters of the illustrated human body tacked to the wall.

"No."

"Or here?" the doctor asked, moving to his spleen.

"No."

Dr. Martin reached up to the lymph glands in Hubbell's armpits."

"How about here?"

"No," Hubbell said. "Nothing."

And that was it – the examination was over. Dr. Martin stepped back and picked up Hubbell's medical chart.

"The absence of any soreness is a good sign, if you're telling me the truth."

"Of course, I'm telling you the truth," Hubbell said.

He watched as Dr. Martin began checking boxes on the printed form clipped to his medical chart.

"I'm going to send you back down to the lab to have some more blood drawn," Dr. Martin said. "Your blood work will tell me exactly how you're doing."

But Hubbell wasn't listening. That was not what he had come to discuss.

"You'll be pleased to know that I've taken an indefinite medical leave from the Chronicle," he told the doctor.

Dr. Martin looked up from the lab form.

"You surprise me, Graydon. I thought you intended to work to the very last. I thought that was your plan, as ill-advised as it might have been."

"The leave wasn't entirely my idea," Hubbell said. "But I didn't fight it."

"I think the decision to take a leave was a wise one, however it came about," Dr. Martin said.

"I have a verification form that I need you to fill out."

"That won't be a problem," Dr. Martin said. "Just leave it with my receptionist."

"I also wanted to tell you that I want to die a natural death," Hubbell said. "No resuscitation, no ventilator, no heroics. When my time comes, just let me go."

"All right, Graydon – I certainly respect your decision."

"My neighbor is going to help me through all this."

"That's good to hear," Dr. Martin said. "And I would strongly recommend that you and your neighbor contact one of the city's hospices. They can be a great source of comfort and assistance at a time like this."

But Hubbell wasn't interested.

"I don't believe I'll be requiring the services of a hospice."

"Dying may not be as easy as you think, even with your neighbor's help," Dr. Martin said.

"I'm sure I can handle it."

"You're a stubborn old fool, aren't you?"

Hubbell did not dignify the remark with a response.

"Will there be anything else?" Dr. Martin asked. "Is there anything else I can do for you?"

"I believe that should do it," Hubbell said.

Dr. Martin extended his hand.

"I'll let you know what the lab tests show when I get the results."

HUBBELL CLOSED the Mustang's trunk and started across the cemetery, walking through the undulating rows of headstones and grave markers. He was sorry to disappoint Dr. Martin, but he had seen no reason to go down to the medical center lab to have more blood drawn. His blood couldn't possibly tell them anything they didn't already know. He didn't need a blood test to know that the number of abnormal white blood cells in his blood and bone marrow was rising, just as he didn't need Dr. Martin to tell him what the increasing tenderness in his abdomen and lymph glands meant. He knew why he was exhausted, a cloak of fatigue draped over his shoulders. His time was running out. It was as simple as that.

With the white roses cradled in his left arm, the metal folding chair in his right, he walked out to the plot where Maria and her family were buried. He set the chair down, then knelt on Maria's grave and arranged the roses in the vase at the base of her headstone, the heavy white flowers poised on the cusp of opening.

When he finished, he looked up into the sky, the sun struggling to burn through the late morning mist.

"Hello," he said. "How are you?"

He laughed at himself. The question was absurd. Maria was fine. Of course, she was fine. She was always fine. He walked over to the folding chair and positioned it at the foot of her grave, then sat down and withdrew a cigar from his coat pocket. After peeling off the wrapper, he struck a match and held it to the tip of the cigar until it was burning evenly.

"Well, it won't be long," he said. "It won't be long before I join you."

He took a drag on the cigar. As he tipped his head back and exhaled, watching the smoke dissolve into the breeze moving in from the ocean, he couldn't help but remember the night Maria died. She was driving back to the city from Stinson Beach, where she had spent the afternoon visiting with a friend from law school. As she drove up out of the small coastal village, climbing the narrow roadway clinging to the sheer face of the cliff, a pickup truck swung wide around one of the tight curves and sideswiped her Volkswagen, sending her over the edge of the pavement, plunging down into a narrow ravine, above the surf crashing on the rocks below.

Late that night, he got the call from the Marin County Sheriff's Department, informing him of the accident, telling him that Maria had been taken to the county hospital in Greenbrae. He drove there as fast as he could, dashing across the parking lot and rushing into the emergency room, only to learn that she had already been pronounced dead. He dropped into a chair in the waiting room, slumping forward with his face in his hands, his whole body trembling, sobs strangling in his throat, the chaplain's hand on the back of his shoulder. It was the worst night of his life, a night from which he would never be fully free, even now, nearly forty years later, even now, as he prepared to depart this life for the next.

He tapped his cigar with his fingertip. As he watched the ash fall into the grass, he had no idea how many times he had visited Maria's grave over the years that followed the accident, how many hours he had spent here with her, consoled by her mere presence, the simple knowledge that she was here, still here, in body if not in soul. It didn't matter. He didn't care. He made no apology. He would never have denied himself the solace he had found here, the refuge he had taken in the cemetery's long silences. But only now, as he leaned back and looked up at the lone white gull gliding overhead, did he realize that he had been coming here not merely to mourn Maria, but to mourn that which had died within him that very same night, indulging his grief solely to insure that he never experienced that terrible pain again, even if that meant spending the rest of his life alone. He couldn't believe how quickly the time had passed, how swiftly the years had slipped away. He couldn't believe how little time he had left, how soon he, too, would be laid to rest.

He rose from the chair and walked over to stand precisely where he was to be buried, merely a patch of grass now, a layer of sod above the bed of soil to be excavated to accommodate his casket. He would lie, like Maria, with his head to the north, and so he turned and looked to the south, gazing down the gentle slope, across the headstones and grave markers planted in the grass below, receding into the hazy distance.

"It's a very fine view, a commanding view," he said.

And he decided, then, to lie down as he would repose in the casket. With the cigar clenched in his teeth, he reached over to the top of Maria's headstone, steadying himself as he sank down onto his knees, then he leaned back and stretched out his legs and lay back on the grass. He reclined there perfectly still in his fine Italian suit, arms along his sides, hands flat against his hips, his feet together, the toes of his new oxfords pointed straight up, staring up into the dissipating mist, a thin ribbon of smoke rising from the tip of his cigar.

"Oh, this is nice," he said. "This is very nice. I'm going to be quite comfortable here."

He closed his eyes and felt himself relax, and he might even have drifted off to sleep – but he wasn't alone.

"Sir, are you all right?"

The voice startled Hubbell. He bolted upright. At the foot of his grave stood one of the cemetery's groundskeepers, a stout fellow in blue jeans and a black, long-sleeve shirt, a red bandanna tied around his neck.

"Yes, of course," Hubbell said. "I'm fine, perfectly fine."

He rolled onto his hands and knees and reached for Maria's headstone to pull himself up to stand. But he had trouble getting his legs underneath him, so the groundskeeper walked over and took him by the elbow and helped him to his feet.

"Thank you, my good man," Hubbell said.

He took a drag on the cigar, but the coal had died out. He waved the unlit cigar across the grass where he had been lying.

"This is where I intend to be buried," he said, as if by way of explanation. "Right here."

The groundskeeper looked down at his mud-caked boots and took a step back, as if to make sure he wasn't standing where he shouldn't.

"Not right now, of course – not immediately," Hubbell said. "But sooner than I would prefer, to be perfectly honest."

"I am very sorry to hear this," the groundskeeper said.

Hubbell turned and looked across Maria's family's plot, admiring the neatly clipped grass, the tracks of the rake across the bare dirt at the foot of the headstones.

"You do nice work, very nice work," he said. "Do you always work in this part of the cemetery?"

The groundskeeper shrugged.

"I work wherever I'm told," he said.

Hubbell struck a match and lit the cigar again, brushing the smoke out of his face.

"Let me ask you this: What would it cost to have you keep an especially close eye on this area?"

The question seemed to puzzle the groundskeeper.

"This is the area I'm referring to," Hubbell said, walking along the perimeter of Maria's family's plot, pointing down at her parents' graves and the graves of her aunts and uncles. "These are the graves I'm talking about."

He stopped and withdrew his wallet and took out a newly printed one-hundred-dollar bill. He folded it in half and extended it to the groundskeeper.

"Please," he said.

"Sir, this is not necessary."

"Of course not. Of course it's not necessary. It's nothing more than a very modest expression of my appreciation for your work."

He stepped up to the groundskeeper and tucked the bill into the pocket of his shirt, then he clapped his hand on the groundskeeper's shoulder.

"I'm not asking for anything extravagant here," he said. "Just take care of me. That's all I'm asking."

He smiled.

"All I'm saying is that I like a tidy grave – what's wrong with that?"

HUBBELL RETURNED to the Mustang, parked along the narrow lane of crumbling asphalt. He was pleased, quite pleased, actually, to have made arrangements for the proper maintenance of his final resting place, and he was sure that Maria and her family would be just as pleased to know that the groundskeeper would be watching over the whole of the family plot. As he placed the folding chair in the trunk, he told himself they could thank him when they were reunited in the afterlife.

He climbed into the Mustang and drove out of the cemetery to return to the city. Traffic was slow for reasons that did not immediately present themselves. As he approached Army Street, he had no idea why the traffic on Mission had slowed to a crawl, and it was there, as he crept along in the right lane, that he noticed the needle on the Mustang's temperature gauge indicating that the engine was about to boil over, a new infirmity that left Hubbell with nothing to do but stroke the dashboard and promise to check the water level in the radiator the next time he filled the tank with gas.

And it is entirely possible, in retrospect, that Hubbell was preoccupied with the potential causes of the Mustang's engine trouble when he started across Army Street, failing to notice that the light had turned red. He never saw the car entering the intersection from the right. He heard only the abrupt blare of its horn, the tires shrieking on the pavement, the heavy thump as the car rammed into the Mustang's right front fender, sending the Mustang spinning through the intersection, eventually coming to a halt in the opposite lane.

Stunned, Hubbell sat back in his seat, his ears ringing, his eyes filled with bursts of light, blood from his nose dripping onto his shirt and tie, splattering his trousers. He tilted his head back and reached for his handkerchief. After pressing the handkerchief to his nostrils, he reached up with his left hand and pinched the bridge of his nose as if that might stem the flow of blood.

A police officer leaned down into the window of the Mustang, his eyes concealed behind his mirrored sunglasses, his ruddy face pocked with ancient acne scars.

"Are you all right in there, Pops?"

Hubbell had to think, taking a quick inventory.

"Yes, I think so, pending a thorough examination."

The police officer opened the door of the Mustang.

"Why don't you climb on out of there," he said.

Hubbell lifted his feet out of the car and placed them on the pavement, then he grabbed the roof of the Mustang and pulled himself up to stand, his head back, the handkerchief still pressed to his nostrils.

"You look all right to me," the officer said.

Hubbell turned and looked across the roof of the Mustang, observing only then that the vehicle that had struck the Mustang was, in fact, a patrol car, its rack of red and blue lights flashing on its roof as it sat in the middle of the intersection, and that did explain how the police had arrived upon the scene of the accident so quickly, the city's finest having earned over the years a richly deserved reputation for taking their sweet time when responding to calls from the public, if they bothered to respond at all.

"Of course, I can call an ambulance, if you think that's necessary," the officer said.

Hubbell turned back to the police officer, peering down the sides of his nose at the nametag on the officer's dark blue uniform. His name was Francis Gillick.

"No, that won't be necessary," Hubbell said.

"That's what I like to hear," Officer Gillick said.

Hubbell made his way up to the front of the Mustang and was surprised to see the extent of the damage – the right headlight shattered, the right front fender crumpled back against the tire, the hood buckled and the front bumper hanging down to the ground, a pool of water spreading beneath the hissing radiator, through the pieces of broken glass. As if to make matters worse, the patrol car, with its flat-iron bumper, appeared to have suffered only minor damage, if it had suffered any damage at all.

"Looks like it might be time to put this old stallion down," Officer Gillick said.

Still holding the handkerchief to his nose, Hubbell turned to the officer, standing directly behind him.

"I thank you for your considered observation," he said.

Officer Gillick shrewdly perceived that Hubbell's expression of gratitude was not entirely sincere.

"Let me see your driver's license," he said.

Hubbell reached for his wallet and handed it to him.

"It's in there, somewhere."

Officer Gillick thumbed through Hubbell's wallet until he found his license. He gave the wallet back to Hubbell and began writing him a ticket.

"You get out much, Pops?"

"As a matter of fact, yes, I do."

"I guess you just didn't see that red light?"

Hubbell did not dignify the question with a response.

"Seventy-six years old – those synapses just don't fire like they used to, do they?"

"Is that your professional opinion?" Hubbell asked.

Officer Gillick tore off the ticket and handed it to Hubbell.

"Actually, this is my professional opinion."

Officer Gillick smiled.

"I called for a tow truck," he said. "It should be here shortly."

Hubbell glanced down at the ticket, citing him for running the red light. He saw the penalty was $360.90.

"Are you kidding me?" he asked.

He looked up, but Officer Gillick was already walking back to his patrol car.

"This is ridiculous," he said. "There's no way I'm paying this. There's no way in hell."

But Officer Gillick paid him no mind.

"Wait a minute!" Hubbell called out after him. "Where are you going?"

When Officer Gillick reached the patrol car, Hubbell started after him.

"Watch this!" he shouted. "Just watch this!"

He began tearing the ticket into pieces, then he heaved the pieces into the air, into the gusting breeze, scattering like confetti across the pavement.

"Did you see that? Did you see what I just did?"

As the patrol car started to pull away, Hubbell stalked after it, shaking his clenched fist.

"Arrest me! I dare you! Arrest me!"

But by then, the patrol car was heading down Mission Street, leaving Hubbell behind, leaving him there to kick at the pieces of ticket and then walk back to the Mustang to wait for the tow truck.

HUBBELL STOOD BACK out of the way as the tow truck eased the Mustang into the garage, watching as the driver guided it into its space along the wall, then slowly lowered the front end, the bumper clanking loudly on the concrete floor. For more than forty years, the Mustang had served Hubbell well, but there was little doubt the Mustang had been mortally wounded in the collision with the patrol car, at least to the extent that Hubbell had the time, much less the energy, to take it into the shop and have it repaired. And that, in turn, Hubbell realized, meant that his days behind the wheel were very likely behind him. He could only shake his head. He had passed yet another depressing milestone on the road to the ever-after.

After the tow truck left, Hubbell climbed the stairs and walked back to the garden. Ms. Gifford was kneeling among her tomato plants. When she heard him behind her, she sat back on her heels and pushed up the brim of her straw hat. He managed a feeble wave as her mouth fell open.

"Dear God, Graydon – what have you done?"

"I'm afraid I had a little accident," he told her.

She stood up and pulled off her gardening gloves, tossing them onto the table as she hurried over to him.

"My God, look at the blood."

Reluctantly, he did as instructed, looking down at his blood-streaked shirt and tie, his splattered trousers, a few stray drops on the lapels of his coat.

"You could have been killed," she told him.

That seemed like hyperbole, but he didn't trouble to dispute her.

"I must have struck my nose on the steering wheel."

"You could have a concussion. You could have brain damage."

He found a smile for her.

"In which case, how bad could it be?"

But his humor eluded her, as always.

"Let's get you inside," she said.

He allowed her to walk him across the patio and in through her open back door. She pulled out one of the chairs and sat him down at the table, then crossed the kitchen and poured a glass of water for him. He picked up the glass and took a long drink.

"Thank you," he said.

She moistened a dishcloth and stood over him, wiping the dried blood from his face, looking him over carefully, even her right eye participating in the inspection.

"I'm worried about you Graydon."

"I'm fine – I'm perfectly fine, all things considered."

But she wasn't reassured. When she finished washing his face, she stepped back to think for a moment, carefully assessing the situation.

"I need to do a shooter," she concluded.

Hubbell certainly had no objection. If Ms. Gifford needed to do a shooter, then, by all means, she should do one. He watched as she walked over to the refrigerator and took down the bottle of tequila, then grabbed a shot glass and returned to the table, sitting down across from him. After pouring herself a generous shot, she cut a thick wedge of lime, then licked the back of her hand and sprinkled it rather generously with salt.

She raised the shot glass.

"To your health," she said.

Hubbell lifted his glass of water.

"To what's left of it, anyway."

She licked the salt off the back of her hand, then threw down the shot of tequila and bit into the wedge of lime, a ritual she had clearly practiced many times in the past. Her eyes watering, she removed the wedge of lime from her mouth.

"Whoa," she said.

She turned and tossed the wedge of lime toward the sink. It skipped across the counter and landed on the stove.

"Where was your accident?" she asked.

"I was on Mission Street, crossing Army."

"What were you doing over there?"

"I was driving back from the cemetery."

"I see," she said.

"That's where I plan to be buried," he said as if to explain.

"Beside your wife?"

"We purchased the plots many years ago," Hubbell said. "It's a very nice part of the cemetery. I'm sure you would like it."

Ms. Gifford picked up the shot glass and tilted her head back, holding the glass above her mouth, allowing the last few drops of tequila to drip onto her tongue. She returned the glass to the table.

"I'm planning on being cremated, if you must know."

"I wasn't aware of that," Hubbell said.

"I don't think I could just lie there in one place for the rest of infinity, or eternity, whichever. I would prefer that my ashes be scattered."

"Do you have a place in mind?"

"Sharon Meadow," she said without hesitation.

"In Golden Gate Park?"

"That's where I slept the first night I was in the city," she said. "That's where I smoked my first pot. That's where I saw the Dead for the very first time."

"I wasn't aware Golden Gate Park held so many special memories for you," Hubbell said.

"I lost my virginity there, too."

"Oh, my."

She stared down at the empty shot glass.

"I don't think I even knew his name," she said.

She looked up and smiled again, her right eye rolling away, as if stricken with embarrassment.

"That's kind of sad, isn't it?"

Hubbell wondered if that might be another of Ms. Gifford's rhetorical questions, requiring no response from him. He couldn't be sure. He was never sure.

"I don't know that I would call it sad," he said, although, of course, it was.

But Ms. Gifford had already moved on, leaving behind the misty recollections of her youth.

"Graydon, do you think your wife would mind if I came out to the cemetery to visit you?"

Hubbell sat back in the chair.

"I certainly shouldn't think so," he said.

"I'd like to come see you, every now and again, if that's all right."

"I would like that," he said.

That seemed to please Ms. Gifford.

"I have a small folding chair that I always take to the cemetery," he told her. "I take it so I can sit there for a while. You're welcome to use it, any time you'd like."

"That's very kind," she said.

"Actually, you can have it," he said. "I don't believe I'll be taking it with me."

"No, I don't suppose you will," she said."

"For that matter, you can have anything of mine you want. You can have it all, for that matter."

But Ms. Gifford shook her head.

"You know I don't want anything."

And that was true. If Hubbell had learned anything about Ms. Gifford over the past few weeks, he had learned that much. That was not what Ms. Gifford wanted. That was not what she needed. That was not what he hoped to share with her in the days that remained to him.

"No, of course not," he said.

She reached for the bottle of tequila and poured herself another shot. But then she stopped herself.

"Maybe the Sinatra," she said. "Maybe your Sinatra albums."

Hubbell liked that. He liked that very much.

"He grows on you, doesn't he?"

"Yes, he does," she said.

HUBBELL STRIPPED OFF his clothes and tossed them into the hamper in the bathroom, then he returned to the bedroom and put on a pair of khakis and an old gray sweatshirt. He walked down the hall to his study, little more than a closed-in porch at the back of his cottage. As he stood in the doorway, he reached in and turned on the light, a single bare bulb dangling by a pair of kinked wires from the porcelain fixture in the ceiling. His desk was pushed up against the opposite wall, beneath a small, four-pane window that looked out upon the neighbor's loquat tree, scrub jays roosting noisily among its gray-green leaves.

He crossed his study to his desk and sat down in front of the old Royal typewriter he had brought home when the newsroom converted to its first generation of computers. It was a splendid piece of equipment. He had written hundreds of stories on it while he covered the Hall of Justice, and he was not ashamed to admit that his attachment to the Royal was largely nostalgic, if not purely sentimental. To this day, he missed the sheer physicality of the manual typewriter, the sharp clacking of the keys on the hard rubber platen, each letter struck with purpose and authority, as if each word was meant to endure. The shallow clattering of computer keyboards simply didn't compare.

He had one last obituary to write – his own, of course. It was not a task he could entrust to the newsroom, not any longer. He knew that Harold would not be replacing him. The Chronicle would no longer have a full-time obituary writer, the position now a luxury the paper's eviscerated newsroom could no longer afford. There was no way to know who might be assigned to write his obituary. He simply couldn't take the chance the assignment might be given to one of his younger colleagues, one of the ignorant pissants who viewed being assigned to write an obituary as a sentence worse than death itself. Which, of course, left him with little choice but to take on that somber duty himself, while he still could, before his hands were stilled and his voice silenced.

He leaned forward and peered into the well of the typewriter and blew the dust from the keys, then he rolled in a sheet of paper. He cracked his knuckles and shook out his aching hands and placed his fingertips on the keys. He began to summon up his lead.

But first, perhaps, a cup of coffee to sharpen what remained of his mind. He was in no hurry. He would take his time, the rest of the afternoon, tomorrow, if necessary. These would be, after all, his last words, his dying words. He wanted to get them right, exactly right. He wanted them to sing.

ACKNOWLEDGEMENTS

Thanks to David Auld, Susan Browne, William Carlsen, Beckie Artis Clevenger, John Curley, Jeff Gillenkirk, Reynolds Holding, Regan McMahon, Steve Proctor, Joan Ryan, David Thomson and Brooks Thorlaksson.

And thanks, above all, to the extraordinary journalists and splendid eccentrics I had the privilege of working with at the Chronicle. This, in so many ways, is their story.

www.ingramcontent.com/pod-product-compliance
Lightning Source LLC
Chambersburg PA
CBHW030818310726
48980CB00006B/540/J

* 9 7 8 0 9 8 5 6 3 1 2 0 8 *